Murder Ink

LORRAINE BARTLETT
with GAYLE LEESON

BERKLEY PRIME CRIME
New York

BERKLEY PRIME CRIME
Published by Berkley
An imprint of Penguin Random House LLC
penguinrandomhouse.com

ISBN: 9780425266014

First Edition: December 2019

Printed in the United States of America
1 3 5 7 9 10 8 6 4 2

Cover art by Chris Beatrice Studio

Acknowledgments

The authors would like to thank Stephen Sikora, MD, for his advice on how an electric shock patient would be evaluated in the emergency room. Any mistakes in accuracy or procedure are entirely our own.

Cast of Characters

Katie Bonner: owner-manager of Artisans Alley, the anchor on Victoria Square

Andy Rust: owner of Angelo's Pizzeria and Katie's boyfriend

Ray Davenport: former homicide detective and owner of Wood U on Victoria Square

Margo Bonner: Katie's former mother-in-law

Rose Nash: jewelry vendor at Artisans Alley and Katie's friend

Vance Ingram: vendor at Artisans Alley and Katie's second-in-command

Nona Fiske: owner of the Quiet Quilter; aunt of Carl Fiske

Seth Landers: attorney and Katie's friend

Don Parsons: co-owner of Sassy Sally's B&B on Victoria Square

Nick Ferrell: co-owner of Sassy Sally's B&B on Victoria Square

Detective Schuler: homicide detective with the Sheriff's Office

Brad Andrews: noted chef, hired to manage Tealicious tea shop

Paul Fenton: tattoo artist and brother of murder victim, Ken Fenton

Fiona Lancaster: guest at Sassy Sally's B&B

Phil Lancaster: husband of Fiona, guest at Sassy Sally's B&B

Regan Mitchell: receptionist at Paul Fenton's tattoo parlor

Mary Jones: sister of Paul and Ken Fenton

Hugh McKinney: retired DEA agent posing as a leather vendor at Artisans Alley

Miles Patterson: blind potter, new to Artisans Alley, former DEA agent

One

~~~

After a day filled with putting out fires—figuratively speaking, of course—Katie Bonner rushed into Del's Diner and headed for the party room in back where she was sure the rest of the Victoria Square Merchants Association was waiting. It wasn't like her to be late, but these days, she was running herself ragged between the business district's anchor, Artisans Alley, and Tealicious, the Square's relaunched tea shop.

"Hi, Katie," said Sandy, the heavyset blonde waitress who was even more of a fixture at Del's than the man himself. "The others have already finished dinner. Did you want me to bring you something?"

"No, thanks. I'll catch something later. Is Andy here?"

Sandy shook her head.

Katie suppressed a sigh. She knew Andy Rust, her boyfriend and owner of Angelo's Pizzeria, hated these meetings, but she'd really hoped he'd be able to make it to this one. They'd been planning on having a night in at her place, and if he wasn't at this meeting, it was likely he was going to have to cancel their date. Dates had been few and far between since she'd bought and reopened the tea shop. Even though Vance Ingram had come on board as assistant manager of Artisans Alley, the former applesauce warehouse turned configuration of artists and vendors, Katie still had many responsibilities there that Vance simply couldn't handle. Plus, her vendors expected her at the helm, and they weren't quite ready to accept Vance's authority.

She entered the party room and was immediately greeted by Gilda Ringwald-Stratton, who owned Gilda's Gourmet Baskets. Gilda kind of reminded Katie of a vampire, with her pale skin and dyed-black pageboy hair. This evening, she exacerbated the comparison by wearing black slacks and a scarlet silk blouse. Gilda made up for her lack of height with her four-inch wedge heels.

"Congratulations on Tealicious," Gilda said. "What a rousing success!"

"Thank you."

"Conrad and I love it now."

Now. Before Katie had bought the tea shop from Francine Barnett six months before, the place had suffered from an admittedly deserved decline in reputation. With it being early June and the tourist season in full swing, Katie was beginning to see a return on her investment.

"I certainly appreciate your patronage," she told Gilda.

"Janine is such a sweet, sweet girl." Gilda rolled her eyes to the left. "Although she seems a bit overwhelmed by it all sometimes, doesn't she?"

"She does," Katie admitted. The tea shop's young manager, Janine Brady, was a conversation for another time. "I need to get the meeting started."

"Of course. We'll talk later."

Katie went to the front of the room. "Hi, everybody. I'm so glad you could make it, and my apologies for being late."

A chorus of *hello* and *hi* echoed back just as Andy stepped in the room. Katie greeted him with a smile. *Yes! Tonight is on!*

"I'll try to make this meeting brief," she told the gathering. "Let's start by talking about Victoria Square's vacant buildings."

A muscle-bound man in gym shorts and a red tank top who'd been sitting in a chair at the back of the room stood. He raised his hand and turned slightly to his left and right, including as many people as possible in his wave and his gaze. He then locked his eyes on Katie. "May I speak?"

"Uh, sure." Who was this Hulk Hogan wannabe?

"My name is Paul Fenton, and I'll be taking care of the problem of one of those vacant buildings within the next few days."

"That's great, Paul," said Katie, amid the subdued greetings offered by the other members of the Merchants Association. "What type of business will you be operating?"

"I'm a tattoo artist," he said.

Katie could see that there was quite a bit of indelible ink on the man's arms and legs. In trying to see what symbols he had and where, she realized she was staring and dragged her eyes away. But, surely, he couldn't have done all of those himself.

"Do you have a partner?" she asked.

"Yes. There are three of us. We're buying the building from Mr. Jones—our closing is set for next week—and we'll be setting up shop immediately after. I'm the main investor, so I came here tonight to join the Merchants Association."

"Hold on," said Sue Sweeney, the owner of Sweet Sue's Confectionery, standing and taking advantage of her height to ensure everyone at the meeting could see her. "I'm not sure a tattoo parlor is right for Victoria Square. We have a . . . well, a *theme* . . . if you will."

"A theme?" Paul demanded. "Whoever heard of a town square having a theme? What do *you* do?"

"I make and sell gourmet chocolates and other exquisite confections," Sue said, sounding annoyed at the challenge.

"And how does *that* fit in any sort of theme?" he asked.

"Well, we're all . . . crafty." Sue looked around for someone—anyone—to back her up.

"You'd probably do better with a tattoo parlor in a location closer to the marina," said Jordan Tanner, owner of the Square's coffee shop and bakery, and whose dignified stance and tone made him appear more like a professor than a baker.

"Why's that?" Paul asked.

"We're just concerned that your business would attract a certain . . . clientele," Gilda offered, her Brooklyn accent more pronounced than usual.

"She means that *our* businesses attract a certain clientele," Gilda's husband, Conrad, corrected quickly. "And she's afraid *your* business would suffer because of it." He forced out a laugh. "Not many little old ladies are getting tattoos, are they?"

Paul spread his hands. "They might after they see our work. My crew and I are renowned artists."

"You do have some nice things there . . . on you," said Charlotte Booth, owner of Booth's Jams and Jellies—ever the peacemaker.

"Thanks." Paul winked at her, causing Charlotte to blush.

Great, thought Katie. *Char will be first in line for a tattoo. I need to do something to get this meeting under control.*

"I think what some of our vendors are concerned about," Katie said, "is that your business won't get the exposure it needs here in Victoria Square."

"So, what are you saying?" Paul demanded, his hands to his hips. "Are you telling me that I *can't* join the Merchants Association, or what?"

Andy stood. "Yeah. Is the Merchants Association going

to push Paul out of the way like it did to *me* during all the years when Ezra Hilton was running the show?"

"This is entirely different." Katie gave him a pleading look meant to tell him to not get involved.

"How?" he asked, clearly ignoring her silent request. "Ezra didn't want a pizza parlor on his precious Square, and now you guys don't want a tattoo parlor. How are the two situations different?"

Katie struggled to come up with a reasonable response. "You have to admit that because Angelo's Pizzeria is located in a vintage building, it isn't your typical pizza parlor."

"Look," Paul interrupted. "Whether you guys want me here or not, I'm here. I don't need your snobby little group to tell me what I can and can't do. I'm buying the building. It's a done deal." With that, he stormed out of the room.

Shaking his head in disgust, Andy left, too.

Ray Davenport, the owner of Wood U, stood as the room erupted in arguments for and against—mostly against—the tattoo parlor. He cleared his throat, and everyone quieted down to look at him. As a retired police detective, Ray knew how to command attention.

"Mr. Fenton said the closing on the building isn't until next week," he said. "That means there might not be any paperwork yet and that someone else could still buy the property."

"Are you going to pony up, Ray?" Conrad asked.

"Not me." He shook his balding head. "I've got one daughter in college and two more to go. I can barely afford to pay attention these days."

"What if the Merchants Association bought the building?" Katie held up a hand to quiet down the furor her question elicited. "Or a consortium of merchants. I realize that not everyone can swing an extra bill every month. But for those who can, imagine the rental income the venture could bring in."

"But even if we buy this building, what's to keep the tattoo guy from simply opening his shop in the other vacant buildings?" Sue asked.

"We could buy them all," Katie said. "I mean, it would at least be worth going to the bank to see what we could do. Don't you think?"

"Count me in," said Jordan. "My daughter still has a couple of years of high school left. Maybe by the time she went to college, I could have the rental income to pay for her education."

"You're making the assumption that the building owner would agree to sell," Ray pointed out. "Maybe he's promised it to Paul Fenton, and that's the way it is."

"Anyone know the owner of the building in question?" Katie asked.

"Harper Jones," Conrad answered.

"Oh, I know Harper," Ray said. "I didn't realize he owned a building on Victoria Square."

"Since you know him, would you please talk to him for us?" Katie asked.

"Sure. I'll be glad to." He winked at her, and she quickly looked away.

Things had been strange between them since Christmas, when he'd kissed her. It was a mere peck, and he'd claimed he did it because he thought she was wearing a sprig of mistletoe on her Dickens Festival costume's bonnet. But their relationship was strained in a way it had never been before.

She addressed the group. "So, Ray will see what he can learn from Mr. Jones, and then we'll call another meeting to discuss the buying of one or more buildings on Victoria Square."

Katie forced a smile and wondered just what kind of mess they were all about to get into.

~~~~~~~

When Katie returned to her cozy apartment above Angelo's Pizzeria, she tried to call Andy, but there was no answer.

Was he busy, or was he angry with her? She should've realized that the situation with Paul Fenton would have brought up memories of Ezra and his attempt to keep Andy out of the Merchants Association. It had been almost two years since she'd taken over both Artisans Alley and the Merchants Association, and it was easy to forget about Ezra's tyranny.

She sighed. Was the Merchants Association following in Ezra's footsteps? He'd certainly have had a conniption at the thought of a tattoo parlor located on his quaint Square. Heck, a pizzeria had been enough to nearly cause him to have a stroke.

After what could only be called a disaster of a day, Katie felt rather frazzled. Upon feeding her cats, Mason and Della, she went in the bathroom to run a tub filled with steaming, scented bubbles. She'd been up since before dawn baking scones and making egg and tuna salads for tea sandwiches before heading to Artisans Alley to tackle her six-month planner, which included outlining advertising for the holiday season. Relaxing in the soothing bath water would be heavenly.

Her phone rang, and her lips curved into a smile. Maybe all was not lost after all. There was room in the big claw-foot tub for two. When she reached for the phone and saw that it was Janine—not Andy—calling, she could've wept. There went not only her romantic evening but her hot bath.

Katie turned off the water, fearing what the conversation might portend. "What's up, Janine?"

"I . . . ju-just . . . ca-can't . . . do-do . . . this . . . anymore!" she sobbed.

The young woman had not seemed this rattled when they'd last spoken only hours before, and Katie forced herself to sound upbeat. "Janine? What is it? What's wrong?"

"Katie, I'm sorry," Janine wailed. "I used to love working at Afternoon Tea with Francine. That was fun. But now . . . now it's not! I have to do *everything*!"

Trying to rein in her sudden ire, Katie counted to ten. Janine did *not* have to do everything. Granted, she had more responsibility than a waitress—and her paycheck reflected that—but she wasn't responsible for the entire running of Tealicious. If that were true, Katie wouldn't be called away from Artisans Alley so much that the vendors had started complaining . . . a lot.

"So, are you telling me you're stepping down as manager?" Katie asked through clenched teeth. "That you'd prefer to be a server?"

"No. I'm quitting. I appreciate you giving me this opportunity, but I no longer feel that my future is in the food industry. I'm going back to school in the fall—with another major."

"You won't even stay on as a waitress until school starts?" Katie asked in disbelief.

"No, thank you. I'll be leaving at the end of this week."

Katie's heart lurched. "Three days? You're giving me three days' notice?"

"I'm sorry!" She didn't sound it.

Katie nearly hung up to avoid having to listen to Janine's racking sobs. Instead, she steeled herself and said, "Well, I wish you the best, and I'll see you tomorrow."

"Th-thank you. Good night."

Katie ended the call and put down the phone, then strode into the kitchen. She could really use a glass of wine to go along with her bath and wondered if even that wasn't strong enough.

~~~~~~~

Katie had just gotten out of the tub and wrapped herself in a white terry robe when a knock came at her door. She looked through the peephole and saw Andy standing there, looking downtrodden. She opened it. "Hello," she said, her voice somber.

"Hello yourself."

They looked at each other for a long moment.

"I'm sorry I walked out of the meeting," Andy said finally, pushed past her, and moved to sit on the sofa. She joined him and he pulled her closer.

"I'm sorry it brought up bad feelings for you." She reached for his hand and squeezed it. "I couldn't help but agree with the vendors, though, that the tattoo parlor would be more successful somewhere near the pier where younger crowds tend to congregate."

"Angelo's Pizzeria is crowded with people of all ages most of the time," he countered.

"That's because you're known far and wide for not only making the best pizza in the area but as the cinnamon bun king of Victoria Square, too." She leaned forward and dropped a light kiss onto his lips.

"What does the Merchants Association plan to do?" he asked, his tone rather flat.

Katie shrugged. "Ray volunteered to talk to the building owner."

Andy scoffed. "I should've known Davenport would throw himself in the middle of the fray."

Katie couldn't help but heave a rueful sigh. Andy had long believed that Ray had a crush on Katie. That was the main reason she'd never told him about Ray's Christmas kiss. It would only confirm Andy's suspicions and further strain the two men's tolerance of each other.

"Could we please stop worrying about Merchants Association business and enjoy the rest of our night?" She wasn't even going to mention the fact that Janine had just up and quit on her. She needed Andy to distract her, not try to help solve her problems.

"I don't know." He sported a crooked smile and ran his hands up her back. "I believe I'm going to need a little more convincing."

She kissed his neck, then pulled back and smiled at him.

"I believe I'm convinced," he said and grinned.

And then the terrible day improved by more than one hundred percent.

Two

~~~~~~

Once again, Katie started the day at Tealicious. The cozy tearoom she'd lovingly redecorated and had spent literally months revamping the menu for was becoming a thorn in her side. Before leaving the house, Katie had printed off flyers announcing MANAGER WANTED and included her cell phone number on them. She placed one of the flyers in the Tealicious front window before heading to the kitchen to prepare more baked goods and salads for what she hoped would be a full lunch crowd, then she made sure everything was in readiness in the tea shop itself. She wanted to make sure standards wouldn't slide now that Janine had turned in her notice.

Katie looked around at the pretty little tea shop she'd bought with the help of her former mother-in-law. The busy wallpaper that had adorned Afternoon Tea had been stripped so the walls could be painted a pale rose. A border stenciled at chair-rail height incorporated pink and blue forget-me-nots and greenery. The tables were white wrought iron, and clear vases filled with pink carnations and baby's breath adorned each one. Matching bouquets of mixed, fresh flowers had been placed at each end of the main display case, too.

At last, Katie climbed the stairs to the second-floor office, gathered some paperwork, and placed it in her briefcase. Yes, she carried a briefcase now. She was a true entrepreneur.

Once back downstairs, she entered the kitchen to check the stock of teas. She was getting low on chai and kava. She made a note of it on her phone.

She raised her head when the door opened and in slumped Janine. Her eyes were red and puffy, and she looked as if she'd barely brushed her hair. Katie ground her teeth together, wondering if there was a way to nicely tell Janine to straighten up and pull herself together. The customers shouldn't see Tealicious's manager looking like that!

"Good morning," Katie said, pasting on a saccharine smile. "Why don't you go on into the ladies' room and fix up a bit before the rest of the staff and the customers start arriving? I'm getting everything ready out here."

"Y-you aren't m-mad at me?"

"Of course not." And, to her surprise, she realized she really wasn't. What good would it do to be angry with Janine? The girl had made her decision. Now it was up to Katie to find a replacement—someone who would, hopefully, be a much better fit for Tealicious—as soon as possible.

"Thanks," Janine said softly. "I'll work as hard as I can . . . you know, for the rest of the week."

For three whole days, Katie thought. "I appreciate that."

Once everything was up and running and Katie was satisfied that Janine wouldn't have a nervous breakdown—at least, not within the next few minutes—she hurried across the Square to Sassy Sally's.

Sassy Sally's Bed and Breakfast was located in a three-story Victorian home originally known as the Webster Mansion. Katie had once dreamed of buying the home with her husband, Chad, and turning it into an upscale bed-and-breakfast called the English Ivy Inn. Unfortunately, Chad invested their savings in Artisans Alley instead, and after his death, Katie was saddled with running the artisans' co-op rather than her heart's desire of a bed-and-breakfast.

That was all water under the bridge now. She'd come to love Artisans Alley, and she felt as if she'd reclaimed some of her former dream when she'd taken over the tea shop. And the fact was she adored Nick and Don, the couple who'd renovated the mansion and turned it into a spectacular inn.

She strode up to the kitchen door and knocked lightly. Nick, his sandy hair still damp from a recent shower, opened it.

"Hey, Katie, what's going on?"

"I need to ask you and Don for some help . . . if you can give it."

"We'll certainly try." He stood to the side. "Come on in. Had your coffee yet?"

"No, and I'd love a cup."

"Coming right up."

Don sat at the island with a steaming mug of joe and the *New York Times* crossword. "Hi, Katie."

"Good morning, Don." She joined him at the island.

Nick placed a cup of coffee in front of her along with a small pitcher of cream.

"Thanks." Katie dumped the cream in the coffee and stirred. "Do either of you know of someone who might be interested in the manager position at Tealicious?"

Don wrinkled his nose. "Janine not working out?"

"No. She called me last night sobbing and said she'd work out the rest of the week but that she no longer thinks a career in food service is right for her."

"Wow, that's a bit extreme."

"Yeah," Nick said. "Thanks for the notice, kid."

"I know, right?"

The bell at the reception desk rang, and Don hopped up off his stool. "I'll take care of that."

Katie sipped her coffee as Nick looked thoughtful. "I think I might know someone," he said at last.

"Really?" She brightened.

"I *might*. I'll give him a call, and then either he or I will give you a call later today."

"Nick, you're the best!"

"I know . . . but, still, don't get your hopes up just yet."

"Can you tell me more about him?"

He shook his head. "Not yet."

"But he's had restaurant—or hospitality—experience?"

Nick nodded. "Oh yeah."

"And why do you think he'd be a good fit?"

"Because he graduated at the top of his class at the Culinary Institute in Hyde Park and also earned a *Diplôme de Pâtisserie* from Le Cordon Bleu in London."

Katie's jaw dropped. "Then there's no way in the world he'd be willing to work in my little tea shop. Talk about hiding your light under a basket."

"Just let me talk to him. The last time we spoke, he was bemoaning the fact that life in Manhattan was simply too stressful for him."

"Manhattan?" Katie shook her head.

"The worst he can say is no, right?" Nick asked. "And, hey, he might say yes. Let me call him."

She raised her palms. "Be my guest."

~~~~~~

As soon as Katie entered Artisans Alley, Liz Meier, the stained-glass artist, practically collided with her and said, "Don't you think it's sweltering in here?"

Liz was working the main cash desk. Her cheeks were flushed and her forehead glistened with perspiration.

"It does feel a bit warm," Katie admitted.

"A bit warm? I heard that a caravan of camels is headed this way because this place is hotter than the Sahara."

Katie laughed. "Have you spoken with Vance about adjusting the thermostat?"

"Yes . . . and more than once. I first spoke with him on Tuesday, and I mentioned it again yesterday. He's apparently choosing to ignore me."

"I'll speak to him about it."

"Thanks," Liz called. "I wouldn't want to collapse from dehydration."

Katie headed toward the back of the building and her office, hoping it wasn't quite as hot in there. She had a fan in her office, and she turned it on as she entered. The heat wasn't unbearable to her but she could understand why Liz was unhappy.

A tap on her door caused Katie to look up to see her favorite vendor, Rose Nash.

"Good morning. I was doing my initial security walk and thought I'd stop in to say hello." Rose made a point of standing in front of the fan, her arms raised so that the circulating air reached under the sleeves of her colorful summer dress.

"Have a lot of vendors been complaining about the heat?"

"Vendors and customers, too," Rose answered ruefully.

Katie sighed. "If you see Vance, will you send him to see me, please? No rush—I'm still putting out yesterday's fires."

"Are you talking about the tattoo parlor guy?"

"You heard?" Katie asked.

"Pretty much everything that goes on in the Square is common knowledge."

That was for sure.

"I *wish* that was my only problem." Katie explained to Rose that Janine had quit the evening before and planned to work through Saturday—period.

"Wow. Nothing like giving you plenty of notice to find someone else." Rose shook her head. "Young people: What're you going to do?"

"Nick Ferrell said he might know someone, and I put a flyer in the window at Tealicious. I'm putting one on the bulletin board in the vendors' lounge and hopefully at a few other spots around town. I thought I'd log on to a couple of online job sites and post the notice there, too."

"If I can think of anyone who might be qualified and is looking for a job, I'll let you know."

"Thanks, Rose."

"I'd better get back to work. I'm power walking on my security circuits."

Katie frowned. Rose usually worked the main cash desk while Liz walked security. Why had they changed tasks?

After Rose left, Katie took a peppermint from the jar on her desk, unwrapped it, popped it in her mouth, and immediately bit it in half. She glanced around her shabby little office—the one at Tealicious was bigger and much more luxurious, but she was used to hanging out here. Plus, the vendors would really think she'd deserted them if she started working from that much more comfortable space. In addition to her desk, she had a file cabinet and one chair that squeaked when she leaned back. One thing she could say about the office—it wasn't conducive to staying holed up in it working all day. It encouraged her to get out and walk around Artisans Alley to see what was going on.

She logged on to her computer and pulled up the first job site on her list. As she stared at the blinking cursor and tried to compose a persuasive ad for a tea shop manager, there came another tap on her door.

Katie called "Come in," and looked up, expecting to see Vance. Instead, Ray Davenport stood in her doorway sporting a swollen eye that was rapidly turning black. For one insane instant, Katie wondered if Andy had punched Ray.

She stood. "Get in here and sit down. What happened?"

"Stop coddling me, woman. The creep got in a lucky shot, that's all."

"What creep? Can I get you some ice?"

He raised his bushy graying brows, and Katie sat back down.

"Suit yourself," she said. "Is this a case of *you should see the other guy*?"

Ray blew out a breath. "No. I was trying to handle the subject of the building sale diplomatically. I saw Harper Jones's pickup truck across the Square and went over to talk to him."

"Wait, I thought Harper Jones was pretty old."

"He is."

"Wow . . . and he can still pack a punch?"

"Harper didn't do this. His brother-in-law, Ken, did. He was there making repairs to the building." He rubbed his forehead. "I asked Ken if Harper would be willing to rescind his offer to Paul Fenton and consider an offer on the building extended by the Victoria Square Merchants Association."

"That *does* sound diplomatic."

"I thought so," Ray said. "But it turns out that Paul Fenton happens to be Ken's younger brother, and he doesn't appreciate the way Paul is being treated by the association. Ken said that sending a representative to buy the building out from under Paul seemed pretty low in his opinion."

"So, you basically went over there and fell into the family viper nest. I thought you knew Harper Jones. How did you not know he was related by marriage to Paul Fenton?"

"For one thing, I believe I told you I was *acquainted* with Harper. I didn't say I knew every member of his family. Heck, I didn't even know the man had a wife until her brother socked me in the face."

"I'm sorry," Katie said. "Again, I'll be glad to get you some ice from the vendors' lounge."

"I'm all right. But, now that we know that Harper and the Fentons are all related, they're not going to budge on selling the building."

"Maybe I can go smooth things over with Ken."

"Good luck. If, after that meeting, *you* need some ice for

your black eye, come on over to Wood U, and I'll see what I can do."

After a quick rap on the door, Vance poked his head inside. "Hey, Katie, Rose said you were looking for me." He glanced at Ray. "But if you did that to Ray, I'll come back later."

"Very funny, Ingram."

"Seriously, Ray, what happened?"

"I found out that there's not a chance the Merchants Association will be invited to put an offer in on the building set aside for Paul Fenton's tattoo parlor."

"Did Paul do that? What happened?" Apparently, Vance was also included in all the Square gossip.

Ray gave Vance an abbreviated account of his visit to Harper Jones's building. "And Katie thinks she might be able to go over there and smooth things over with Ken."

"No offense, Katie, but the man is obviously a loose cannon," Vance said. "You can't go over there by yourself."

"I can, and I will. I think he might be more amenable to a woman." She shrugged. "Maybe he thought Ray was trying to threaten him."

"Oh, yeah . . . *I* was threatening *him*." Ray stood. "If you'll both excuse me, I need to get back to work."

When Ray left, Katie mentioned to Vance that she'd been getting complaints all morning about the heat. "Could you please adjust the thermostat so the heat pump will kick in and make it a little cooler in here?"

"I'll see what I can do. But you know how expensive that will be? Giving in to the whims of a few menopausal women?"

Katie cringed at the remark. "It's more than that," she said evenly. "Rose said several of the vendors *and* customers have complained."

"So, this is coming from Rose?" Vance demanded, rather unreasonably, Katie thought. The two of them had always gotten along so well.

"No. The first person who mentioned it to me this morning

was another vendor. I asked Rose if anyone else had complained."

"I'll tell you what it is," Vance declared. "A lot of these people are jealous of the position you've put me in, and they're doing everything they can to undermine my authority."

Katie frowned. "I hope that's not the case, but if you'd please turn down the thermostat, I'd really appreciate it."

"Fine." Vance threw his hands up in the air and stalked off in a huff.

What the heck? Katie thought. She was the one who paid the bills. Why was he taking the situation so personally?

She shook her head and turned her attention to the computer. She had other, bigger dilemmas to solve.

~~~~~~

After a morning filled with far too many problems, Katie was due to meet Andy for their regular lunch date at Del's. But first, she decided to swing by Harper Jones's vacant building to have a word with Ken Fenton.

As she walked up to the frame building, Katie was greeted by the sound of a hammer pounding wood. Gingerly, she stepped inside the building and called, "Hello!"

Katie's great-aunt Lizzie would have said Ken Fenton was built like a fireplug, and, honestly, he was the first person for whom she thought that description was accurate. The man was short and looked as if he was tough as nails. A red bandana was tied around his head, and the intimidating expression on his stubbly face could best be described as grim.

"What can I do for you?" he asked, still clutching a hammer rather than putting it into the holster on his tool belt.

"I'm Katie Bonner, head of the Victoria Square Merchants Association. I came to apologize for Mr. Davenport's visit this morning. I think the two of you must've misunderstood each other."

Fenton straightened, looking none too friendly. "I think I made my position pretty clear."

"Yes, sir, but I just wanted you to know that the Merchants Association doesn't want to run your brother out of business. In fact, we want to make sure his business is successful . . . and we're afraid he won't get the kind of traffic he needs here on Victoria Square."

"Why don't you let him worry about that?"

"We just want to see him succeed," Katie reiterated, hoping he'd notice the sincerity in her voice.

"Yeah, sure you do." He dropped the hammer into the loop on his tool belt and picked up a circular saw. "I need to get back to work."

"I understand, but—"

He turned on the saw to drown out her words. Immediately, his smirk changed to a look of horror. As his body began to shake, Katie looked for the power cord. Maybe if she—

Wham!

The next thing Katie knew, she was sitting against the wall on the other side of the room from Ken . . . Ken, who'd turned on the saw and then . . .

Ken!

She struggled to sit up. Where was he? Why was her body trembling so badly? She could see Ken lying on the floor. Her purse had been spilled, so she crawled toward it and rummaged through the contents until she found her phone. She'd missed two calls from Andy, but she called 911 first.

When she was assured the ambulance was on its way, she called Andy.

"Hey, where are you?"

"I'm . . . I'm at Harper Jones's vacant building on the Square. Andy, I got shocked . . . and I think K-Ken might've been . . . electrocuted."

Andy's voice was taut. "On my way."

Three

Katie shuddered as she eased forward on the edge of the hospital gurney. She nestled as closely into Andy's strong arms as she could. "Hold me tighter," she whispered.

"I've got you, Sunshine." He kissed the top of her head.

"I want to go home."

"I know. We'll get you there. Just be patient."

A tall male nurse wearing light blue scrubs pulled back the curtain and entered the cubicle. Andy took a step back but held Katie's hands.

"Ms. Bonner, I'm going to hook you up to this EKG machine," said the nurse. "We're going to do a little cardiac monitoring. I'm also going to take a blood sample, and I'll need you to empty your bladder into this cup for a urinalysis. Can you do that?"

Katie nodded.

"I'll help you stand," Andy said.

"Still trembly?" the nurse asked.

"Yeah, she has been for nearly two hours now." Andy helped Katie to her feet.

"That'll pass soon. Or it should."

Katie took the cup and went into the bathroom. She returned with the urine sample, and then the nurse asked her to lie back on the gurney. He proceeded to fill two tubes with blood before attaching electrodes to her torso and hooking her up to the EKG machine. With the promise that he'd be right back, the nurse left the room.

Andy pushed a rolling stool over to the gurney, sat beside her, and took her hand. "Are you okay?"

"I hope so." She sighed. "Ken . . . did he—?"

"I don't know."

Katie closed her eyes. She was still too jittery to relax, let alone sleep, and within a few minutes, she could hear shuffling noises inside her room.

"Is she asleep?" Rose asked.

Katie opened her eyes and gave her friend a wan smile. "No."

Vance must have gotten over his pique from that morning and had accompanied Rose to the hospital. They were both standing uncomfortably close to the gurney. Katie knew it was thoughtful of her friends to come and check on her, but at the moment she didn't want to be with anyone but Andy.

"How are you feeling?" Rose asked softly.

"Ready to go home," Katie said. "Please . . . have a seat. You, too, Vance. You both look way too concerned, and it's a little disconcerting."

"Well, um . . . we were worried," Vance said, placing a hand on Andy's shoulder. "When we heard what happened, we got here as quickly as we could."

Katie wondered if her stab of guilt would spike the EKG readings. "How's Ken?"

Rose looked around the room, found a chair, and quickly moved to sit against the wall.

"He didn't make it," Vance said. "That's the main reason we were so concerned about you."

"What happened?" Katie asked. "Was it faulty wiring?"

Andy squeezed her hand. "We'll talk about that later. Right now, you need to be calm so the hospital can get an accurate reading on your EKG."

"Vance, we should get back to the Alley," Rose said. "Without Katie there to run business, someone needs to hold down the fort."

"Yeah . . . we'll go. Katie, let us know if you need anything."

"Oh, and I'll look in at Tealicious to make sure Janine doesn't need any help and that she knows what's happened. After all, you've had quite a shock." Rose laughed at her own joke. Her laughter quickly died when she realized she was the only one laughing.

"Thank you," Katie said. "I appreciate your coming by."

Vance and Rose retreated, and Katie closed her eyes as a frown settled across her features. "I hope I didn't appear rude, but they *did* kinda add to my stress. There are so many things I need to take care of, both at Artisans Alley and at Tealicious."

"All of it can wait. Provided they don't admit you to the hospital, I'm planning on taking care of you the rest of the day and night."

Katie shook her head. "You have a business to run, too."

"Already taken care of. I called Erikka on the way here, and she's handling Angelo's for the night."

Erikka. Wonderful, beautiful Erikka . . . She worked for Andy because Katie had regretfully suggested he hire her as his assistant manager. And now she'd become invaluable to him.

Of course, Katie had also suggested Erikka apply for a part-time secretarial position with the school system to get her away from Andy, but that had only served to make Andy angry with Katie . . . especially after Erikka got the job. But, then, the woman assured Andy that she'd never leave him.

Swell.

A woman wearing scrubs and a white lab coat came into the room. "Hi, Ms. Bonner, I'm Dr. Casey. I've looked at your bloodwork, urinalysis, and EKG, and I think you're going to be just fine. You're incredibly lucky." She walked over, turned off the monitor, and took the sensors off Katie's body. "I'm going to let you go home, but if you feel any pain in your extremities, feel anxiety, suffer from memory loss, insomnia, or chest pain, I want you to return to the emergency department as soon as possible."

Katie's head spun as she sat up too quickly. "I will."

"She will," Andy said simultaneously.

Dr. Casey smiled. "I'll initiate the paperwork for your release."

"Thank you," Katie said, looked at the clock on the wall, and then turned to Andy. "Can we get something to eat on the way home? I'm starving."

He smiled and planted a kiss on the top of her head. "Anything you want, love." He wrapped his arms around her shoulders, and Katie felt loved and secure. And then her thoughts returned to the memory of Ken Fenton lying dead on the sawdust-covered floor, spoiling her sense of relief.

~~~~~~~

After a leisurely late lunch in a much-too-expensive restaurant not far from the hospital, Andy drove them back to McKinlay Mill and Victoria Square. He'd entered the lot via the east entrance and they drove slowly past the now-shuttered building where Ken Fenton had met his maker. Yellow crime tape cordoned off the front of the building, the sight of it causing Katie to shudder.

Andy pulled his white Ford truck into a parking space in front of Angelo's Pizzeria, now bathed in shadows, and parked in his designated space. She leaned forward and squinted. "Who's that?"

"Who's what?"

"There's someone standing by the stairs to my apartment. I think it's Ray."

Andy wrenched open the door of the truck. "Davenport! What are you doing here?"

"I was going to tape a note to the door," Ray called, as he walked toward them. He squinted into the cab of the truck. "How are you, Katie?"

"I'm—"

"Who dotted your eye for you, Davenport?" Andy said and snickered.

"I'm fine," Katie said, with a sharp glance at Andy.

"That's good," Ray said. "I . . . everyone . . . has been worried about you."

"Thanks."

"You didn't answer my question," Andy said, his tone sharper than necessary. "Who gave you the shiner?"

"Ken." Ray shoved his hands in his pockets and looked down at the pavement.

"Ken? As in, Ken Fenton? The recently deceased Ken Fenton?"

Ray brought his gaze back up to glare at Andy. "Yes, *that* Ken Fenton."

Andy scoffed. "You didn't tamper with that saw, did you?"

"I didn't, as I've been explaining to Detective Schuler for the past few hours."

Katie gasped. "The sheriff's office questioned *you*? Why?"

"Schuler found it a strange coincidence that Ken died so soon after he and I argued, especially since Ken's death has been deemed suspicious."

"Suspicious," Katie repeated, "but not a homicide?"

"Not as of yet," Ray said.

Katie got out of the truck and walked around to the side where Andy and Ray stood.

Andy put his arm around her, more possessive than protective. "Steady."

"I'm all right. Ray, did Detective Schuler give you any indication as to why Ken's death seemed suspicious?"

"No. He's playing his cards close to his vest. If he winds up charging me with anything, he wants to make it stick."

"Oh, come on! That's ridiculous!"

Ray shook his head. "Not to him, it's not."

"We'll see you later," Andy said dismissively, and led Katie to the stairs.

She didn't like feeling like a pull-toy in the teeth of a couple of pit bulls.

Andy insisted on steadying Katie as they walked up the stairs to her apartment. She unlocked the door and her two cats—Mason, a noble-looking black-and-white cat, and Della, a timid tabby—came mewing to wind around her and Andy's legs.

Katie loved the little one-bedroom apartment. Sure, it was tiny, and it could get noisy during peak hours when Angelo's was pumping out scores of pies, but it was cozy, a stone's throw away from Artisans Alley, and it had everything she needed.

"I'll feed you two in just a minute," Andy told the cats. "Let's get Katie settled on the sofa first."

"I'm not an invalid, Andy. I'm perfectly fine."

"I know. But taking care of you makes me feel manly, so humor me . . . please?"

She laughed. "All right. I'll allow you to get us some wine and maybe some popcorn, but I'm feeding the cats."

"Great. I'll even let you pick the movie tonight."

"Ooh . . . this is big." It was, after all, Andy's night to choose. "Let me think of the mushiest, gooiest, sappiest—"

He swept her into a bear hug. "You know what's sappy? That killer clown movie. I've heard it's really romantic."

"No, it is not!" She was laughing when the doorbell rang.

"Hope it's not old Slugger Davenport again," Andy griped. "I'm ready for some alone time with you."

"Me, too. Whoever it is, get rid of them."

"My pleasure." Andy went to the door as Katie weaved through the maze of cat legs to the kitchen.

When he spoke again, Andy's voice was grave. "Katie, Detective Schuler is here."

She stifled a groan and emptied the can of cat food in the bowls, setting them on the floor as Andy led Schuler through to the living room. She returned to the room and sank onto the sofa. "Hi, Detective."

Andy sat down beside her, and Detective Schuler lowered his lanky frame onto the seat near the window.

"How are you feeling?" Schuler asked, taking a notebook and pen from his suit pocket. "I hear you suffered quite a jolt when Ken Fenton turned on that saw."

"Not like he did," Katie said, slipping her hand in Andy's.

"Thank goodness for that. But you got a clean bill of health from the hospital?"

"I did."

"Do you feel like answering a few questions?"

Not particularly. "Sure."

Schuler flipped open his notebook. "I understand you were the last person to see Ken Fenton alive. Is that correct?"

"I don't know . . . I guess so. I was there when . . . when the accident occurred."

The detective scribbled something in his notebook. "Tell me exactly what happened, please."

Katie squeezed Andy's hand.

Andy leveled his gaze at the detective. "If you're not feeling up to this, I'm sure Detective Schuler can speak with you tomorrow."

"I'd prefer to get it over with," Katie said. She took a deep breath. "This morning, Ray Davenport stopped by Artisans Alley to tell me that, as requested by the Victoria Square Merchants Association, he went by to speak with the building owner but found Mr. Fenton there instead."

"What was the subject of the discussion?"

"The possibility of selling the building to the Association."

"Go on," Schuler encouraged her.

"It seems Mr. Fenton wasn't receptive to the idea and they had words. I thought it might be a good idea if I—as head of the Association—tried to smooth things over with Mr. Fenton."

"And how did that go?" Schuler asked.

"Mr. Fenton was angry because he felt we had treated his brother unfairly. I tried to explain our position, but Mr. Fenton didn't want to talk to me. To stress his unwillingness to have a talk about it, he picked up his circular saw, turned it on, and . . . and that's when it happened."

"When Mr. Fenton was electrocuted?"

"Yes, Detective Schuler, when the man was electrocuted."

Scribble, scribble, scribble.

"You maintain that at that time the current arced off Mr. Fenton and hit you. Is that correct?"

"I don't know exactly what happened," Katie said. "All I know is that I saw a huge spark and was thrown backward."

"All right. And what do you know about Ray Davenport's altercation with the deceased?"

"Only what Ray told me—that he asked if Mr. Jones would consider selling the building to the Merchants Association, and Mr. Fenton punched him."

Scribble, scribble.

"Do you know whether or not Mr. Davenport has any prior history with the deceased?" Schuler asked.

"I don't think they'd ever met before today."

"Do you have actual knowledge of this alleged fact, or did Mr. Davenport give you this information?"

Katie blew out a breath. "It's what Ray told me. Could we please finish this up? I've had a rough day, and I'm tired."

"Sure. I think I have what I need," Schuler said. "But don't go anywhere without letting my office know. You might

be called as a material witness in a homicide investigation."
He got up and sauntered out of the room.

Andy saw Schuler to the door then returned to the living room. Looking quizzical, he said, "Is it just me, or does it seem like Schuler is enjoying this investigation way too much?"

Four

~~~

By the next morning, it seemed every Artisans Alley vendor—and just about everybody else Katie had met since arriving on Victoria Square—wanted to talk about the "accident." The Alley's landline kept ringing, and the texts to Katie's cell phone kept coming like a nonstop interrogation. Finally, she asked Rose to handle the calls and "tell them whatever you think will make them go away." She also turned her cell phone to vibrate and gained instant peace and quiet.

A gentle knock at the doorjamb caused Katie to look up. Sue Sweeney stood in the doorway, white-knuckling the handle of a small basket filled with an assortment of cellophane-wrapped candies. Sue's pallid face stood out against the dark hair that framed it.

Katie pushed her chair away from her desk and stood. "Sue? Is everything all right?"

"I just feel so awful. This whole mess with Ken Fenton's death is my fault."

Katie directed Sue to the chair beside her desk. "What are you talking about? What mess?"

"If I hadn't put up a fuss about the tattoo parlor at the Merchants Association meeting on Wednesday evening, none of this would have happened. Ken would be fine, and we'd all be going about our business."

"Sue, you don't know that," Katie said, patting the woman's arm. She sat back down. "Why do you feel that way?"

"If I hadn't piped up and complained, Ray wouldn't have gone over to the vacant building and gotten in a fight with Ken. And now Ken is dead." She shook her head. "And the truth is that I couldn't have cared less about a tattoo parlor—it was Paul Fenton I didn't want here on Victoria Square."

"So . . . you know Paul Fenton?" Katie took a peppermint from the jar on her desk and offered one to Sue, who declined. And why not? She made her own, which were infinitely better than the commercial mints Katie kept on hand. Katie unwrapped hers and popped it in her mouth.

"Not personally," Sue said. "But he dated my niece about a year ago. She broke up with him when he became an abusive jerk."

"Oh no. Sue, I'm sorry to hear that." Katie didn't say so, but it appeared to her that a hair-trigger temper ran in the Fenton family. Of course, she hadn't been there when Ken had punched Ray, but she knew Ray wouldn't have gone to speak with Ken in an aggressive manner.

Sue released her death grip on the basket in order to raise a hand to wipe a stray tear from the corner of her eye. "I feel responsible for Ken's death."

"Sue, we have no idea what happened with the saw Ken was using. Unless you know something I don't."

"I know the police have questioned Ray."

Katie ground the peppermint between her molars. "That doesn't mean Ray is guilty."

Sue shrugged. "It doesn't mean he's innocent, either." She stood and placed the basket on the corner of Katie's desk. "For what it's worth, I don't think Ray would've wanted you to get hurt."

"And he wouldn't have wanted Ken to get hurt, either," Katie said. "I know Ray Davenport, and he's not a killer."

Sue nodded, shoved the basket into Katie's hands, then turned and left.

Katie stood. "Wait, you—" Her phone vibrated. For an instant, she was torn between wanting to further defend Ray and the impulse to answer her phone. She glanced at the number. Caller ID said it was unknown, and Katie hoped it was an answer to one of her classified ads for the tea shop manager.

Holy crap! She'd completely forgotten about the tea shop and hadn't gone over to get things ready for the lunch trade. She grabbed the phone. "Artisans Alley. This is Katie; can I help you?"

"Good morning. My name is Brad Andrews. Nick Ferrell told me you're looking for someone to manage your tea shop."

"Yes, Mr. Andrews, I am."

"Are you available to see me at Tealicious in one hour?" he asked.

Relief coursed through her. "I'll be there."

~~~~~~~

The instant Katie saw the tall, broad-shouldered, blond man standing in the center of the dining room at Tealicious, Pachelbel's Canon in D major began to play. She thought she was imagining the tune because the man was downright beautiful. But, no, the music was coming from *him.*

"Mr. Andrews?" she asked.

"Yes." He held up his phone. "Lovely classical music— that's what should be playing in here. Not this soft pop drivel."

"Okay." Katie had allowed Janine to choose the music

because the young woman had lobbied so hard for it, it had made her happy, and the customers appeared to enjoy it. Katie had to agree, however, that the song streaming from Brad's phone was much more pleasing than the one currently playing over the tea room's speakers.

"I'm glad we're in agreement. Otherwise, I'd have to turn down your job offer." He smiled, shut off the music, and returned the phone to his pocket.

"I've not yet made you a job offer, Mr. Andrews."

"Call me Brad. And you know you're going to offer me this position because no one is more qualified than me."

"That remains to be seen." She nodded toward the stairs and her attic office. "Follow me."

As they passed the door to the kitchen, Katie saw that Janine was peeking through the small glass window, watching them. Had she been eavesdropping as well?

Within five minutes of meeting him, Katie had moved past Brad's arrogant demeanor and had downgraded him to self-assured. Within fifteen minutes, he'd impressed her so thoroughly she was ready to offer him the job.

But first, she had to know: "Why do you want to work at Tealicious? With your credentials, you could work at any five-star restaurant or hotel in the country."

"True, and as you can see from my résumé, I *have* worked for some of the finest establishments in the state. But the stress nearly killed me." He lowered his gaze to his hands. "I began drinking . . . too much and too frequently."

"Did your drinking interfere with your job performance?" Katie asked, keeping her voice neutral.

He let out a breath. "It was starting to . . . so I quit and checked myself into rehab." He met her gaze again. "I'm one-hundred-twenty days sober."

Katie gave him what she hoped was an encouraging smile. "Congratulations."

He looked at her steadily, his dark blue eyes never wavering. "Well?"

"Welcome to Tealicious. Why don't we go meet the staff?"

Janine had stationed herself near the tea room's register. Her ponytail was gone, and her dirty-blonde hair hung around her shoulders. She'd also put on a fresh coat of lipstick.

"Ah, Janine. I'd like to you meet Tealicious's new manager, Chef Andrews."

Janine's eyelids fluttered and she offered her hand. "Very nice to meet you."

"My pleasure," Brad said.

Katie was about to turn away when Janine spoke up. "Uh, Katie. I just wanted you to know that I've been thinking it over and I may have been a little hasty in my decision not to stay on as a server. I'll be more than happy to remain here in the shop until school starts in September."

Katie gave the young woman the warmest of smiles, and said, "That's all right, Janine. We'll be just fine."

~~~~~~~

Katie couldn't help but breathe a sigh of relief as she returned to Artisans Alley. Brad would be starting on Monday, and she felt confident he would be a wonderful asset to Tealicious. Plus, as petty as it was to admit, after Janine had quit so abruptly, Katie wasn't about to allow her to stick around and make doe eyes at Brad.

As soon as she walked into Artisans Alley, however, a gray cloud settled over her usually sunny disposition. Detective Schuler stood by the main cash desk waiting for her.

"Detective Schuler, are you finding everything okay?" She knew he wasn't at Artisans Alley to shop, but she couldn't resist goading him a bit, especially since he seemed so eager to point a finger of guilt at Ray Davenport.

"I'm afraid I'm here on official business, Ms. Bonner. May we speak in your office?"

"Of course." Katie ignored Rose's worried frown and led Detective Schuler through the Alley's main showroom to her office.

"It's kinda warm in this place, don't you think?" Schuler asked as they walked. "Don't you guys have air-conditioning?"

"We do, actually, and it's not as hot today as it was yesterday."

Once in her office, Katie turned on the fan and sat in her office chair. Schuler refused her offer to let him sit in her visitor's chair.

"Our tech team has examined the saw that killed Ken Fenton," he said with no preamble. "Someone tampered with it. It was rigged to shock him as soon as he turned it on."

"I wish you'd mentioned that before I switched on the fan," Katie said and glowered. "We might have a serial electrocutioner in Victoria Square."

"Oh, I don't think *you* have anything to worry about, Ms. Bonner, because you're friends with . . . well, with a lot of people who have extensive knowledge of electrical processes."

"Such as?"

"Such as Ray Davenport, Vance Ingram—"

"Hold on. Just because Ray and Vance are skilled woodworkers doesn't mean they're expert electricians."

"True," Schuler agreed. "But who else do you know who had a grudge against Ken Fenton and might have sufficient electrical knowledge to rig that saw to kill him?"

"For one thing, I don't know a single soul who had a grudge against Ken Fenton. Furthermore, I couldn't even begin to fathom how much electrical proficiency one would have to have in order to purposefully electrocute another person."

"So, you're saying you don't know?"

"That's exactly what I'm saying."

Schuler took his notebook from his breast pocket. He removed the pen he'd clipped to it and dictated as he wrote: "Friday at eleven twenty-two a.m. Katie Bonner denies knowledge of any personal grudges against Ken Fenton and-slash-or anyone with the ability to weaponize electrical current." He replaced the pen and slipped the notebook back in his pocket. "You *will* call me if you're enlightened about either of those circumstances, won't you, Ms. Bonner?"

Katie's eyes narrowed. "Immediately."

He stood. "See that you do. And, in the meantime, I'd check all my electrical cords before turning on anything," he said, seeming to change his tune. "You just never know."

~~~~~~

Nearly forty-five minutes after speaking with Detective Schuler, Katie was still fuming. Briskly walking the three blocks to Del's Diner hadn't quelled her ire. She had actually *liked* the deputy before he'd been promoted.

The diner's interior was cool and a welcome change from the harsh noon sun and Katie slid in the booth just as Andy walked through the door. He came over, leaned down, and gave her a brief kiss.

"How are you, Sunshine?"

"I'd say I'm ready for the weekend, but since we don't have Saturdays and Sundays off like regular people, would you consider running away with me?" Katie asked.

Andy plunked down opposite her. "Your morning has been that bad?"

"It didn't start out that way." That wasn't entirely true, but she told him about hiring Nick's friend to be Tealicious's new manager. "And he'll start on Monday, so that's fantastic. But when I returned to Artisans Alley, Detective Schuler was there. Ken Fenton's death has officially been ruled a homicide since it was evident that someone tampered with the saw's wiring so it would shock Ken when he turned it on."

"After yesterday, we were expecting that, though. Weren't we?"

"We were. But this morning, Schuler asked me who I

knew who had both a grudge against Fenton and knowledge about electrical processes. I said no one."

"He's going after Davenport in a big way."

"Not only Ray. He mentioned Vance, too," Katie said.

Andy blinked. "Vance? No way."

Katie started. "So you'd believe Ray is actually capable of murder, but not Vance?"

Andy didn't have an opportunity to answer because Sandy, the waitress, arrived to take their order. After requesting a grilled cheese sandwich and a slice of coconut cream pie, Katie decided that if Andy didn't pick the thread of their conversation back up, neither would she. The thought of either Vance or Ray killing anyone was laughable, so she didn't feel the topic was worth debating.

That said, when her lunch arrived, Katie didn't feel like eating. Still, she managed to choke down half the sandwich during their innocuous chitchat, and then asked for the rest of her order to go. And she insisted on picking up the check. At that moment, she wanted nothing from Andy other than goodwill—and right then, she wasn't at all sure he was willing to give it.

~~~~~~

Katie declined Andy's offer to drive her back to Artisans Alley, and instead power walked the distance—her mind set on her next course of action. Instead of returning directly to Artisans Alley, Katie went to Wood U to talk to Ray. Even though Schuler had included Vance in his suspect list, he'd made it clear the evening before that he believed Ray was responsible for Ken Fenton's murder. Or, even if he didn't entirely believe it, he *wanted* Ray to be guilty. Katie wondered what had happened to cause such animosity between the two men. Maybe Ray would tell her. Either way, she felt she should warn him.

When she entered the building, Ray's balding pate shone

under the halogen lighting as he bent over an intricate carving of an eagle.

"Be right with you," he said, without looking up.

"Take your time," Katie said.

Sasha, Ray's youngest daughter, came out of the back with a small chisel in hand. "Dad, is this the one you need?" The teenager abruptly stopped upon seeing Katie.

"Hi, Sasha," Katie said.

Sasha didn't reply until Ray prompted her to do so.

Six months before, Katie had been wildly popular with the three Davenport girls. Then Katie had discovered Sasha was taking diet pills and had informed Ray. The middle daughter, Sadie, had decided that Katie was trying to take their mother's place. And all it had taken for Katie to lose the oldest girl's affection was to hire Janine as the manager of Tealicious. Katie hadn't known that Sophie and Janine had played on different high school volleyball teams and were bitter rivals. Sophie had, at one point, been eager to do her summer internship at Tealicious. But, thanks to Katie's hiring Janine—which turned out to be a horrible decision anyway—Sophie was interning elsewhere. Katie had forgotten how easily the admiration of teenage girls could be won or lost.

Now Sasha glared at Katie as she handed the chisel to her father.

"Ray, since Sasha is here to watch the shop, could you walk with me for just a minute?"

Sasha rolled her blue eyes and blew out a breath.

Ray arched his brow in his daughter's direction, as though to admonish her, before turning to Katie. "Sure. I could use a break. Let's go."

Once they were in the parking lot, Katie said, "I'm sorry to pull you away from your work like that, but I didn't want Sasha to hear this."

"Let me guess—Schuler paid you a visit?"

"Two, actually. One last night and another this morning.

Ken Fenton's death has been ruled a homicide. The saw was rigged to shock Ken as soon as he turned it on."

"Yeah, I already knew that from one of the guys I used to work with at the Sheriff's Office."

"Why is Schuler so . . . ?" She trailed off, not quite knowing how to finish that sentence.

"Why is he so determined to pin this murder on me?"

"Yes."

Ray sighed. "Before I retired, the sheriff asked me if I thought Schuler would make a good replacement for me. I said no. He didn't have the necessary experience. It was my honest opinion."

"Then how did he get the job?" Katie asked.

"His family has some clout with the county executive. The guy I recommended for the job wound up quitting and going to another county in the Southern Tier."

"But would Schuler hold such a huge grudge against you that he'd try to pin a murder rap on you? That doesn't make sense."

He shrugged. "People seldom if ever make sense, Katie."

"I can believe that. Sue Sweeney came by my office this morning. She said the real reason she didn't want Paul Fenton opening a shop in Victoria Square was that he was abusive to her niece when they were dating."

"The loose-cannon gene must be hereditary . . . and it appears to run on both sides of that family," Ray said with chagrin.

Katie frowned and turned to see the heat shimmer off Victoria Square's vast asphalt parking lot. "Why do people have to be so mean?" She heard Ray sigh and turned her gaze back to him.

"It's human nature," he said simply.

"That's not the way I was brought up—the way I feel," she declared.

He sported a cockeyed smile. "You're a good person, Katie. You want—and expect—the best of everyone."

"Is that unreasonable?"

Ray shrugged. "These days . . . maybe."

Katie frowned. "I'm not about to change the way I operate—no matter what kind of world we live in."

Ray grinned. "And I wouldn't expect anything less of you."

Five
~~~~~~

Before heading back to Artisans Alley, Katie took advantage of the beautiful sunny day to walk to Sassy Sally's, intending to thank Nick for recommending Brad for the manager's position at Tealicious. She was glad to see Nick sitting on the front porch with a glass of lemonade in one hand and a book in the other.

"Katie—how are you?" he called, as she neared the porch.

"Not as good as you," she teased.

"Want some lemonade?"

"No, thank you." She mounted the steps and took a seat on the wicker couch beside him. "I came to say I owe you a debt of gratitude. Your friend Brad starts work at Tealicious on Monday."

"I appreciate your letting me know. I'll give him a call.

Maybe Don and I can have him over for dinner one day next week."

"You're a good friend," Katie said, watching as a monarch butterfly landed on a bright red geranium in the wooden planter near her. "I have to ask, though, why would Brad be content to hide away in Victoria Square when more prestigious venues are bound to be clamoring for his services?"

"He provided full disclosure, right?" Nick asked.

"He told me he'd gone to rehab and was one hundred and twenty days sober. But that still doesn't explain why he'd want to work at Tealicious rather than a much more prestigious venue."

"Suffice it to say that Brad really does long for a calmer life, and that his ex-girlfriend is nutty."

Girlfriend? Katie shook her head and ignored the mention. "Then you think Brad will stick around for a while?"

"I believe Tealicious will be perfect for Brad—and vice versa. But even if Brad should ever decide to leave, I can promise you the man will give a minimum of two weeks' notice."

Katie sighed. "I guess I can't ask for more than that."

Nick cocked his head, studying his friend. "Are you okay?"

Katie sat up straight. "Me? Of course."

Nick shook his head. "You look . . . sad."

Katie forced a grin. "Not at all. I just have a lot on my mind."

"If you say so."

Katie stood. "I need to get back to work. Thanks again for steering Brad my way."

"You're welcome. And if you need to talk—you know where to find me."

Katie gave his knee a pat. "Of course. See you later." She headed back down the stairs.

Did she need someone to confide in? To spill her innermost thoughts to?

Maybe. Maybe not.

~~~~~~~

When Katie returned to Artisans Alley and saw a scowling older man standing by the cash desk, she made a mental note to never use the front entrance again. Sure, that idea would fly out the window in a day or so, but for now, she didn't appreciate the second surprise guest in a row. First Schuler and now this short, balding gentleman. By the looks of him, he might be Grumpy from the Snow White fairytale.

"Katie, this is Harper Jones," Rose said, raising her eyebrows as though in some sort of telepathic warning. "He's been waiting to see you."

Harper Jones, the owner of the vacant building where Ken Fenton was electrocuted.

"Mr. Jones, I'm Katie Bonner. It's nice to meet you." She held out her hand, but he didn't shake it—just stared at her. "If you'll follow me, my office is this way." She strode toward her office, assuming he trailed behind her. If he was too ornery to shake her hand, she was too stubborn to look back to see if he'd accompanied her.

Katie unlocked her office door, pushed it open, and turned on the fan . . . which, thanks to Schuler's warning, gave her pause. When she turned back toward her door, Jones had shuffled into the office and settled on the chair by her desk.

Katie closed the door and took a seat. "What can I do for you, Mr. Jones?"

"You can buy my building, that's what you can do," he huffed. "First, you send Ray Davenport over to bully Ken, then Ken gets killed and Paul backs out of his contract. My wife is heartbroken, and your fancy Merchants Association has cost me a profitable business deal. You people need to make this right!"

"I'm sorry you felt Ken was bullied. It was, in fact, Mr. Davenport who left the conversation with a black eye."

Mr. Jones shrugged. "Ken wasn't ever one to pull his punches, figuratively or literally. You always knew where you stood with him. That said, he didn't deserve to die like he did."

"I agree. No one does."

"So, you'll make things right, then?"

"Mr. Jones, the Victoria Square Merchants Association is not at fault for Ken Fenton's death or for Paul Fenton breaking his contract with you to buy your building," Katie said. "However, we might be willing to acquire the property, if you make us a fair offer." She slid a notepad and pen across the desk to him.

He squinted, picked up the pen, wrote a figure, and pushed it back across the desk.

Katie turned a skeptical glance at the man. "You've got to be kidding. That building has been empty for at least two years. There's no way it's worth this much. It wouldn't have been even if Ken had completed the renovations, and we both know he was far from finished." She pushed the paper back. "You'll have to do better than that, Mr. Jones, for me to even consider taking an offer to the Merchants Association."

He ground his teeth together, making veins pop out in his jaw as well as his forehead, as he wrote down a second figure. He shoved the paper at her. "Final offer."

Katie glanced down. The figure was still too high, but it gave her a starting point with the Merchants Association. At least now they could make a reasonable counter.

"I'll call a special meeting of the Merchants Association and be back in touch with you as soon as I know something," Katie said. "Do you have a card?"

"No." He retrieved the paper and scribbled his phone number beneath his final offer.

"Thank you, Mr. Harper. I'll be in touch by early next week."

"See that you do. I don't want to be kept hanging." He got up and left the office.

He left the door standing open, and Katie had to get up to close it before awakening her computer. As she logged in to her email account, she thought about Paul Fenton. There had to be more to the story of why he'd backed out of buying Jones's building. He hadn't struck Katie as the kind of man who would give in or scare easily. So what was going on?

She composed a message to the Merchants Association, asking them to convene for a quick meeting at Del's in the party room at five thirty that evening. "I'll make it quick—I promise," she typed. "It's about the vacant building."

Rose rapped on the door before popping her head into Katie's office. "I'm just making the rounds and wanted to say hi. That old man looked mean. Who was he?"

"Harper Jones, the man who owns the vacant building where Ken Fenton was killed."

"Oh. Did he come to apologize for your almost getting . . . you know, fricasseed?"

Katie chuckled. "Mr. Jones was not in the least concerned about my health. The only thing he seems to care about is that Paul Fenton backed out of buying his building, and now he wants to sell it to the Merchants Association."

"Well, he wasn't at all nice to me or to anyone else while he was waiting on you. I'd think twice before committing to a deal with a man like that." Rose began marching in place. "Are you feeling okay? No aftereffects from being electrocuted?"

"Not unless I'm hallucinating your walking in place."

"Nope, you're not hallucinating. I *am* walking in place," Rose said. "It's good exercise. But I did an Internet search, and I know what sort of weird symptoms you might have. If you hallucinate anything, let me know."

"Will do. And why are you walking in place?"

"I'm training for a marathon."

Katie's eyes widened. "You're running in a marathon?"

"No," Rose admitted, "but I'm *walking* in a five-K for charity."

"Good luck. Let me know if there's anything I can do to help."

"Is there a chance the Merchants Association could sponsor me?" Rose asked.

"I don't see why not. Get me something in writing that I can present to them at tonight's meeting."

"You're meeting tonight?"

"Thanks to Mr. Harper, we are."

Rose smiled. "You bet!"

After she left, Katie decided it was time to do some Internet searching of her own. She Googled Paul Fenton. From a social media site, she learned that the man was currently working as a tattoo artist in Rochester. The place was called Ink Artistry.

Katie took a peppermint from the jar on her desk and then pushed back her chair. It was Friday. Everything seemed to be running smoothly at Tealicious and at Artisans Alley. And she was going to get nothing done today for wondering what was up with Paul Fenton. She bit the peppermint in half. It was time for a trip to Rochester.

~~~~~~

Ink Artistry wasn't what Katie expected. She wasn't a hundred percent sure what she *had* expected, but a cross between a doctor's waiting room and a beauty salon was not it.

"Hello. How may I help you?" asked a young woman with spiked blue hair, gauges in her ears, a thin steel bar through her right eyebrow, and a large rose tattoo on her left arm.

"I'm . . . uh . . . I'm here to see Paul." Katie looked around the room and saw the man. He was drawing on a woman's forearm with what looked like an electric pen of some sort—she'd never seen a tattoo needle before and was guessing that's what it was. "Um . . . hi. I—"

"I'm with a client," he said coldly. "You can wait over there, or you can leave."

Customer service was obviously not his forte.

"I'll wait."

"Good." His steely gaze seemed hard enough to cut through stone. "Pick out your design."

"My design?"

"For your tattoo. If you're here, that must be why."

The spiky-haired woman pointed to a portfolio on a table.

Katie raised her chin. "Very well." She went over to the sofa and picked up the open book of patterns. She had no intention of actually getting a tattoo—she was getting queasy by simply seeing the woman at Paul's workstation get hers. Every so often, he used a tissue to wipe away the blood that pooled under his unrelenting needle. Still, it wouldn't hurt to pretend until she had the opportunity to speak to him.

"Would you like a water?" Spiky-hair asked.

"Yes, thank you."

The woman walked to a refrigerator, took out a water bottle, and brought it to Katie. Katie thanked her again.

"No problem. I'm Regan, by the way. Let me know if there's anything else you need."

"Thanks." Katie began flipping through the design book when she saw a paw print with a little crown at the top. The image brought sudden tears to her eyes as she was mentally transported to when she was a little girl.

"Are you okay?" Regan asked.

"Yeah." She nodded. "It's just . . . this design . . . makes me think of a wonderful cat I had when I was growing up. I called him my little prince."

The woman shrugged. "I'm a dog person . . . but I get what you're saying."

On the one hand, it seemed like forever before Paul finished with his client. But when Katie realized this big, angry man wanted to give her a tattoo now, it seemed like a matter of seconds before the woman was paying Regan and Paul was looming over her.

"Come on back." Paul led the way to his freshly sanitized station.

Katie still clutched the book of designs, and she took it with her. Paul nodded at the chair, and she sat.

"What've you decided on?" he asked.

"I'm sorry about your brother."

For a moment Fenton looked startled, then his facial expression settled into what she thought of as indifference.

"Thank you." He nodded toward the book. "Your design?"

"Shouldn't you have taken today off?" Katie asked. "I know how hard this has to be for you."

"You don't know anything about me . . . or anyone else in my family." A muscle worked in Fenton's jaw as he leaned in toward her. "There's nothing I can do for my brother now, and his funeral isn't until tomorrow."

"Mr. Jones came to see me. He said you've backed out of buying the building on Victoria Square."

"You must be thrilled."

"I'm not. I'm confused. Why don't you want the building anymore? Is it because your brother died there?"

Paul narrowed his eyes. "How about this, huh? My partners and I decided you and your cronies were right—we'd get more business somewhere closer to the marina."

"I think your decision had less to do with location and more to do with your brother."

He clenched one fist. "Look, do you want a tattoo or not?"

"Who do you think killed your brother, Paul?"

His gaze was icy. "You tell me. Now, if you don't want a tattoo, then get the hell out of my chair."

Katie gave him a hard look and did just that.

~~~~~~

Katie didn't want to wait until she returned to McKinlay Mill before making what she considered an important call. As soon as she got back to her car, she rolled the windows down and pulled out her cell phone.

"You'll never believe what I just did," she said, as soon as Ray answered his phone.

"Try me."

"I went to Paul Fenton's tattoo parlor in Rochester."

"You're right," he said. "I don't believe it. You're not that stupid."

Katie was silent. To avow that she really had gone to see Paul would confirm to Ray that she was indeed *that stupid.*

"Katie?" he prompted.

"Maybe you're confusing bravery for stupidity," she said.

"Two sides of the same coin." He blew out a breath. "Sue Sweeney flat-out told you that Paul Fenton was abusive toward women. Please tell me you didn't let him anywhere near your . . . your body . . . with a tattoo needle."

"Of course, I didn't. *Do* you think I'm stupid?"

"No, I don't. But the thought of you being near people with mean streaks like the Fentons scares me. Ken was sneaky and brutal. I can easily imagine his brother would be the same way."

A smile quirked Katie's lips. "Aw, you're worried about me."

"This isn't something to joke about," Ray said sternly.

"I know. But, gosh, Ray, I didn't arrange to meet the man in a dark alley. I met him in his place of employment, and there were other people around."

"People who would take his side against yours."

"You don't know that," Katie huffed.

"And you don't know they wouldn't. I'm only asking you to be careful." He paused. "I have to wonder if you'd even be pursuing this if it wasn't for me."

"You're not the only person with something at stake here." The very idea that she was trying to be Ray's savior in this was laughable . . . wasn't it? "I could've been killed at the same time Ken Fenton was."

"You think I don't know that? You think I haven't imagined your being there . . . being close to him . . ." He sighed. "It makes me sick."

She needed to change the subject. Fast. "Here's what I think—Paul Fenton is scared. Now, you and I both know a man like that probably doesn't scare easily. I believe he thinks that whoever killed his brother is going to come after him next. And I highly doubt he thinks it's a member of the Victoria Square Merchants Association."

"No. If Fenton thought I did it, he'd have been in my face by now . . . probably beating it to a pulp."

"Exactly. So who is Paul frightened of? When we find that out, we'll find out who killed his brother."

"No, Katie. No *we*. Let Schuler do his job."

"If Schuler does his job, you'll be the one rotting in prison for this. And who's going to take care of your girls?"

Ray swore under his breath. "I'll have my friend in the Sheriff's Office look into it."

"Can you trust him to keep it from Schuler until we have something more tangible to go on than a gut feeling?" she asked.

"Yeah. I can trust him."

Katie certainly hoped so.

Six

Katie parked her car in the lot behind Artisans Alley and walked over to Angelo's Pizzeria to talk to Andy. The take-out restaurant was a flurry of activity, and one of Andy's delivery guys brushed past Katie with a pizza—pepperoni, if her nose was correct. The aroma reminded Katie that she'd only eaten half a sandwich that day.

Andy held up a finger to let her know he'd be with her as soon as he could.

She shook her head. "I know you're busy!" she called. "I'll talk to you later."

"I can cover for you," Erikka said, bumping her shoulder against Andy's. "Go on and take a break. You deserve it."

"Thanks." Andy grinned at Erikka before stepping out from behind the counter to lead Katie into his office. Once there, he gave her a lingering kiss, pulled back, and beamed at her. "How are you feeling?"

She grinned. "Much better now." Her stomach growled. She closed her eyes in mortification while Andy laughed.

"I'll get you something to eat before you leave," he said.

"Maybe we could grab something together before the Merchants Association meeting."

"No can do, Sunshine. I'm not going to be able to make the meeting. We've been slammed all day—we had two guys call in sick—and we're expecting extra traffic tonight after that concert in the park."

"Oh yeah. I'd forgotten about that."

He brushed a strand of hair off her face. "I'm sorry to disappoint you."

"You're not disappointing me. I was afraid you wouldn't be able to make it—in fact, there might be a lot of absentee members since I called the meeting on such short notice. If the association decides to buy the building, are you interested in buying in?"

"I'll consider it, provided the terms are good *and* that the Merchants Association doesn't dictate too harshly who can or cannot lease the building."

"That's why you need to be part of the decision-making," Katie said, standing on her tiptoes to kiss his lips. "You won't let that happen."

"You're very persuasive."

"I try. You know, I was shocked that Paul Fenton abandoned his plans so easily." She paused. "In fact, I drove to Rochester earlier to speak to him about it."

Andy stiffened. "You what?"

"I went to talk to him."

"And how'd that go over?"

"Truthfully, not well. He would only say that he and his partners decided they could do more business in a better location, but I don't think that's why they backed out of the deal."

"So, what's your theory, Nancy Drew?" Andy asked.

"I think Ken's death scared Paul."

"Paul doesn't strike me as the type of person who'd be frightened into abandoning his plans. There must be some other reason."

"Maybe, but if that's the case, I'd sure like to know what that reason is."

Andy pulled her into a tighter embrace. "It's not important, Sunshine. You have more pressing concerns."

Katie smiled up at him. "Not since I hired Brad. With his credentials and experience, he could be working anywhere and for a lot more money than I'm paying him. But I'm not about to question my good fortune. I mean, I don't expect him to stay long-term, but when he does leave, I'm sure he'll do so in a professional manner."

"What—Janine giving you only three days' notice wasn't professional?" he teased.

"Oh, Andy, it was priceless. After seeing Brad, Janine *suddenly* decided she *could* stay on as a server until school started back in the fall. I told her that wasn't necessary." She scoffed. "As if I'd keep her on merely to let her make goo-goo eyes at Brad all summer."

"So, he's handsome, then."

"He is," Katie admitted. "As a matter of fact, Nick mentioned Brad had an ex-girlfriend. I thought maybe Brad and Erikka might hit it off . . . I mean, if Erikka isn't seeing anyone at the moment."

"Um . . . I don't know whether she is or not, but I don't think it's a good idea to play matchmaker."

"Well, we won't set them up on a blind date or anything. Maybe we could simply invite them both to lunch . . . on Sunday when Tealicious is closed . . . you know, as a friendly outing. We could see if Nick and Don would like to join us. What do you say?"

Andy scowled. "We'll see."

She giggled. "I'll take that as a yes."

~~~~~~

Before she left the pizzeria, Andy made Katie a pepperoni calzone and she took it back to Artisans Alley to eat at her desk. Once she'd finished her lunch/dinner, she called Nick and told him about her plan for lunch with Brad and Erikka on Sunday.

"Ah, I see what you're doing here. You think if you can get Erikka interested in Brad, she'll take her hooks out of Andy."

"I didn't say that," Katie said evenly. "I'm only trying to welcome Brad to Victoria Square and introduce him to a few people." There was no way she'd admit to Nick that there was some truth to his accusation. "I thought that since you're already friends with him, you and Don might want to join us."

"That's really a lovely idea," Nick said. "Why don't Don and I host the luncheon here at Sassy Sally's?"

"No, I couldn't possibly impose on you like that."

"It's not an imposition. You know how I enjoy entertaining, and I'd love to show off the B and B to Brad. We could invite Seth and his beau, and there's an older couple staying here who might like to join us. They're regulars. Fiona is usually up for anything, but Phil can be a curmudgeon."

"Are you sure?"

"Sure that everyone will come on such short notice? No. Sure that Brad will be interested in Erikka so soon after breaking up with his girlfriend? Also, no. But I *am* sure that I want to host a luncheon welcoming Brad to the neighborhood. So, let me hang up and get in touch with everyone—after talking with Don, of course—and I'll call you with the deets when I have them."

"Thanks, Nick. You're the best."

"Don't I know it?"

Katie was still grinning from her conversation with Nick when Vance arrived at her office door. "Got a minute?"

"For you? Always."

He sat on the chair beside her desk and rubbed his forehead. Was the stress of being a manager taking a toll on him?

"What is it, Vance?"

"One of the new vendors—Hugh, the leather-goods maker—is upset because he thought Artisans Alley was responsible for the security of his tools and the items he crafts for sale."

"That's ridiculous. The vendor contract clearly states that any items left in the booths are there at the vendor's risk and that Artisans Alley is not responsible for any loss."

"I tried to explain that to him, but he says he must've missed that section of the contract."

Katie went to the file cabinet and retrieved the agreement Hugh had signed. She took it back to her desk, sat down, and flipped through the pages. "There's the clause, and there's his signature. You can take that and show it to him if you think it'll help."

"I did that already. It didn't help."

She blew out a breath. "Maybe you could offer to have some of the other vendors reassure him. You'd need to tread carefully so it doesn't appear to Hugh that his concerns aren't being properly addressed, but if he learns that others have been here for years and have never had any problems—"

"I did that, too," Vance interrupted. "And I assured him that, other than a few rare instances of shoplifting, we've never suffered any major losses due to theft. I'm at the end of my rope, Katie. He still isn't happy."

"Then the only thing you can do is offer to terminate his contract. With it being tourist season, we won't have any trouble renting out his booth." She took a peppermint from the jar on her desk and offered one to Vance. "I believe Hugh is simply angling for some sort of special treatment. Call his bluff, and he'll either go or he'll stay. I'm guessing he'll stay because it appears he's doing a good amount of business."

"A lot of people seem to gather around his booth," Vance admitted. He stood. "Thanks, Katie."

"Wait. Before you go, there's something else you should

know." She told him about Detective Schuler's suggestion that he or Ray could have rigged the saw to electrocute Ken Fenton. "I don't think you need to be too concerned about his allegations since Detective Schuler made it abundantly clear that he suspects Ray, but I wanted you to be aware."

"I appreciate that. I'm not worried about Detective Schuler, though. Sure, I have the knowledge necessary to have rigged that saw, and I figure Ray does, too. Heck, there are probably several more Artisans Alley vendors who could do that sort of thing if they wanted to."

"Whatever you do, don't mention that to Detective Schuler," Katie said emphatically.

Vance chuckled. "I won't . . . although he probably already knows it. I can't help but wonder, though, who *did* kill Ken Fenton."

"You and me both. I'd never noticed him around the Square before. Did you know the man?"

"No . . . but I'll ask around to see if any of the other vendors knew him."

"Thanks, and keep me posted," Katie said as Vance left her office.

He gave a wave. She watched as he walked through the vendors' lounge and disappeared into the showroom. She had Googled Ken Fenton's brother—but not the dead man. Typing the name into the browser's search box brought up nothing. So, Ken Fenton had not left his mark on the Internet. She could only wonder what any of her vendors knew about the man.

~~~~~

It was only five twenty and Katie was pleased to see that she was the first to arrive at Del's Diner but apprehensive that she might be the only member of the Merchants Association to do so. Not long after, a number of the merchants wandered in.

At five thirty-five, Katie figured everyone who was going to arrive had already done so and called the meeting to order.

"We've got to make this meeting short and sweet. Del has the room booked for another event in half an hour. I'd like to start by announcing that Rose Nash has asked the Merchants Association to sponsor her in a charity five-K walkathon." She handed a stack of flyers to Sue Sweeney and asked her to pass them around to the other merchants. "As you can see from the flyer that will be coming your way, it's for Alzheimer's research, and Rose is excited to be a part of this event. She's training hard. Do I have a motion?"

"I'll make the motion that we sponsor Rose with fifty dollars from petty cash." Sue looked around the room to see if the others were in agreement.

"I'll second the motion," Gilda said.

The vote to sponsor Rose was unanimous.

"And now for the reason you're all here—I spoke with Harper Jones. I'm passing around the piece of paper on which he wrote his offer." Katie waited while each merchant looked at the note before passing it along to a neighbor.

Ray frowned at the paper. "This is too high, Katie. I realize I don't have a dog in this fight, but Jones is asking more for this building than I paid for Wood U . . . even though Wood U is bigger than this place." He handed the note to Conrad.

"Well, I certainly agree with Ray," he said.

"Then let's come up with a counteroffer I can present to Mr. Jones," Katie said.

After dickering for a few minutes, the merchants reached an offer Katie felt confident everyone could live with.

"I've picked up enough legalese from attorney Seth Landers over the years to present this offer to Mr. Jones contingent upon the Merchants Association being able to obtain a loan to buy the property." She smiled at the group and was ready to close the meeting when Sue spoke up.

"I'd like to inject a caveat to the conversation, which was brought to my attention by Charlotte Booth."

"Of course, Sue. Go ahead."

Sue stood. "As some of you know, Charlotte couldn't be here because she's babysitting her grandson tonight, but she brought up an excellent point to me. She said that since not all of the merchants would be participating in buying the building, those participating should form a separate partnership for this endeavor."

"I agree," Katie said. "But let's not get ahead of ourselves. If Mr. Jones accepts our offer, *then* we can form a partnership. If he doesn't, then it won't matter. Of course, we will need a partnership agreement in place before we approach the bank, so if Mr. Jones does accept, I'll send out an email to everyone in the Merchants Association. Those interested in buying the building can let me know, and I'll set up a meeting with Seth Landers."

Everyone seemed happy with that arrangement, and Katie adjourned the meeting just as the people celebrating a major birthday began to arrive. She slunk out of the function room feeling nothing but relief.

~~~~~~

After the Merchants Association's meeting, and before Katie went up to her apartment, she glanced in the direction of Angelo's Pizzeria. She had planned to wave to Andy, but he stood at the counter, shoulder to shoulder with Erikka. They were laughing at some shared joke. Katie frowned, her stomach doing a little flip-flop. She *really* hoped Erikka and Brad would hit it off.

She climbed the steps to her apartment, fed the cats, and settled onto the sofa. She wasn't in the mood to watch television or to read, so she thought she'd call Margo and update her on the latest happenings at Tealicious. Her former mother-in-law should be thrilled that Katie had landed a world-class chef to manage the tea shop.

Margo answered on the first ring. "Hello, Katie. I don't have but a minute—I'm getting ready to go out with friends. What's up?"

"I just wanted to let you know that I've hired a new manager for Tealicious."

"How nice. The teeny-bopper didn't work out, then?" Her voice had an *I told you so* quality that made Katie even gladder she'd called to tell Margo about Brad.

"No, but it's all worked out for the best. The new guy—Chef Brad Andrews—starts on Monday."

"There was a fabulous chef named Brad Andrews who used to work at that fantastic French place in Manhattan, but that couldn't be the same person."

"Actually, it is." Katie doubted she'd kept the smugness from her voice. "Brad graduated from the Culinary Institute in Hyde Park and also earned a *Diplôme de Pâtisserie* from Le Cordon Bleu in London. He has extensive credits in Manhattan . . . *including* that fantastic French place."

"How delightful for you! I must get down there soon, so I can sample this Chef Andrews's wares."

"Right." That was a development Katie hadn't foreseen. Hopefully, Margo wouldn't come for a visit *too* soon.

"I have to be off now, dear. Love to Andy."

"Have fun, Margo."

"I always do." And with a trilling laugh, she hung up.

Katie set her phone down feeling disconcerted. Margo was going out with friends, Andy was fraternizing with Erikka, and Katie sat in her overly warm apartment—alone.

Mason jumped up on the couch, sashayed over, and stood on Katie's lap.

Okay, she wasn't *entirely* alone.

"Thanks, little butt. You're not my little prince, but you *are* my darling boy."

"Purrbt," Mason said and nuzzled Katie's chin.

She wrapped her arms around the cat, whose purring went into overdrive.

At that moment, it was exactly what she needed.

Seven

Upon awakening on Saturday morning, Katie realized she'd been neglecting her exercise of late because she'd been so busy and stressed out. But then, she'd recognized that not getting her walking in was merely exacerbating her stress. So the first thing she did that morning—after feeding the insistent cats, of course—was to dress, lace up her sneakers, and head out into the bright morning sunshine. There was still enough nip in the air to be bracing, but Katie knew that after a couple of laps around the Square, she'd be sweating and in need of a shower.

Walking was the perfect time for reflection. Now that she'd hired Brad, Katie felt like things were looking up. Upon completion of her walk, Katie would need to make tea cakes and salads for sandwiches. Then she needed to call Harper Jones and present the Merchants Association's counteroffer . . . That could wait until she was ensconced in her office at Artisans Alley.

As she approached Wood U, Katie saw Sadie Davenport getting ready to go inside her father's shop. Katie raised a hand in greeting. Sadie looked directly at Katie, her expression sullen, and continued inside the building. Katie felt a pang of disappointment over the girl's conduct, but that disappointment quickly turned to indignation. She'd never been anything but nice to the Davenport daughters. If they'd chosen to spurn her friendship, so be it. She passed Wood U keeping her chin up and her face forward. She wasn't about to give Sadie the satisfaction of seeing her venturing a glance at the shop window.

She'd walked only a few feet from Wood U when she heard Ray call her name. She turned around but didn't move back toward the shop. Ray trundled down the stairs and jogged to where Katie stood.

"Have you spoken with Harper Jones yet?" he asked.

"No. That's on my to-do list for later today." She didn't say so, but she wondered why Ray would even ask about the call since he'd already said he wasn't interested in going in on the property. Had he seen Sadie snub her and called out to her as an excuse to talk?

"I know you're dying to know why Fenton went back on his deal to buy the building from Jones," Ray said. "I'm thinking Jones can give you a better idea of what happened than Fenton was willing to divulge."

"You could be right. It wouldn't hurt to ask."

"Maybe you could present the question to Jones as if some of the members are concerned there might be something wrong with the building since Paul pulled out so abruptly. Ask about the wiring, since his brother was electrocuted."

Katie nodded. "You're pretty good at this, Davenport. You should be an interrogator."

"Ha, ha," Ray deadpanned. "Even if Jones doesn't know the real reason Paul Fenton decided not to buy, raising these concerns might make Jones more amenable to your counter-offer."

"Entirely plausible," she admitted. "Are you sure you won't reconsider going in on the building with us? The more merchants who are willing to participate, the less each person's payment will be."

"I realize that, but if Schuler has his way about it, I'll need to be saving every cent I've got for legal fees. Don't even get me started on what a trial would do to Sadie's and Sasha's college funds."

"There's not going to be a trial, and you're not going to have to pay legal fees." Katie hoped.

Ray merely shook his head. He obviously didn't feel as if he'd get through Schuler's investigation unscathed, and Katie was afraid he might not, either.

Sadie poked her head out the door of Wood U. "Dad! It's time for your class to start!"

"I'll talk to you later, Ray, and I'll let you know what Harper Jones says about Paul Fenton's backing out of their deal."

Ray gave her a curt nod and headed back inside Wood U.

He'd given Katie a tactic she could use in her negotiation with Jones. Now to hope the man would be receptive to it.

~~~~~~

Three circuits later and drooping after her walk, Katie was reinvigorated by showering with an energy-inducing aroma-therapy gel. She towel-dried her hair and put it up with a tortoiseshell clip. She slipped on jeans and a short-sleeved button-down white shirt, and off she went to Tealicious.

As she toiled in the industrial kitchen, she wondered what it would be like to work alongside Brad. She'd neglected to speak to him about her arriving in the mornings to prepare some of the sandwich spreads and baked goods. Would he welcome her presence, or would she feel Katie was being too intrusive or watchful of him? More likely, as a trained chef, he simply wouldn't need her help. If that was the case, she'd miss the work. She enjoyed baking and preparing food for others to enjoy. Still, she needed to come up with a good way to discuss the matter with Brad at the first opportunity.

Once she had the food prepared, she entered the dining room to make sure the front of the house was in order. Janine came in as Katie was adding water to the flower vases.

"Good morning, Katie. You're up and at 'em early, as always."

Good grief. She'd been up for hours. Why was Janine trying to kiss up to her now? As if she didn't know. Katie buried her unpleasant thoughts and gave Janine a cheery hello.

"I just want you to know that even though this is my last day . . . you know . . . as manager—"

"Well, it *is* your last day," Katie said. "You'll certainly be missed." She wondered if she should've done something nice for the girl, but under the circumstances by which she abruptly quit, Katie thought not. Still, a small gift wouldn't hurt.

"About that," Janine said. "I just wanted to let you know that I can help out whenever you might need an extra set of hands . . . at least until school starts."

"Thanks."

"I appreciate the opportunity you gave me, and I've enjoyed helping you launch Tealicious."

"I'm glad." Katie preferred not to bring up the fact that Janine had never seemed all that happy to be managing the tea shop. "What do you plan to study when you return to school in the fall?"

"Business administration. I think I might enjoy opening my own retail shop one day. Maybe here on Victoria Square." She smiled. "If not that, I feel I'd do well in human resources."

As difficult as it was, Katie managed to return Janine's smile. "Good luck." She'd certainly need it. She couldn't have chosen any careers she'd be less suited for.

~~~~~

Reneging on the promise she'd made herself to refrain from going through the front door at Artisans Alley, Katie strode through the lobby on her way to her office. A flash of blue caught her eye. Turning to her right, she saw Regan, the girl from Ink Artistry.

"Hello!"

Regan turned and squinted for a second. "Oh, hello. You're the woman who left Ink Artistry without getting a tattoo."

"I am. Katie," she supplied.

"Katie . . . right."

"And you're Regan . . . ?"

"Regan Mitchell. So, why'd you leave the tattoo parlor?"

"If you want the truth, Paul Fenton scared me. I don't think he likes me."

Regan laughed. "Paul comes across as gruff, but he's a really nice guy when you get to know him. And he's an excellent tattoo artist. If you reconsider, I'm sure he'd do a good job for you."

"Have you known him long?"

She shrugged. "Since I went to work for Ink Artistry, so . . ." She looked at the ceiling as she calculated. "Just over three years now."

"Are you an artist, too?"

Regan laughed. "Me? No. I'm working as the office manager. I'm taking classes at night to become a tax accountant." She held out her arms to show off a number of tattoos, which included a parrot and an ivy vine. "I might need to change my image a smidgen when I start looking for work in the button-down world, don't you think?"

"Maybe, maybe not." People from all walks of life seemed to have tattoos these days.

They both laughed.

"Do you come to this place often?" Regan asked.

"Every day. I'm the manager."

"Oh, cool. It's my first time here, and I don't know where to begin exploring."

"It all depends on what you're looking for—we have everything from lace to leather and stained glass to woven items." She jerked her head toward the stairs. "Why don't I give you the grand tour?"

"Lead the way."

"Do you live nearby?" Katie asked as they worked their way toward the west end of the building.

"I live in the town of Greece."

"That's where I'm from," Katie said.

"The rest of my family lives here in McKinlay Mill. I came to Victoria Square today to have lunch with my brother before he starts his shift."

"Where does your brother work?"

"Angelo's Pizzeria," Regan said.

"What a small world! My boyfriend is Andy Rust, the owner."

"Andy's been wonderful to Roger—my brother. He got in trouble for possession of drugs and spent time in juvenile detention. Roger's now on probation, and he's lucky Andy was willing to hire him."

"Yeah," Katie said. "Andy's a great guy."

"Roger is also fortunate that when he told Andy how much he loves building, Andy introduced him to a contractor. Thanks to Andy's influence, Roger is already working with the contractor when he's not working at Angelo's Pizzeria. When Roger graduates from high school next year, he'll be able to join the apprentice program and work for this contractor full-time."

"That's fantastic."

As they neared the cabinet that contained Ida Mitchell's handmade lace, Ida, who'd been hovering nearby, narrowed her eyes behind the thick glasses perched on the bridge of her skinny nose and gave her head enough of a shake that it made the massive wart on her cheek wobble. She clearly disapproved of Regan's punk-rock appearance.

Still, Regan surprised Katie—as well as Ida—when she approached the shelf and carefully picked up a piece of Ida's intricate lace. "Oh, wow! This is incredible work."

"You . . . you *like* it?" Ida asked. It was so rare that she sold a piece that she seemed even more astounded than Katie.

"I love it," Regan said. "It's such exquisitely delicate work. Did you make it? How do you do it?"

Ida smiled and placed a hand at her chest. "Oh, my dear, once you get the hang of it, it isn't as hard as it looks. In fact, it can be quite relaxing."

"I read an article about it online and was fascinated," Regan said, still fingering the lace. "I'd love to know more about the art."

Ida practically beamed.

"And I'd be glad to tell you all about it."

"On that note, I'll leave you two ladies to discuss it," Katie said. "Regan, if you get a chance before you meet your brother, please stop in my office. And, if not, I hope to see you again soon."

"Good-bye, Katie," Ida said. "Regan, is it? Come around here, and I'll tell you all about my process."

Regan grinned and waved to Katie. It was all Katie could do not to shake her head in amazement. Regan with her wild blue hair and gleaming piercings had tamed the dragon that was Ida Mitchell. Good for her!

As she passed through the vendors' lounge, Katie poured herself a cup of coffee, entered her office, and closed the door firmly behind her. The tiny room wasn't yet an inferno, so she didn't turn on the fan. She sat down behind her desk, sipped her coffee, took a deep breath, and dialed the number Harper Jones had given her the day before. He answered on the third ring, had her repeat her name twice, and then asked if she'd called to accept his offer on the building.

"No, sir. I'm calling with a counteroffer."

"You're what?"

Katie raised her voice. "I'm calling with a counteroffer."

"What is it?"

Not sure whether he was asking her again why she was calling or asking what the counteroffer was, Katie went with the latter. Harper Jones might have been hard of hearing, but he understood well enough that he wasn't getting the amount of money he was asking for. As he blustered on about how the deal was unfair, Katie tapped a pen against her desk pad.

"Please look at the situation from our perspective," Katie said, as soon as she could get a word in. "A man was electrocuted in that building."

"I know. Ken *was* my brother-in-law, for pity's sake!"

"I realize that, Mr. Jones. Has the wiring been tested to ascertain that it's up to code?"

"You think it's *my* fault that Ken is lying dead in that morgue?"

"Of course not," Katie said. "I'm sure Mr. Fenton's accident was in no way your fault."

"Accident my left eye," he muttered. "Ken was murdered, and everybody knows it. You Merchants Association lot are simply trying to take advantage of a grieving old man."

"Then perhaps we should talk about this when you've had more time to process your loss. I only took your offer to the Merchants Association because you approached me about buying the building."

"Yeah, yeah," the old man groused.

Katie didn't know if Jones really thought she and the other merchants were trying to take advantage of him, or if he was using his grief as a bargaining chip. She decided to find out.

"Mr. Jones, perhaps you should take a step back, continue renovating the building, and then see if you can find a buyer willing to pay your asking price."

"Aw, now don't go getting your knickers in a twist," Jones said. "Well, I guess . . . I guess I'll accept your offer."

Katie blinked, taken aback. She hadn't expected Jones to cave—at least not without more of a fight.

"Does that mean you're willing to accept the offer proffered by certain members of the Victoria Square Merchants Association provided a loan for the property can be expediently obtained?"

"Don't think you can hoodwink me with your legal mumbo-jumbo, missy," Jones huffed. You people have a month to bring me the money. Any longer than that and the offer is thereby rescinded. See? I know legal words too."

"One other thing," Katie said. "Why did Paul Fenton go back on his promise to buy the building?"

"Would you want to go do work every day where someone you loved was killed?"

Katie opened her mouth to answer, but Jones didn't give her a chance.

"No, you wouldn't." With that, he hung up.

Katie replaced the receiver and hadn't fully recovered from the conversation's abrupt end when the phone rang once again. For one wild second, she thought it might be Jones calling back to apologize for hanging up on her. Instead, it was Nick, and he barely gave her time to say hello before he began rattling off his plans for the next day's luncheon.

"Of course, I've got a confirmation from Brad. You and Andy will be there. I've invited Seth and his SO—significant other, but you know that . . . Wait. Why are you being so quiet?"

"I'm sorry. I just had a strange conversation with Harper Jones," she said.

"The mean old man who owns the building where his brother-in-law was killed? Hmm . . . might need to look a little closer at Mr. Jones's alibi for the time of the murder."

"No, it isn't that. I got the feeling Paul Fenton had been scared off from buying the building . . . that maybe he believed that whoever killed his brother might be coming after him next."

"Why?" Nick asked. "What's so special about that old building? I mean, no offense to you or to the other merchants on the Square, but I can attest to the fact that these old buildings are money pits. Don't get me wrong—Don and I love Sassy Sally's, but it's constant upkeep. It's not like the walls are made of gold or anything."

"You're right," Katie mused. "The building shouldn't have anything to do with Ken Fenton's death or with Paul Fenton's decision to back out of buying it . . . you know, other than the fact that his brother was killed there."

"Yeah, sweetie, don't worry about that. One of my guests told me the other day that Ken Fenton was involved with some shady people at one point."

"What kind of shady people?"

"I don't know. My friend Fiona can tell you more about Ken. She'll be at the luncheon tomorrow. Maybe you can ask her then."

"Maybe so. Thanks, Nick."

After speaking with Nick, Katie sent an email to everyone in the Merchants Association asking that interested buyers meet her on Monday at noon at Tealicious. They had a contract to pound out.

Eight

Not long after Katie sent the email to the Merchants Association, there was a tap on her door. She called for her visitor to come in and was glad to see it was Regan.

"Hi, there," Katie said. "How did you and Ida get along?"

"Great. She's going to teach me how to tat lace."

Katie's eyebrows shot up. "Really? That's wonderful."

"Yeah. So, I was wondering if you'd like to join me and Roger for lunch."

"I'd love to." Katie put her computer to sleep, grabbed her purse, and led Regan out the side entrance.

"I'm proud of Roger," Regan mused, as they walked to Angelo's Pizzeria. "He's come so far."

"He's lucky to have such a supportive sister."

"I'm lucky, too. He's a good kid."

They walked into Angelo's and Andy came out from behind the counter to greet Katie with a kiss.

"To what do I owe this pleasant surprise?" he asked.

"We're here to have lunch with Roger," Katie said. "Have you met his sister Regan?"

"I have." He smiled at Regan. "Good to see you again."

"Nice to see you, too, Mr. Rust."

"Please call me Andy." He looked back toward the counter. "Erikka, can you manage without me for a few minutes? I want to have lunch with this rowdy crowd."

"You got it, boss." Erikka gave him a wink and a smile. "By the way, Katie, Nick invited me to his luncheon tomorrow welcoming your new Tealicious manager."

"I hope you can make it. Brad's a terrific guy . . . easy on the eyes, too."

"Uh-oh . . . sounds like Andy had better watch out," Erikka said.

"Hardly. Andy has nothing to worry about." Katie smiled up at her boyfriend, hoping Erikka hadn't put crazy suspicions in his head. Of course, he already knew Katie was hoping Erikka and Brad would hit it off.

A lanky boy with dark hair and large brown eyes came up and draped his arm around Regan's neck. "Hey, kiddo."

"Hey, yourself. Katie, I'd like you to meet my brother Roger. Roger, this is Katie. She's Andy's girlfriend, and she runs the artisans' arcade next door."

"Cool." He stuck out a hand.

Katie gave his hand a shake. "It's a pleasure to meet you, Roger. I've heard good things about you."

Roger gave his sister a teasing grin. "You been lying to this woman?"

"Nope. Everything I told her was a hundred percent true."

"Regan is very proud of you, Roger," Katie said.

Andy asked if everyone liked pepperoni, and when they said yes, he asked Erikka to make them a large pizza. "Roger, you and I can get the drinks. Ladies, sit wherever you'd like."

"Very funny," Katie said. There were only two small tables in the place.

Regan took a seat and she and Katie faced each other. The men returned with cans of pop and sat down beside the women.

"So, Katie," Roger said, after taking a long drink from his pop, "how do you know Regan?"

"I met her yesterday at Ink Artistry."

"Awesome. What did you get?" he asked.

Katie laughed. "Scared off. I turned into a complete chicken."

"I, for one, am glad about that," Andy said.

"Why did you change your mind?" Roger asked Katie.

"Paul intimidated her," Regan said.

"Aw, he's an all right guy." Roger took another drink of his pop. "He can come across as a butthead sometimes, but he's cool."

"I'm sure he is . . . and that he's an excellent tattoo artist . . . but I don't think he likes me very much," Katie said. "It's my own fault. I told him I was sorry for his loss—you know, his brother just died—but then I went on to ask him some questions that were none of my business."

"Like what?"

"Roger," Regan chided her brother.

"No, it's okay," Katie said. She lowered her voice. "Paul's brother was murdered. I wanted to know who might've wanted him dead. I mean, I *was* there when Ken was electrocuted."

"She's lucky she wasn't seriously injured . . . or worse," Andy added gravely.

"Whoa, that's mega," Roger said. "I'm glad you're okay. For what it's worth, there are probably a lot of people who wanted Ken Fenton to take a dirt nap. The guy was an A-number-one jerk." He looked at his sister. "I'm sorry to say that about Paul's brother, but it's true."

"Why? What did he do?" Regan asked.

"He totally screwed over the contractor I work for when I'm not working here with Andy."

"What did he do to John?" Andy asked.

"He got inside info to undercut John's bid on a big project," Roger said.

"That sucks," Andy said.

"It's terrible," Katie said. "John must've been furious."

"He was." Roger shrugged. "He said it wasn't that Ken got the job but that he cheated to get it."

"I agree. I've heard Ken didn't have a good reputation." Katie sipped her soda. "It's surprising how completely different siblings can be." Although, given what Sue had said about her niece and Paul, Katie wondered if Ken and Paul really were all that different. "What about Harper Jones's wife? She's Paul and Ken's sister. What is she like?"

Erikka brought their pizza then, and Roger got up to grab another can of pop, so Katie's question went unanswered. It was then Katie decided she should pay Mrs. Jones a visit and see for herself what the Fentons' sister was really like.

⁓⁓⁓⁓⁓

After lunch, Katie strolled over to Wood U to get a small gift for Janine. It was the girl's last day, after all, and Katie decided she should do something to commemorate Janine's all-too-brief tenure at Tealicious.

As she entered the shop, Katie was relieved that none of Ray's daughters were around. Ray greeted her and, since there was another customer in the shop, Katie browsed around the store.

After the other customer had paid for his purchases and left, Katie commented, "I failed to mention it when I saw you this morning, but your eye is looking better. At least, the swelling is going down."

"Thanks. Are you just here to comment on my ugly mug?"

"No. I actually came by to get a gift for Janine."

"I heard she up and quit on you. Did she change her mind? Is that the reason you're giving her a gift?"

"No, she didn't change her mind. The gift is a good-bye-and-good-luck present."

Ray scoffed. "You're goofy."

"Maybe so, but I don't want to burn bridges. Besides, Janine might have done me a favor in the long run. I've hired a highly qualified chef who'll be taking over on Monday." She selected a small ornate plaque on which Ray had carved "Live, Laugh, Love." She took it to the counter to pay for it.

"I could carve you up one that says 'Thanks for Nothing' in about an hour if you'd like."

Katie laughed. "I think I'll stick with what I've got. Can you gift wrap it, please?"

She was still smiling when she left Wood U and crossed the parking lot to Tealicious to deliver Janine's gift.

"You're giving me a present?" Janine asked and immediately teared up upon seeing the small gift-wrapped box.

"Of course. Thank you for everything you've done to help get Tealicious off the ground."

"You're being awfully generous. In retrospect, I didn't do all that much. You're the one who got Tealicious off the ground," Janine said ruefully. "I'm sorry things didn't work out."

"Me, too." Katie gave Janine the briefest of hugs and wished her well. As she turned to leave, she smiled to herself that the pop music she heard from the speakers would be changed to classical on Monday. She was looking forward to working with Brad. She had a good feeling about him, anticipating that she'd learn a lot with his guidance.

She remembered how Erikka had winked and smiled at Andy at the pizzeria earlier. It would be terrific if Brad and Erikka fell in love at first sight.

As she made her way back to Artisans Alley, Katie thought about what Roger had said about Ken and about Regan's opinion of Paul. True, Sue had said that Paul was abusive to her niece, but Regan had worked with Paul for quite some time. Surely, she'd have had occasion to see him at his worst at some point. Could Paul be that adept at hiding his true nature? Or had Paul asked Regan to befriend Katie to discover what she could about the members of the Merchants Association and what they might know about Ken's death?

She wasn't sure she liked that idea.

~~~~~~~

The longer Katie sat in her office at Artisans Alley and tried to work, the more she thought about the Fenton siblings. Despite the fact that Ken Fenton had been buried that morning, Katie decided a visit to Harper Jones's wife could wait no longer. She used the phone number Jones had given her to track down his home address, and then Katie headed for Sweet Sue's Confectionery to buy a box of candy.

The bells over the door tinkled cheerfully as Katie entered the shop.

"Hello, Katie. What brings you by?" Sue greeted her.

"I'd like a two-pound box of assorted chocolates to take to Harper Jones's wife. I thought I should do something to express my condolences."

"That's nice. Do you want to choose them yourself or do you trust my judgment?"

"Yes, please choose. You know what your customers enjoy most."

Sue nodded, pulled a pretty gold-and-white box from under the counter, and began selecting various candies.

"You mentioned your niece once dated Paul Fenton. How long ago was that?"

Sue tilted her head as she gave the matter some thought. "Well over a year ago. Why?"

"It's just that I met someone who sings the guy's praises, and I wonder if it could be possible that he's changed."

"I highly doubt that," Sue said with a snort. "But Paul Fenton isn't the first man I've ever known with the ability to fool people, and I doubt he'll be the last."

"That's true."

"My best friend's first husband was a controlling, abusive jerk," she continued, warming to her subject matter. "At least, that's what he was behind closed doors. To the rest of the world, the man came across as Mr. Terrific. In fact, when my friend finally got the courage to leave him—mind you, this was after he'd held a loaded gun to her head—everyone who knew them blamed her for the breakup. They couldn't understand how she could leave such a wonderful man."

"You're kidding!"

"I wish I were. My friend was so devastated that she had to move away and start her life over elsewhere."

"What a shame," Katie said. "Talk about your Dr. Jekyll and Mr. Hyde!"

"Yep. And Paul Fenton is cut from that same cloth. Even my sister thought Paul was perfect for my niece until she saw the bruises on her daughter's arms. I'm just glad she managed to be rid of him before the violence escalated."

Katie had known women who'd been abused and hadn't been so lucky.

Sue rang up the sale and Katie paid for her purchase. "See you later," Sue called as Katie exited the shop.

As she approached her car, Katie wondered about the timing of her visit. Was it too soon? After all, Ken Fenton's funeral had only happened hours earlier. Still, she was the last person to be with and talk to the man.

As Andy had said, she was lucky she hadn't been killed, too.

~~~~~~~

When Katie arrived at the Jones's contemporary ranch, she was relieved to find Mr. Jones wasn't at home. Fortunately, the lady of the house was there.

"It's nice to meet you . . . although I'm sorry it's under such sad circumstances," Katie said, after introducing herself to Mrs. Jones.

"Thank you." The woman accepted the chocolates and invited Katie inside. "I'm Mary, by the way."

"I'm so terribly sorry for your loss."

Mary leaned closer, squinting at Katie. "Wait . . . I recognize you from the newspaper report. You're . . . you're the one who was with him . . . Ken . . . when he . . . when he died."

"Yes, I am."

Mary led the way to the living room, then turned to face Katie. "Please tell me—did he suffer?" Before Katie could answer, Mary turned away, as if she couldn't bear the answer to her question, and placed the candy box on the coffee table between the sofa and an overstuffed chair.

"I don't believe he did," Katie said softly. "I was knocked unconscious as soon as I was struck by the current, and I feel certain that Ken must've been, too." Actually, Katie wasn't sure of anything, but she wanted to give this woman some peace and reassurance about her brother's death. After all, there was nothing anyone could do to change it.

"Why were you there?" Mary eased over to the sofa and sank back against the cushions. "Please have a seat."

Katie perched on the edge of the chair, which turned out to be a rocker, not especially wanting to get comfy and stay awhile. "I'd gone by to see Ken in order to clear up any misunderstandings he might've had about the Victoria Square Merchants Association's feelings about Paul's shop."

"What feelings did your hoity-toity association have about my brother's tattoo parlor?" Mary asked, her voice hardening.

"Well . . . while the Merchants Association would never assume to know what was best for Paul and his business, we felt he would get more foot traffic if he opened his shop closer to the marina," Katie said.

"Why did they send you there after they'd already sent that other man to strong-arm Paul into selling them the building?"

"No one was sent to strong-arm Paul," Katie said emphatically. "Mr. Davenport simply dropped in to speak with your husband about reconsidering the sale of the building. He didn't realize who Ken was or that he was Paul's brother."

"Right." Mary's eyes narrowed. "It seems to me that your Merchants Association would have done anything to keep my brother from opening his tattoo parlor on Victoria Square. And I'd even believe you people might have had something to do with Ken's death if it wasn't for that other—" She broke off and lowered her eyes.

"That other what?" Katie prompted.

"Nothing." Mary stood. "I'm feeling tired now and need to lie down. Thank you for dropping by with the chocolates. I'm sure you can see yourself out."

Katie blinked at the abrupt dismissal. She stood. "Again, I'm so sorry for your loss, Mary."

"Like hell."

Katie had nothing more to say and found her way out. She felt glad she hadn't had to run into Harper Jones as she got in her car and backed out of the driveway.

She took one last look at the house and saw Mary watching from the window, and wondered who it was that the woman was afraid to mention.

Was it the same person her brother Paul feared?

Nine

As she drove back toward Victoria Square, Katie used hands-free calling to phone Rose. As usual, Andy worked Saturday evenings—his busiest night of the week—and after Katie's unsettling visit with Mary, she decided she needed some company.

"Artisans Alley, this is Rose speaking. Can I help you?"

"Hi, Rose. It's Katie. I was wondering if you're free to-night if you'd like to have dinner with me at Del's."

"I'd love to."

"Great. I'm on my way back to Artisans Alley. When I get there, we'll walk over together."

"Sounds like fun. It's so tiring to eat alone night after night."

Katie grimaced. She groused about how seldom she and Andy had time alone together when Rose, a widow, spent every night on her own.

Once back at Artisans Alley, Katie left the closing of the business to Vance, and she and Rose set off for the diner.

At Del's, Betty, the nighttime waitress, recommended the freshly made lemonade. Katie and Rose accepted and then decided to throw dieting and nutrition to the wind and indulge in cheeseburgers and fries.

"Thank you for convincing the Merchants Association to sponsor me in the walkathon," Rose told Katie.

"They didn't need convincing. I simply told the group what you were doing, and everyone was eager to support you."

"Well, I certainly appreciate their vote of confidence, and I hope none of the merchants come by and see me pigging out."

Katie laughed. "Given the intensity with which you've been training, I'm sure you don't have anything to worry about." She sipped her lemonade. "How are things going between Vance and the vendors? Any better?"

Rose looked thoughtful. "For the moment, but the vendors sure miss having you around, Katie. It's not just your management style, but your presence. The vendors not only respect you, but they care about you."

"That's nice to hear, but they've always liked Vance, too."

"As a peer," Rose pointed out. "Now that he's been officially placed in a position of authority over them, some of the vendors resent it."

Katie frowned. "Do you think I should call a meeting of the vendors to address the matter?"

Rose shook her head. "No. I believe it's going to take some time, that's all."

"It's been almost six months," Katie pointed out.

Rose grinned. "Apparently, it's going to take longer than that."

"I hope I'll be able to spend more time at the Alley once Brad gets the hang of running Tealicious."

"I hear the new chef is a looker."

Before Katie could respond, Betty brought out their meals.

"Do you two need anything else at the moment?"

"I'd like a refill on my lemonade," Katie said.

She waited until Betty brought the pitcher over, refilled her glass, and had gone back to the kitchen before telling Rose that she went to visit Harper Jones's wife earlier.

"I wondered where you'd gone," Rose said. "How'd it go?"

"Not well. In fact, Mary Jones said she wouldn't be surprised if someone from the Merchants Association was responsible for her brother's death if it weren't for that other thing."

Rose raised her eyebrows. "What other thing?"

"I have no idea. When I asked, she told me to leave."

"Have you told Detective Schuler this?"

"Not yet," Katie said. "I was a little shaken by the whole encounter and wanted to clear my head first." She dipped a fry into a small paper cup of ketchup. "I plan to call him when I get home. Maybe he can figure out what this 'other thing' is."

"And, hopefully, it'll get Ray Davenport off the hook." Rose carefully removed the onion slice from her burger.

"Yeah, that's the only part that worries me about putting the responsibility for discovering this mysterious other thing in the hands of Detective Schuler. He doesn't seem to *want* to get Ray off the hook."

"Still, he has to uphold the law," Rose reminded her. "It's his sworn duty no matter how he feels about a suspect. By the way, I heard you visited Paul Fenton at his tattoo parlor yesterday."

"You heard correctly."

Rose leaned forward. "What was it like? Was it seedy?"

"Not at all," Katie said with a laugh. "It was kind of a cross between a salon and a doctor's waiting room. Everything was clean, organized, and professional."

"And did you . . . you know . . . get inked?" Rose asked eagerly.

"I did not. Frankly, I wouldn't let Paul Fenton anywhere

near me with a needle. The man doesn't like me at all." She inclined her head. "Did you see the girl with me at lunchtime today?"

"The one with the spiky hair and the piercings?"

Katie nodded. "Her name is Regan, and she works at Ink Artistry. She thinks Paul is a great guy. Sue Sweeney says he has people fooled. Her niece dated him, and Sue says he was abusive."

"I can believe it. The girl—Regan?—she seemed nice."

"She is. She's interested in lacemaking and made friends with Ida."

"Good Lord—she must be exceptional."

"Her brother Roger is working with Andy."

"It's so good of him to mentor all those at-risk kids," Rose said. "You've got a wonderful man there, Katie."

She smiled. "Yes, I do."

~~~~~~~

When Katie returned home, she fed Mason and Della before pouring herself a glass of white wine. She considered doing another power walk around the Square to work off the heavy meal she'd just eaten, but she decided she was too tired. She'd fit in an extra lap the next morning.

She placed the wineglass in the center of the stove, where she was fairly certain the cats wouldn't turn it over, and went to take a shower. She'd told Rose she was going to call Detective Schuler when she got home but decided she'd rather wait until morning. There was no need to make him think it was some sort of emergency or that she had vital new information when she really had nothing concrete to give him.

Katie got out of the shower, towel-dried her hair, and slipped into her favorite summer pajamas—light blue satin shorts with a matching short-sleeved button-down top. She snagged her book off the bedside table, retrieved her wine as she passed through the kitchen, and headed for the living room sofa. She placed the glass on a coaster, snuggled against the sofa cushions, and welcomed Della and Mason. Now that the cats' bellies were full, they were ready for some cuddle time.

There was a rap on the door. Guessing it was Andy coming to see her during a quick break from work, Katie didn't bother going back to the bedroom for her robe.

She walked to the door and said, "Is that you?"

"Yeah."

Katie's eyes widened when she opened the door and saw Paul Fenton standing there. He looked her over and sneered. "If you've been trying to get my attention, you've got it."

She tried to slam the door shut, but he pushed it open wider and stepped inside.

"I have not been trying to get your attention. If you'd like to talk, please meet me downstairs at Angelo's Pizzeria," she said. "I'll go get dressed."

"Not necessary. What I have to say won't take long." Paul pushed the door closed with his foot and barged through her kitchen, striding into the living room. She followed a few steps behind and was taken aback when Paul lunged at her and grasped her by her upper arms.

Katie struggled and accidentally knocked the lamp off the table. The light went out. Had Katie not left the light on in the kitchen, she and Paul would've been plunged into darkness. As it was, the living room was too dark for comfort.

Paul pinned her against the wall.

"Let me go, or I'll scream."

"Who's gonna hear you over the noise from the pizza place?"

"What is it you want from me?"

"I want you to leave me and my family alone."

She opened her mouth to speak but closed it again.

"What? Were you going to deny sending that old man to talk to Ken? That you sought me out at Ink Artistry and interrupted my work? That you visited my sister today? Mary's been sick, by the way . . . and she's grieving the loss of our brother."

"And I went to visit your sister to offer my condolences," Katie said.

"If that's true, then why did Mary call me in tears after you left?"

"I don't know. Maybe she didn't care for the chocolates I brought her. Or maybe she's terrified over that thing that got your brother killed."

Fenton paled. "I'm warning you for the last time to stay away from me and my family." He gave her a rough shake before tossing her aside. He tramped through the kitchen to the open door and stalked down the steps.

With shaking hands, Katie pushed the door closed and locked it. Then she rubbed her arms, wishing she could stop trembling. Feeling suddenly cold, she moved to the sofa to contemplate her next move. Fenton's visit had lent credence to the argument that there was something far more sinister than the Victoria Square Merchants Association behind Ken Fenton's death, and that his sister knew it.

She picked up the phone to call Detective Schuler. Her "it can wait until tomorrow" could no longer wait.

Suddenly there was a pounding on her door.

"I'm calling the police right this instant!" she yelled. "Just stay where you are, and the arresting officers won't need to come looking for you!"

"Katie, it's Ray! What's going on?"

Katie hurried to the door. She was surprised to see that Ray was holding one of her cats.

"Mason!" she cried, upset to think she'd nearly lost her darling boy. She gathered the cat in her arms. "He must've got out when Paul muscled his way in."

"Paul Fenton?" Ray demanded.

Katie nodded and then became uncomfortably aware of her state of undress. "I need to grab a robe." She gave Mason a kiss on the top of his head and set him on the floor before she went into the bedroom to get a calf-length white robe to slip on over her pajamas. She was relieved to see Della peeking out from under the bed, looking anxious. She'd probably run into the room when Paul had arrived. Katie breathed a prayer of thanksgiving to know that both cats were now safe.

When she returned to the still-dark living room, Andy and Roger had arrived. Roger was trying to get the lamp to work.

Andy hugged her. "What happened?"

Katie hesitated. She didn't want to say anything damaging about Fenton in front of Roger, but then, he deserved to know what a jerk his sister's boss really was.

"Paul Fenton came to speak with me," Katie said. "And I accidentally knocked the lamp off the table." She looked at the three male faces crowding around her. "Why are you all here?"

"I came to pick up a pizza for dinner and saw Mason," Ray said. "I wasn't completely sure it was your cat, but I thought I'd better check. I brought him here to see."

"I'll never be able to thank you enough," Katie said sincerely.

"When I saw Davenport with Mason, I knew something was wrong," Andy said. "You'd never let Mason slip outside, and if you did, you'd be racing after him."

Roger smiled. "I came back from a delivery and saw Andy running up your stairs. I followed to help with whatever was going on with my boss."

"What did Fenton want?" Andy asked, his voice hard.

Katie glanced at Roger.

"Hey, don't mind me," the young man said. "I know Regan thinks the world of the guy, but I barely know him. He's always struck me as kinda sketchy."

"When he knocked on the door, I thought it was you," Katie told Andy. "He muscled his way inside, and I told him that if he wanted to talk to me, I'd get dressed and meet him downstairs at the pizza parlor. He said what he had to say wouldn't take that long, and then he warned me to stay away from him and his family."

Andy stiffened. "Did he hurt you?"

She shook her head. "Still, I was getting ready to report the incident to Detective Schuler when Ray brought Mason home."

"I think you should go ahead and call him." Andy nodded at Ray. "And you should probably get on home with that pizza before your girls send out a search party."

"Yeah," Ray said. "I guess so."

"Thank you again for bringing Mason home."

"No problem. Call if you need me." Ray nodded to the men and then departed.

"I'd better get back to work, too," Roger said. "Don't want to get in trouble with the boss. By the way, Katie, your lamp seems to be shot. I'll be happy to take it with me and see if I can fix the socket."

"Are you sure? That sounds dangerous."

"I actually enjoy that kind of stuff."

"Then I'd appreciate your looking at it," Katie said. "Thank you, Roger."

"Hey, Rog, let Erikka know I'll be there as soon as I can, all right?"

"Sure thing, boss." Roger took the lamp and left.

As soon as they were alone, Andy pulled Katie to him for a warm embrace. "Are you sure you're all right?"

"Positive. Especially now that I'm in your arms."

"Did Fenton put his hands on you?"

"He grabbed me by the biceps, but it was no big deal. He didn't hurt me." Katie downplayed her fear and the fact that her arms were sore from being in Fenton's grip. She didn't want to put Andy in danger should he decide to confront the thug. "You ought to get back to work. Now that it's dark, I'm going to read in the bedroom."

"And call Schuler."

"That, too," she agreed.

"I'll be up to check on you after work." Andy kissed her and she watched him go, locking the door behind him.

Katie allowed herself a few long moments to collect her wits before she took her wine, book, and phone into the bedroom. After making sure the cats were in the room with her, she closed the door.

She turned on the overhead light and then flipped on the bedside lamp. She hesitated before turning out the overhead light, then slipped out of the bedroom to double-check that the back door was locked. When she returned to the bedroom, Katie called Detective Schuler.

"Schuler," he answered crisply.

"Oh, hi, Detective, it's Katie Bonner. I was expecting your voice mail. I'm calling because Paul Fenton just left my home, after issuing a threat."

"Interesting. I just got off the phone with Mr. Fenton, who was complaining about you harassing him and his family. He told me that if you go near him or anyone in his family again, he's going to have you arrested for trespassing."

Katie gave a chirp of indignation. "I beg your pardon? I took a box of chocolates to his sister today to express my condolences for her loss. While I was there, she said something cryptic about Ken's death. She said she thought it had to do with 'that other thing.' I believe you should pursue the matter further to find out who Mary Jones thinks killed her brother and why."

"Mr. Fenton informed me that his sister, Mary, is in poor health and probably doesn't know what she's talking about."

"Isn't it possible he's manipulating you so you *won't* investigate further?"

"Investigate what, Ms. Bonner? Some mysterious 'other thing'?" he asked, his tone mocking. "That makes no sense. What does make sense is that you're making yourself a nuisance to Paul Fenton and his family, and I will not tolerate it. Consider *this* a warning."

All traces of fear were now gone. In its place was seething anger. Katie had no idea what other thing Mary Jones was talking about, but now, more than ever, she was determined to find out.

Ten

~~~~~~

Katie arose early on Sunday morning, quietly got dressed, and kissed a sleeping Andy on the forehead before she fed the cats and headed out for her power walk around the Square. As she walked, she breathed in the fresh air and admired the pink and white impatiens overflowing from wooden flower barrels spaced along the edge of the walkways in front of the shops.

The beauty and peace of Victoria Square helped Katie to compartmentalize her anger at Paul Fenton. The fact that he'd come to her apartment and practically threatened her and then turned the entire situation around on her when she related the incident to Detective Schuler still caused her blood to boil, but she knew she had to set that anger aside if she was going to be able to learn the truth about Ken Fenton's murder.

Finding out what Mary suspected to be responsible for

her brother's death and avoiding getting arrested for trespassing was going to be a problem. Katie remembered Nick telling her that someone familiar with Ken's "shady past" would be at the luncheon. Hopefully, she would get some answers there.

Andy was still sleeping when Katie returned from her walk. She hopped in the shower. When she emerged from the bedroom showered and wearing a knee-length floral dress, she found Andy in the kitchen.

"The scent of cinnamon hit me the instant I opened the bathroom door," she told him, placing her arms around his waist as he stood at the counter drizzling icing onto warm cinnamon rolls.

"I thought you could use something sweet after what you had to deal with last night, Sunshine."

She laughed. "I thought my something sweet was you."

"Well, yeah . . . that's true." He turned and dropped a kiss onto her lips. "Wow. You look beautiful."

"Thank you. I wanted to dress up a little for the luncheon."

"Either way, you'll be the most beautiful woman there, but you've certainly sealed the deal now," he said.

She hoped that meant he thought she was more beautiful than Erikka. She wasn't, but she certainly wanted Andy to think so.

"I might have to walk again this evening after having one of these for breakfast."

He held a cinnamon roll to her lips. "Taste this and tell me it isn't worth it."

She did and moaned with delight. "That is beyond delicious . . . and worth every step I'll need to take to work it off."

Andy openly appraised her figure in the dress. "You've already worked it off this morning. You're really rocking that dress. Do you *have* to go to work before heading to the luncheon?"

"You know I do. Will you have trouble making the luncheon?"

"Nope. You, Erikka, and I can walk over together. I'm leaving Roger in charge of the pizzeria."

Katie blinked in surprise. "Roger? Are you sure he's the best choice?"

Andy's face tightened. "Yes, I want to give him the opportunity to prove himself . . . both to me and to himself. It'll be good for him."

"It's just that he's so new." And he'd been in even more trouble than some of the other high-risk boys Andy had employed at the pizzeria.

"True, but I'll be right across the Square if he needs me. And besides, there are two other guys in the shop. They've all had their turn at being in charge. It helps them build confidence."

She nodded. "Okay."

He tweaked her chin. "Just because *you're* a control freak doesn't mean everyone else is," he teased.

She smiled, but she was thinking that, yes, she was careful about whom she left in charge of Artisans Alley, as well as Tealicious, but she didn't hire people who'd just gotten out of juvenile detention, either. She guessed Andy must see something special in the young man.

~~~~~~

When Katie entered the vendors' lounge at Artisans Alley, she found herself looking at an unfamiliar face. A short man with buzz-cut steel-gray hair, brown eyes, and a long, thin scar on the left side of his forehead was turning from the refrigerator with a bottle of water in his hand.

He nodded. "Good morning."

"Good morning. We haven't met. I'm Katie Bonner."

"Hugh McKinney." He strode over to shake her hand.

"You're the new leather goods vendor, aren't you?" Vance had taken care of the paperwork when McKinney had arrived.

"Yessiree."

"I'm sorry I haven't yet had a chance to visit your booth, but I've seen your products go through the checkout and they're beautiful."

"I understand. You've been busy. Would you like to see it now?"

She didn't really have time, but she didn't want to be rude to a new vendor—especially one who had a beef with the place. "I'd love to."

Katie accompanied Hugh McKinney up the stairs to his booth. His space was neat and tidy, with the majority of his merchandise strung together and secured to his table with cord reels. The smell of leather and tobacco made Katie feel that, if she closed her eyes, she could be in a gentleman's study.

"You must smoke a pipe," she mused.

"Not on Artisans Alley property, ma'am," he said. "But, yes, I do. And I keep a pouch of tobacco here. Is that all right?"

"Of course. The scent complements the leather nicely."

He smiled. "Charlotte told me the other day that I have the best-smelling booth in the building."

"I'm inclined to agree."

Katie looked over the wallets, eyeglass cases, belts, and toiletry bags. "These are beautiful."

"Thank you. I can make larger items as well as custom-ized items upon request. And, if you see anything you like, I keep most of my merchandise in locked boxes fitted with alarms beneath the table."

The area under the table was blocked from view by a black cloth.

"And when I'm not here giving a demonstration, I keep my tools hidden, too. It's always better to be safe than sorry."

"That's true." Katie remembered Vance telling her about Hugh's inquiries and concerns about loss prevention. "How long have you been leather crafting?"

"My father taught me when I was about fifteen years old. Now that I'm retired from the postal service, I can pursue my hobby full-time."

"I'll have to get a customized wallet for my boyfriend, Andy, closer to his birthday," Katie said. "I'm really glad you seem to be fitting in with Artisans Alley so well. Do you have any questions about anything while I'm here?"

"Not . . . not really." He grinned. "I'm glad you turned up the air conditioner."

"I think we're all happy about that. But I get the impression there was something else you wanted to ask about."

"Well . . . I just wanted to tell you I'm sorry for what you went through."

At Katie's frown, he continued.

"Seeing that man get electrocuted . . . and then getting hurt yourself."

"I just got knocked down . . . and out," Katie said. "I'm sorry for Mr. Fenton . . . and his family."

Hugh nodded. "I appreciate your stopping by. Be sure and let me know when you want that wallet—I'll give you the friends and family discount."

"I appreciate that."

Katie returned to her office and was looking over the spreadsheet for Saturday's receipts when Ray called.

"Hi, Katie. Sorry to disturb you, but I wanted to make sure you're all right after your visit from Paul Fenton."

"Yes, Ray, I'm fine. Thanks again for bringing Mason home."

"I'm glad I was able to catch him so easily. He's not that familiar with me."

"He's more reasonable than Della. She makes a person work for her affections. But I appreciate your returning him. Had he gotten in the road . . ."

"You *did* call the police on Fenton, didn't you?" he asked.

Katie let out an exasperated breath. "Yeah and a fat lot of

good that did me." Katie told Ray how Fenton had been able to change the narrative on her.

"I hate to admit it now, but I once saw you as a buttin-ski, too."

"What changed your mind?" she asked.

"Who says I've changed my mind?"

"Fine. Then I'll let Detective Schuler send you up the river for a crime you didn't commit."

"Gee, thanks for the vote of confidence," he scoffed. "I was a detective longer than you've been alive."

That was almost the truth.

"You *were* a detective. You aren't anymore, and it's some-one on the inside who's trying to pin Ken Fenton's murder on you."

"Nobody has convicted me yet."

"'Yet' being the key word. Paul went ballistic because I went to see his sister, Mary, and she told me about some . . . other thing . . . she believes is responsible for Ken's death. I believe that whatever this *other thing* is, it's the key to solv-ing Ken's murder."

"Stand down, Nancy Drew. I don't need anyone sticking her dainty little neck out for me."

"I'm not. I'm doing this for myself and for the Merchants Association. Before we decide to invest in buying that build-ing from Harper Jones, we need to find out if something about that building had anything to do with Ken Fenton's murder."

"Now why on earth would anyone kill a man over a half run-down building that didn't even belong to him?" Ray asked.

"I don't know—I'm grasping at straws."

"I don't think you have anything to fear as long as you stay away from Paul and Mary. Let the Sheriff's Office han-dle the case."

"If the Sheriff's Office handles the case, you'll wind up in prison," Katie said.

"Will you tie a yellow ribbon around the old oak tree for me?"

"You won't think this is so funny if Sadie and Sasha end up living with their grandparents while Sophie finishes school."

"Katie Bonner! You really don't have any confidence in my sleuthing abilities at all, do you?"

"I do . . . but I care about you and want to help."

"Ha! I knew you were sticking your neck out for me."

"We're friends, Ray. Wouldn't you help me under the same circumstances?"

"You know I would. I . . ." He cleared his throat. "I've got a customer coming in. I'll talk to you soon."

~~~~~~~

Just before eleven o'clock, Katie walked over to Angelo's Pizzeria to see if Andy—and Erikka—were ready to go to Sassy Sally's for the luncheon.

"Hey, Katie!" Roger called when she walked in. "I got your lamp fixed this morning before we started work. Andy said he'd bring it up to you when you get back from lunch."

"Thank you, Roger. How much do I owe you?"

"Aw, you don't owe me anything. Andy has done more than enough for me already."

"I appreciate that, but I want to pay you something for your work."

"We'll talk about that later," Andy said, walking up and draping an arm around Katie's shoulders. "We need to head over to Nick's place or we're going to be late."

"Hi, there, Katie," said Erikka, approaching Andy from the opposite side. "Don't you look cute?"

"Thank you." She gritted her teeth to do it, but she managed to return the compliment. "You look nice, too."

"Oh, you're sweet. I wasn't sure I should go since I didn't dress up or anything, but Andy said I never look bad." Erikka giggled. "Isn't he the sweetest thing?"

"Just like sugar," Katie said, trying desperately to keep an edge from her voice.

"Roger, be sure to call me if you need me for anything," Andy said.

Katie wondered if he'd really felt the young man needed a reminder or if Andy simply wanted to break the growing tension between the women.

"Everything will be fine, boss," Roger said. "And, if it's not, I know you're only a phone call away. Go on and enjoy your lunch."

Andy rolled his eyes, and when he saw that Katie saw, he grinned sheepishly and kissed her temple.

"It'll be fun," Katie said. "I really think you'll like Brad."

"I've heard he's model handsome," Erikka said, with a sidelong glance at Andy. "But I'm sure he won't be any competition for this one."

"Not at all," Katie said and smiled sweetly.

"Good to know." Andy stepped out from between the two women and opened the door. "After you."

Erikka motioned for Katie to step through the door first. Katie did so. Again, Erikka put Andy between the two of them. This time, she took his arm as if he were her escort. "You'll make everybody jealous, Andy . . . a striking man with his two best gals at his sides."

Katie ground her teeth together and firmly took Andy's other arm. Erikka definitely needed a man in her life . . . just not hers. She hoped the floozy—*ahem*—the woman and Brad took one look at each other and fell head over heels in love.

She wasn't sure what she'd do if they didn't.

Eleven

~~~~~~~~~~

When Katie, Erikka, and Andy entered Sassy Sally's beautifully restored foyer, Nick was there to greet them before giving Katie a kiss on the cheek.

"Thank you so much for hiring Brad," he said. "We love having him here—and you're going to love working with him." He turned and nodded toward the left corner of the room, where Don and Brad were engaged in conversation.

Don waved to them, and Brad turned. Upon seeing Katie, he excused himself and hurried over to join the newcomers.

"Katie, I'm so glad you brought your friends," Brad said. "And what a lovely couple they are." He extended a hand to Andy. "I'm Brad Andrews, the new chef and manager at Tealicious."

"Andy Rust." He shook Brad's hand. "I'm with Katie." He jerked his head toward Erikka. "This is Erikka Wiley, the assistant manager at my pizzeria."

Brad smiled. "Ah, so the two of you are in the restaurant business as well. I'm sure we'll have lots to talk about."

"I'm sure we will." Erikka shook Brad's hand, covering his with her free hand as she did so. "I'd love to hear all about your work." She shot Andy a venomous glance, but he didn't seem to notice.

Andy kissed Katie's cheek. "Nick, what do we have to drink?"

"Talk to Don. He's the bartender."

"I'll do that."

As Andy strode toward Don, Nick took Katie's arm. "Come with me."

Katie allowed Nick to propel her toward an older woman with snowy white hair wearing a dove-gray waist-shirt dress and several strands of pearls.

"Fiona, I'd like you to meet Katie Bonner. Katie, this is Fiona Lancaster."

"Mrs. Lancaster, it's a pleasure to meet you." Katie gently shook the woman's delicate hand.

"Please call me Fiona." The woman had a scratchy voice that suggested she'd once been—perhaps still was—a smoker. She wore a flowery scent, possibly because she'd once wanted to mask the odor of cigarette smoke. Fiona frowned. "Dear Nick said you were in the building with Ken Fenton when he was electrocuted."

"That's right," Katie said.

"How dreadful for you! Are you all right?"

"I'm fine, thank you."

"You're lucky, darling. I was acquainted with Ken Fenton, and he had a lot of enemies. I'm surprised one of them was clever enough to make the man's death look like an accident."

"You talk as if you might know who some of these enemies were," Katie said innocently.

Fiona shrugged. "I hired Ken to renovate an apartment building I own in Rochester. One evening while Ken was working, someone drove by and threw one of those home-made explosives—you know, where they put a cloth in the top of a liquor bottle—"

"A Molotov cocktail," Nick interjected.

"Yes, right. Anyway, someone threw one of them at the apartment building. The bottle broke a window and set one of the apartments ablaze. Despite my having good insurance, the repairs cost me a fortune . . . and that was on top of the planned renovations."

"Were the police sure the perpetrators were targeting Ken Fenton?" Katie asked. "They didn't think it was random?"

"I'm not sure whether they're sure or not, but I was absolutely positive. I'd overheard Ken on the phone telling someone he'd make sure they got their money by Thursday. It was on a Friday that the explosive was thrown at the apartment building." Fiona raised her carefully filled-in eyebrows and spread her hands. "And *I* certainly don't have any enemies."

"Was anyone hurt in the fire?" Katie asked.

"Fortunately, no."

Katie started as a large hand landed on her shoulder. She turned to see that it belonged to Brad.

"May I please steal Katie away? I want to show her some dishes I've prepared. I hope she'll like them enough to feature them at Tealicious."

"Of course." Fiona smiled up at Brad. "I'm utterly and completely charmed by this man," she told Katie. "I can hardly wait to visit Tealicious and see what he'll be serving."

"It was a pleasure meeting you, Fiona. I hope we'll have time to chat some more." Boy did she ever, but Katie allowed Brad to lead her to the kitchen. There he presented her with an assortment of beautifully prepared goodies: champagne cookies, a charlotte russe, and peach marmalade.

"Naturally, I can't give you a taste of the charlotte russe until lunch is served," he said. "But, here, try this." He handed her a champagne cookie.

She bit into the cookie and closed her eyes as the sweet, slightly tart flavor engulfed her taste buds. She moaned.

"What's going on?"

Katie's eyes popped open at the sound of Andy's voice. "Oh, Andy, you have to taste these cookies. They're wonderful."

Brad proudly offered Andy the cookie tray. Andy looked at Brad and then back at Katie before selecting a cookie. He tasted it and proclaimed that it *was* really good.

"Thank you," Brad said. "Katie and I are going to make a great team, don't you think? Hopefully as good a team as you and Erikka."

"Yeah," Andy said, his voice flat.

"Now, you must both taste this peach marmalade. Katie, it will be wonderful with scones."

At that moment, Nick stuck his head through the kitchen door. "Are you guys ready? Because lunch is."

"I'm starving," Andy said, placing his hand on the small of Katie's back and directing her toward the door. "Let's go."

Nick had placed Katie between Andy and Brad with Erikka on Brad's other side. Directly across from Katie was Seth Landers, Katie's lawyer but also her friend, who was more like a brother to her. On one side of Seth sat his partner, Jaime, a broad-shouldered young man with chestnut-colored hair, green eyes, and an open smile. Seth and Jaime had been together for a little over six months now, and Katie had never seen Seth happier. Fiona Lancaster sat on the other side of Seth, and the seat beside her was empty. Nick and Don sat at either end of the huge Neo-Renaissance table.

"Fiona, where's your husband?" Katie asked.

The older woman waved her hand dismissively. "Phil tied one on last night and is still sleeping it off. Hopefully, he'll be down before you leave."

As a waiter served their drinks, Nick explained that he'd met Brad while living in an apartment on the Upper West Side.

"I had three roommates," Nick said, "but they were all out when I decided to heat up a chicken casserole my aunt Sally made for me on her last visit."

Don smiled slightly and shook his head. He'd undoubtedly heard this story before.

Brad picked up the thread. "Apparently, poor Nick didn't realize he needed to allow the dish to thaw before placing it in the preheated oven."

"Oh no," Katie said, squeezing her eyes shut in dread.

"Oh *yes*. That casserole dish exploded! And I went screaming into the hallway." Nick dissolved into laughter.

"He nearly ran over me!" Brad said, grinning at the memory. "I took him by the shoulders and asked him what was wrong. He said he thought he'd just blown up his kitchen."

"I really thought that!" Nick said as everyone laughed. "You should've heard that *sound*!"

"We went inside, where I went to the kitchen and turned off the oven," Brad said. "There was, of course, no way he was having a chicken casserole for dinner—at least, not that one—so I invited him to have dinner with me and my . . . well, the woman who was my girlfriend at that time."

"It was the best meal I'd ever eaten." Nick looked at Don. "But I never told Aunt Sally that. Best of all, Brad even came back to my apartment with me and helped me clean up the oven. I knew right then we'd be friends for life."

Brad raised his glass to Nick. "And I knew I'd never let you cook in my kitchen!"

~~~~~~~

It was lucky Nick had prepared the feast, and everyone was generous with their compliments. After the dishes had been cleared away, Katie took Brad aside.

"That charlotte russe was delicious," she said.

He inclined his head. "Thank you. Do I hear a 'but' coming?"

"Certainly not. I think you're going to bring a lot of variety and poise to Tealicious. Janine, the former manager, did very little in the way of baking." Katie shrugged. "I've been used to going to the tea shop every morning to make some sandwich spreads, scones, and tea cakes."

"And you've continued working another job as well?" He shook his head. "How on earth have you managed it all?"

She laughed slightly. "Not terribly well, I'm afraid."

Nick overheard Katie's comment and came to drape an arm around her neck. "Don't let her fool you. She's a real dynamo. But, I'm glad you're here now so she won't have to run herself ragged anymore." He backed away. "Feel free to resume your private conversation now."

Brad chuckled. "You gotta love that guy."

"Yes, you do," Katie said. "Anyway, I was wondering . . . actually, I'd like to still come into the kitchen in the mornings. I don't want to get in your way or anything, but if I can help . . ."

"You're welcome anytime," Brad said. "After all, it *is* your kitchen."

"Well, yes, but I don't want you to think I'm looking over your shoulder."

"You could never do that—you aren't tall enough."

Katie looked at him with mock umbrage. "I could get a stepstool!"

He laughed again. "Join me in the kitchen anytime. It'll be fun."

"Then I'll see you first thing tomorrow morning," Katie said.

"I'm looking forward to it."

Katie turned back around to where the other guests were standing and noticed Andy glaring toward her and Brad. She smiled and winked at him.

Was he actually jealous of Brad? If so, good. Maybe now he could understand how *she* felt about Erikka.

She'd intended on walking over to where Andy was talking with Seth and Jaime, but Fiona Lancaster intercepted her.

Taking Katie by the arm, Fiona said, "Phil has finally decided to join us. Come meet him."

Phil looked as if someone had magically transformed an English bulldog into a human. His hair was white and spiky, his hooded brown eyes were slightly bloodshot at the moment, and his jowls nearly hung to his collar.

"Phil, I'd like you to meet Katie Bonner. Katie, this is my hungover husband."

"Woman, I told you to tell these people I had a *headache*, not a hangover!" He flattened his lips and shook his head at his wife before offering his hand to Katie. "Nice to meet you, young lady."

"It's a pleasure to meet you, Mr. Lancaster. I hope your headache is waning."

"It is, thank you. What do you do, Katie?"

"She owns that fabulous tea shop, Tealicious," Fiona said. "I was telling you about it last night. See that dapper young man right over there?" She pointed to where Brad was standing with Don and Nick. "He's the new chef there. I can hardly wait to try his food."

"How wonderful," he said. "Katie, that was an excellent ventriloquist act you did with my wife. I'm sure she wouldn't be so rude as to answer your questions."

Katie laughed. "She wasn't being rude at all. I'm delighted Fiona is excited about Tealicious."

"Katie also runs Artisans Alley," Fiona said. "It's an arts-and-crafts arcade."

"Hmm. Are the artisans all painters, or are there other kinds of artists there?" Phil asked.

"We have dollmakers, woodworkers . . . we just added a leather goods artisan."

"Leather goods?"

"Yes, sir. The artisan's name is Hugh McKinney, and he has some beautiful things on display at his booth."

"McKinney, eh? I wondered where he'd land after the post

office made him take early retirement. It's good he had a backup plan."

Katie frowned at Phil's words. "I didn't realize the post office made him retire. That's too bad."

"Well, it would've been worse if they could've proven what they believed about him," Phil said.

Fiona placed a hand on her husband's arm. "Phil, darling, stop. I don't want Katie to think we're criticizing her artisans."

Phil shrugged. "I'm not criticizing anyone."

"Well, it rather sounds that way," Fiona said. "If you'll recall, Katie is the one who was with Ken Fenton when he was electrocuted."

Katie hated that Fiona had changed the subject. She was rather curious to know why the post office had made Hugh McKinney take early retirement and what it was they believed Hugh had done. She'd hate to think that the first vendor Vance had signed up on his own turned out to have a shady past.

"Ken Fenton." Phil's voice boomed, and Katie resisted the urge to look around to see if anyone else had heard him. "That one certainly was a piece of work. I'm surprised he lasted as long as he did."

"Phil shares my low opinion of the man," Fiona said.

"He was nothing but trouble," Phil continued. "He did shoddy work, he was into loan sharks for money, and it was rumored that he was a drug dealer."

"Wow . . . I had no idea." Okay, she had *some* idea but she didn't realize Ken had been in so much trouble. "What about his brother, Paul? Do you know anything about him?"

"Big guy? Runs a tattoo parlor?" Phil asked.

Katie nodded.

"I don't know the man personally, but I'd stay away from him if I were you. He and Ken seemed to be closer than two front teeth. When Ken was working on our apartment building—"

"Before he nearly burned the place down, and we threw him out," Fiona interrupted her husband.

"—Paul came to see him sometimes twice in the same day," Phil continued. "I'd imagine that whatever Ken was involved in, Paul was, too."

Before Katie could question the Lancasters further, Andy came and took her by the arm. "Erikka and I need to get back."

"And I'm hoping there are some leftovers from lunch," Phil said, heading toward the kitchen.

"I'll walk back with you," Katie told Andy. "Fiona, it was wonderful meeting you and Phil."

"Likewise, dear. We'll be to see you at Tealicious—and at Artisans Alley—as soon as we can."

~~~~~~

When Katie returned to her office at Artisans Alley, she immediately phoned Ray. He answered with a seemingly distracted "Hello."

"Hi, Ray—it's Katie. Is this a bad time?" she asked.

"Um . . . I've got a minute. What's up?"

Katie debated whether or not to continue the conversation. Ray was obviously distracted. "It can wait."

"No," he said. "Go ahead."

"I simply wanted to tell you that Nick introduced me to a woman named Fiona Lancaster, who told me that while Ken Fenton was working for her, she overheard him speaking on the phone with someone about money he owed them. She said he told the person he'd have the money to them by Thursday. On Friday, someone threw a Molotov cocktail at her building."

"Is she sure she wasn't the target of the assault?" he asked.

"*She* is. From what she told me, I don't think the police were convinced. But, given everything we've heard about Ken Fenton, it couldn't hurt to see if he was a gambler or—"

"Katie, please stay out of this investigation. I don't want you to find yourself on Schuler's bad side."

"I can take care of myself."

"I know that, but—" He sighed. "I need to go. The girls are waiting for me."

He ended the call before Katie even had a chance to say good-bye. She wondered what was going on with them. Hopefully, not more drama. Ray had enough problems of his own at the moment without having to help teenage girls deal with their either real or—more likely—imagined crises.

She'd just put her phone back into her purse when there was a light tap on her door. "Come in." She expected it to be Rose and was surprised to see that her visitor was Regan.

"Hey."

"Regan, hi," Katie said, with a smile. "What brings you by?"

"I was in the tag room with Ms. Mitchell having my first lesson in tatting lace."

Katie tried to keep her face from crumpling in a grimace as she asked, "How did that go?"

"Well, I knew it would be delicate work, but I didn't realize how hard it would be. Ms. Mitchell loaned me a shuttle, but I'll need to get my own before our next lesson."

"A shuttle?"

"Yeah." Regan took a piece of plastic from her pocket that was shaped sort of like an elongated guitar pick with holes at each end. "You wind your thread through the shuttle and around your fingers and then you make loops . . . oh, and knots—can't forget the knots."

"That sounds way too nerve-racking for me. I'll have to leave the lace tatting to you and Ida."

Regan chuckled. "I feel sure you could get the hang of it if you wanted to."

"What made you want to learn to tat lace?" Katie asked.

The younger woman shrugged. "I like to see people reviving or continuing historic arts." She looked down at her high-top sneakers. "But I didn't stop in to tell you about my lesson with Ms. Mitchell. Roger told me about Paul coming to see you."

"He was really angry that I'd gone to see his sister. I . . . I took her some chocolates . . . but I suppose I *did* ask too many nosy questions."

Regan met Katie's gaze. "Paul's a good guy—he really is. I'm sure he was just feeling extra protective of his sister. I mean, their brother died only a few days ago. I'm sure the whole family is a wreck over that."

"I imagine they are," Katie said. "Did you know Ken at all?"

"Not really. I mean, I'd met him a time or two, but I wouldn't say I knew him. Why?"

"At lunch today, I met a couple who said they'd hired Ken to do some work for them. They said someone threw an incendiary device that set their apartment building on fire during the time Ken worked there."

"And they thought Ken had something to do with it?" Regan asked.

"No, but they believed that whoever threw it did so as a threat to Ken. They thought he was in trouble with someone financially."

"But that's dumb. Why would someone throw a bomb or whatever at this couple's building if they were threatening Ken? Wouldn't it make more sense to throw the bomb at Ken's house? Or even his truck?"

Katie frowned. "It makes a lot of sense."

Regan nodded. "It seems to me that someone had a grudge against this couple rather than with Ken. You say they owned an apartment building?"

"That's what they said."

"Then maybe they'd evicted someone or raised the rent or something, and this was that person's way of getting back at them," Regan said.

"You're absolutely right," Katie said, not pleased that her theory could have holes blown through it with so little thought. She needed to look further into Fiona and Phil Lancaster's story before taking it at face value.

"And about Paul . . . I know he can get angry sometimes—especially where his family is involved—but he really is a sweetheart. I can't help but think the two of you got off on the wrong foot. If you got to know each other, I believe you'd be friends."

"I'd like to think so," Katie said. "By the way, thank Roger again for me for repairing my lamp. He did a great job."

"I will. He's always been handy at fixing things, even before he took that electricity class at vocational school." She smiled. "Even when we were little kids, he'd take something apart just to see how it worked. Then he'd put it back together again."

"And did it work when he got it reassembled?"

"More often than not, it did."

"You sound really proud of him."

"I am," Regan said. "Yeah, he got in some trouble, but overall, he's a great kid . . . and an awesome brother. Do you have brothers or sisters?"

Katie shook her head. "I'm afraid not. I always wished I did have, but my parents died when I was young."

"That's rough. Our old man bailed on us, and our mom works two jobs. I want to be able to help her someday . . . make it to where she doesn't have to work so hard. Roger wants that, too."

"You're good kids. Your mom is blessed to have you."

"We're the ones lucky to have her," Regan said. "Well, I guess I'd better get going. Ms. Mitchell is expecting me to have a row of picots by the next class."

"Good luck."

"Thanks. I'm sure I'll need it." She left, pulling the door closed behind her.

Katie sat at her desk and ruminated on what Regan had said about Fiona Lancaster. It did make more sense that a person targeting Ken Fenton would threaten him at home. Maybe the Molotov cocktail attack *was* aimed at the Lancasters. But, then, Ken was the one who'd been murdered.

Twelve

After feeding the cats the next morning, Katie skipped her own breakfast and practically ran to Tealicious. She unlocked the door and called, "Hello!"

"Good morning!" Brad's deep voice trumpeted from the kitchen overtop the classical music that was already streaming from the speakers.

She smiled as she strode into the kitchen. "It smells heavenly in here."

"And wait until you taste." He took a batch of pistachio scones from the oven and placed them on a wire rack.

Katie's mouth nearly watered as she watched Brad drizzle the scones with a vanilla glaze.

"I've made coffee if you'd like a cup," he said.

"I'd love one." She didn't admit to him that she'd been so eager to get to work that she'd run out of the apartment without coffee or breakfast. She was afraid, however, that given the tantalizing aromas, her stomach would growl and clue him in.

She poured herself a cup of coffee and added milk. "May I top off your cup?"

"Please." He plated one of the scones. "See what you think."

Katie took a fork and cut into the crumbly scone. She was uncomfortably aware of Brad watching for her reaction when she brought the fork to her mouth, but he wasn't disappointed. When she closed her eyes and moaned with pleasure, he laughed.

"I was hoping that's what you'd think. In fact, I hope that's what *all* our customers will think."

"You've got a hit with these scones."

"I very much enjoyed lunch yesterday," Brad said. "It was kind of Nick and Don to host it for me." He chuckled. "Nick has come quite a way from his casserole-bursting days."

Katie laughed. "He must have been horrified to have made such a mess while his roommates were out. Thank goodness you were there to help him."

"Katie!"

It was Ray Davenport, calling to her from the dining room. She excused herself, put her plate on the counter, and went to speak with Ray.

"Hey," she said. "What brings you by?"

The former detective craned his neck, trying to see into the kitchen. "Sounds like you were having fun back there. You and the new manager must be hitting it off."

There was something odd about his tone. Something she'd heard in Andy's voice way too often. Jealousy? And how did Ray even know she was here at Tealicious?

"Yes, we are. Brad is great. But I'm sure that's not why you're here. Is something wrong?"

"Oh, no. I just wanted to come by before going to my shop and apologize for blowing you off when you called yesterday. Both Sadie and Sasha were in the room and, well . . ." He trailed off.

Every muscle in Katie's body tensed. "And they hate me for various reasons." Something in Ray's face hinted at a new reason to fan his children's dislike. "Wait. Do they blame *me* for the trouble you're in with Detective Schuler?"

"You know how unreasonable teenagers can be, Katie . . . especially overprotective daughters."

Those tense muscles weren't about to relax. "You're the one who volunteered to speak with Harper Jones—it wasn't my idea."

"Hey, I don't blame you for anything," Ray said defensively. "But yesterday, the girls and I were having a nice day and I didn't want to ruin it."

"By talking with me," Katie finished uncharitably.

He shrugged.

Katie ground her teeth, wishing she had a peppermint to pulverize. How could Ray's daughters be so unreasonable? And Ray! He simply blew her off yesterday when all she was trying to do was help him get out from under suspicion of murder! If none of them wanted her help, so be it.

Ray cleared his throat, but Katie refused to look at him, preferring to gaze out the window at the sun already heating up the pavement.

"I had my friend in the Sheriff's Office look into that Lancaster incident," Ray said. "The investigating officer couldn't pinpoint who was actually targeted—if anyone. However, the Lancasters had only recently purchased the apartment building and it had been vacant for a couple of years prior, so they had no disgruntled tenants—former or otherwise. And since Ken Fenton had dealings with some shady characters, the officer suspected Ken was the target."

"Fine," Katie said flatly.

"Katie, please."

"No . . . that's fine. They believed he was the target, but they had no suspect and no proof. Got it." Why did she feel so angry?

"I . . . uh . . . doubt I'll be getting any other inside

information for a while," he said. "My friend said he was sticking his neck out for me to get the information about the Lancaster incident. The department has been instructed not to talk to me anymore—unless it's in an official capacity—until the conclusion of the Ken Fenton murder investigation."

Katie finally dragged her gaze back to Ray and saw that he was distressed about the fact that his friends could lose their jobs for even talking with him now. "I'm sure everyone in the Sheriff's Office will still work hard to prove your innocence."

"Well . . . I hope you're right." He sighed and his gaze dipped. "I have to get to work, but I'll go by the post office later to find out what I can about Hugh McKinney."

"Don't bother. I'll take care of that myself. Your girls are right in their belief that I rely on you too much."

"That's *their* belief, Katie, not mine. Friends help each other."

"True, but I need to go to the post office anyway. I—"

The kitchen door opened. "I'm sorry to interrupt," Brad said, his tone making it clear he wasn't sorry in the least. "This is a new recipe, Katie, and you simply must give me your opinion." He held a white petit four between his gloved index finger and thumb and lifted it to her mouth.

Katie allowed Brad to give her a bite of the cake. She chewed slowly, allowing the taste of coconut and white chocolate flavors to linger on her tongue. "Oh, wow . . . Ray, you need to try this."

Brad offered him the rest of the tiny pastry.

Ray shook his head. "No, thanks. I'll pass."

"Sorry," Katie said, realizing the men hadn't before met. "Ray, this is chef extraordinaire Brad Andrews. Brad, this is Ray Davenport. Ray owns the Wood U gift shop across the Square."

"It's a pleasure to meet you," Brad said, his smile about a mile wide.

Ray looked more than a little uncomfortable. "Yeah . . .

it's . . . uh . . . it's nice to meet you, too." He glanced at his watch. "I've got a business to run. See you later." With that, Ray turned and left.

Katie wasn't sure how to interpret what had transpired during the previous five minutes except that there'd been way too much tension. But then her stomach growled, reminding her that she hadn't yet filled it.

She pointed to the petit four Brad still held. "Any chance I can have the rest of that?"

~~~~~~~

After working steadily together, Katie and Brad had assembled the buffet table, which was filled with mouthwatering treats for the Square's merchants arriving for the meeting, including an assortment of pastries and sandwiches.

Nick and Don were the first to arrive. Nick went to say hello to Brad, and Don told Katie that it looked as if things were working out well with Brad.

"So far, so good," Katie said, holding up her crossed fingers. "He welcomed my input and didn't seem to mind my being in the kitchen this morning. Of course, I tried to give him plenty of space. And he *did* tweak my chicken salad recipe, but I have to admit, it's even better than it was before."

"I know Nick enjoys having him around," Don said. "And Brad seems like a nice guy."

"Yes, he does. I thought he was a bit full of himself at first, but once you get to know him, it becomes part of his charm."

Don grinned. "That's probably one of the things he and Nick have in common."

"Good point," Katie said. "By the way, did Brad say anything about Erikka last night?"

"Not a word," Don said. "I know you're hoping those two will hit it off, but I wouldn't bet the tea shop on it."

Not what Katie wanted to hear.

"Oh, my!" Sue Sweeney exclaimed, helping herself to one of the petit fours. "These look marvelous."

"So do you," Katie said. Sue wore a bright, predominately yellow dress decorated with cute white flowers, and she looked very . . . well . . . sunny.

Sue blushed at the compliment. "Aw, thanks." She lowered her voice. "I have a date later."

"With whom?" Katie asked.

Before Sue could answer, Andy came over to check out the tray. "These look great." He gave Katie a quick kiss, grabbed a plate, and took a chicken salad sandwich.

By the time Katie had turned back to where Sue had been standing, the woman had wandered off to talk to Charlotte Booth.

Once everyone had arrived and had a plate of food, Seth presented the group with a preliminary partnership agreement stating that all partners would share equally in the expense as well as the profit from buying and leasing the Victoria Square property.

"I'm going to pass around a notepad," he said. "After you've had a chance to read the contract, should you still wish to be a partner in this venture, please print your legal name on the pad and pass it to the person next to you. That way, I'll have the names of all the partners when I draw up the final agreement."

"What if we're having second thoughts?" The question was raised by Nona Fiske, who Katie was, frankly, surprised to see at the meeting in the first place.

"If you've decided not to enter into the partnership, simply pass the pad along without adding your name," Seth said.

When the pad was returned to Seth, Katie could see that these names were on it:

Katherine Bonner
Andrew Rust
Conrad Stratton

Gilda Ringwald-Stratton
Susan Sweeney
Jordan and Ann Tanner
Charlotte Booth
Nona Fiske

Katie raised her brows at Seth when she saw Nona's name at the bottom, but he merely smiled. It was so like Nona to waffle. Katie only hoped the woman didn't intend to back out once the deal was underway.

Seth announced that he'd draw up the final contract and then schedule a time when they could all meet at his office to sign the paperwork and prepare the necessary documentation to take to the bank.

After the meeting, everyone but Andy filed out of Tealicious. He put his arms around her and pulled her close. "Are we still on for tonight?" he asked against her hair.

"You bet." She raised her head for a kiss.

"I need to get back to Angelo's. Erikka doesn't come in until later this afternoon, and Roger is holding down the fort again."

"It sounds like Roger is getting really good at fort holding," Katie said.

"He is."

"Good. Maybe now that you have a full staff you'll be able to take more time off."

He chuckled. "Are you angling for a vacation?"

"Maybe one of these days . . . if we can keep ourselves from over-entrepreneuring!"

"Is that even a word?"

"It is now," she said. "Can you think of one that more adequately describes our sickness for new ventures?"

"*Your* sickness. You're the one with all these irons in the fire."

"I saw your name on that pad, too."

"I know." He kissed her again. "Still . . . a vacation does

sound good, doesn't it? A beach somewhere . . . tropical breeze . . . no clock-watching."

She sighed. "It sounds wonderful." Still, Katie wondered if either of them would ever take enough time off work to enjoy such a trip together.

After Andy left, Katie returned to her upstairs office to check her email before uploading photographs of the display case and the day's specials on Tealicious's website. Then she went downstairs to stroll around the dining room. She was pleased to see Fiona and Phil Lancaster had arrived for lunch.

"Hello! I'm so glad you could make it."

"We wouldn't have missed it," said Fiona, dressed casually today in a bronze maxi dress and turquoise jewelry. "We're leaving Sassy Sally's tomorrow, but we hope to get by Artisans Alley before we go."

"We'd planned on getting by there today, but it wasn't opened," Phil added.

"Yes, we're closed on Mondays but will be open at ten tomorrow morning," Katie said.

"Good." Fiona smiled. "I'm looking forward to browsing around."

"I'll try to make it—I'd like to see what Hugh McKinney is crafting out of leather." Phil barked out a laugh. "He's lucky he's not making license plates."

Fiona scoffed. "Oh, Phil. I don't think they even do that in prisons anymore . . . do they?"

Katie shrugged, having no idea where or how license plates were made. "I need to run a quick errand, but I'll look forward to seeing you tomorrow. Just ask for me at the cash desk, and I'll come out and give you the grand tour."

Why on earth would Phil Lancaster believe Hugh McKinney was lucky not to be in prison? Katie felt it was more imperative than ever to discover exactly who the man was who'd so recently leased vendor space from her. After all, if he'd been up to something shady before and was now continuing his activities from Artisans Alley, couldn't Katie—and perhaps even the vendors—get in trouble as well?

~~~~~~~

Katie hadn't realized it, but it seemed like after a day off, Mondays were the post office's busiest workday. After standing in line for several minutes, she asked the clerk if she could speak with a manager.

The clerk looked wary. "May I tell him what it's about?"

"It's about a former employee," Katie said.

The clerk called for the manager and then instructed Katie to stand to the side so she could wait on the next person in line. "He'll be with you in a moment."

The manager was a tall, imposingly built man with a shaved head. He opened a locked door and then lifted his hand and motioned Katie toward him with two meaty fingers.

Katie swallowed nervously and then followed him through the door and down the hall to his office. He allowed her to go inside first, and then he came in behind her and closed the door.

She didn't know why she found the man intimidating. But there was something about—she read his nametag—B. Martin that made one feel that he had a short fuse.

"How may I help you?" he asked brusquely.

"My name is Katie Bonner, and I run Artisans Alley, the converted apple—"

B. Martin rotated his wrist in a wind-it-up gesture.

"Uh, I need to ask you about a former employee—Hugh McKinney," she blurted.

"What about him?"

"He's a vendor at Artisans Alley. I was busy with another project and didn't personally vet the man's application like I usually do, and it's come to my attention that Mr. McKinney might've been forced to leave his employ at the post office."

"I can only confirm to you that Mr. Hugh McKinney was indeed an employee of the United States Postal Service. Anything else in Mr. McKinney's personnel record is strictly confidential and cannot be divulged barring a court order."

"But . . . if you were me . . . would you feel comfortable having this man in your business?"

"All information about postal employees past or present is confidential."

It was obvious that Katie had wasted his time. She stood. "Thank you for your time."

B. Martin nodded, his expression devoid of emotion, his eyes as dark and forbidding as a shark's. "See yourself out."

～～～～～

Dinnertime arrived, and Andy appeared in front of Katie's office door. "Let's go!" he said and escorted her to his truck. He drove to the new Mexican restaurant that had just opened near the marina. Over a dinner of beef fajitas for him and a chicken taco for her, she told him about the post office incident.

"The manager looked more like a prison warden than the manager of a post office," Katie said. "It wasn't as if I was asking him to give out confidential information. I just wanted to know if he thought Mr. McKinney was okay to have as a vendor at Artisans Alley."

Andy rolled his eyes. "You were *so* asking him to give out confidential information. You wanted to know if Hugh McKinney was indeed forced to take early retirement, and if so, how it would affect his working at Artisans Alley."

"Okay, fine. But wouldn't you be concerned if you were me?"

"Not really. I trust my instincts. For instance, I seriously doubt there's a single teacher or former employer who would give Roger a glowing recommendation, but he's one of the best employees I have. Just because the PO manager wasn't singing Hugh McKinney's praises doesn't mean the man wasn't an excellent employee. Maybe the early retirement— if he was, in fact, forced into it—was due to his age."

"Maybe," Katie said. "But he's the only person I haven't vetted myself since I took over Artisans Alley."

"And Vance thought he was fine. Are you allowing the gossip of a man who was too hungover to attend the luncheon yesterday to cast a shadow over both Vance's judgment *and* your new vendor?"

Katie frowned. "You're right. But I *do* want to get to know the man and see what my instincts tell me."

"Fair enough."

Katie's gaze lifted as a couple strolled behind the hostess and into the dining room. "Speak of the devil," she murmured.

"What?"

Katie smiled as Sue Sweeney and her date, Hugh McKinney, passed their table. "Hi, Sue. Fancy seeing you here."

Sue paused. "It seems everyone on the Square is trying out the new restaurant, I guess," she said and giggled. "Hugh, I believe you know Katie."

Katie said hello and introduced Hugh to Andy.

Cordialities dispensed with, Hugh and Sue gave a wave before the couple was shown to their table.

Andy took Katie's hand and leaned in close. "That man is a stone-cold killer if I've ever seen one," he deadpanned. Katie blinked and then, unable to keep a straight face any longer, Andy burst out laughing.

Katie threw her napkin at him. "Ha, ha." But she wasn't feeling jovial. Her gaze drifted to the table where Sue and Hugh sat. Why did it feel so weird to see the two of them together?

Thirteen

First thing Tuesday morning, Sue stopped by Katie's office at Artisans Alley. Once again, she had taken more care with her appearance than she typically did, and she looked pretty in her wine-colored peasant blouse and denim skirt. Katie told her so.

"Thank you," Sue said, taking a seat on the chair by Katie's desk. "I stopped by to say hello to Hugh and to thank him again for last night before I head over to the shop."

"I take that to mean that your date went well."

Sue giggled. "Oh, Katie, it did. I know he's a bit older than I am, but what's that old saying? I'd rather be an old man's darling than a young man's welcome mat?"

"That's a new one to me." Katie shrugged. "But I'm glad you and Hugh hit it off."

"We did. He's so kind and attentive." She flattened her palm to her chest. "He asked me so many questions—how long I've lived in this area, where I grew up, what led to my love of candy-making . . . He even asked if I'm one of the merchants buying Harper Jones's building."

"Really?" Katie decided there was a fine line between being interested and being far too nosy on a first date. "Why did he ask you about that?"

"Out of concern, I guess. When I confirmed that I am going in on the building, Hugh told me to be careful. He said that nasty business with the Fentons might not be over yet."

"I wonder what he meant by that." Did Hugh McKinney know something about Ken Fenton and, possibly, his death?

"I imagine he heard something about how the building was going to be bought by Paul Fenton before his brother was killed there. I mentioned to Hugh that my niece had dated Paul and that Paul was a horrible piece of work." She smiled. "It's nice to have someone worry about me."

Katie nodded. "It is."

She wasn't satisfied with Sue's answer, though. Still thinking Hugh knew more than he was saying, she decided to speak with Hugh herself and determine just what he knew about the Fentons' "nasty business" that might not be over.

Katie's phone rang. She looked down at the screen and saw that it was an in-house call.

"Excuse me, Sue, I need to answer this."

"Of course! I need to get to work anyway." She stood. "Can't sit around mooning over a man all day, can I?" She waggled her fingers at Katie as she went out the door.

Katie waved back as she answered her phone.

"There's a couple here to see you," Rose said.

"The Lancasters. Tell them I'll be right there." She ended the call and hurried out to the cash desks, where Fiona and Phil Lancaster were waiting.

Fiona looked lovely and sophisticated, wearing light-blue seersucker pants, a white eyelet blouse, and navy pumps. A sapphire-and-diamond necklace-and-earring set capped the outfit. In contrast, Phil looked rumpled in his wrinkled khaki slacks and a red polo shirt. Katie was beginning to think that Phil was always in a bit of disarray and that he'd look downright disreputable if it weren't for Fiona.

"I'm so glad you made it," Katie said, as Fiona gave her a warm hug.

"We wouldn't have missed it," Fiona said. "I can hardly wait to discover all the treasures you have here."

Katie took them on the promised tour. Fiona appeared to be delighted by everything, especially Liz Meier's stained glass. She bought a lovely suncatcher to hang in her dining room window.

Phil, on the other hand, didn't care for anything except for Vance's furniture. He even took Vance's card so he could commission Vance to make the Lancasters' granddaughter a rocking horse for Christmas.

As Katie and the Lancasters strolled by Hugh McKinney's booth, Phil stopped and rocked back on his heels. Hugh sat on a cobbler's bench, tooling yet another piece of leather.

"McKinney, I'm glad to see you landed on your feet." Phil squinted at the assortment of goods Hugh had for sale. "Some of these look pretty good."

"They all look good," Hugh said. "You old codger." His face broke into a smile. "What're you doing in these parts?"

"Fiona likes to visit from time to time. She says it's quaint." He shrugged. "So, how come you set up a leather goods shop?"

"I had to do something after retiring from the post office."

"Retired, eh?" Phil chuckled. "I heard there was a little more to it than that."

"Well, they were downsizing, and I was getting close to retirement age," Hugh said. "They offered me a nice severance package if I'd go ahead and leave."

"Huh. I've been kicked out of a few places before, but nobody has ever paid *me* to leave," Phil said, and he and Hugh shared a laugh.

"What a small world," Fiona mumbled. "Excuse me, dear. I'll be right back."

As Fiona hurried over to speak with the older woman she'd recognized, Katie hung back to watch Phil continue to verbally spar with Hugh. After a moment, Phil looked around, realized Fiona was missing, and asked Katie where she'd gone. Katie nodded in the direction of Fiona and her friend, and Phil went to join them.

"So, how do you know Mr. Lancaster?" Katie asked Hugh.

"We were privates together at Fort Gordon." Hugh grinned. "Phil and I were always trying to outdo each other."

Katie nodded, then spoke again. "I apologize for changing the subject, but I spoke with Sue Sweeney this morning." Katie watched Hugh's face to see his reaction, but there was none. "She mentioned that you cautioned her about buying Harper Jones's building."

The corners of his mouth turned down. "Just making an observation, that's all."

"Do you think Mr. Jones was involved in whatever led to Ken Fenton's death?"

"I couldn't say. All I know is that Ken was involved in some nasty business and that his brother was up to his neck in it, too. Either way, If I were you, I believe I'd let everyone know that Paul Fenton is in no way still affiliated with the building."

"Why do you think Paul was involved in whatever trouble Ken was in?" Katie asked.

"Because you never saw one when the other wasn't far behind."

Before he could say anything more, Phil and Fiona returned.

"Ladies, we'd better continue this tour," Phil said. "We need to get on the road before too much longer."

"I know, I know," Fiona said, rolling her eyes at Katie. "Always so impatient."

They said their good-byes to Hugh and continued walking until they'd reached Chad's Pad.

"I saved this one for last," Katie said. "There's nothing for sale here, but it's where my late husband's artwork is showcased."

"Oh, Katie!" Fiona enveloped her in another hug and then went to explore each painting in the cramped room.

"These are breathtaking." Fiona held a painting of a magnolia blossom at arm's length. "It's so lifelike you almost feel as if you could lean in and smell it. Don't you, Phil?"

When she got no response from Phil, she turned and looked around the room. No Phil.

"Where'd he go?" Fiona asked Katie.

"I haven't a clue. I didn't even notice him leave."

"Neither did I." Fiona chuckled. "I suppose we'd better try and find him."

Katie nodded and closed and locked the door once more.

"You must miss your husband so much. How long has it been since you lost him?"

"A little over two years."

Fiona shook her head sadly, and Katie hoped she wouldn't ask for more details. She didn't want to discuss her private life with a woman she'd only just met. Fortunately, they quickly found Phil, and their conversation was abruptly halted. Unfortunately, he was in what appeared to be a heated argument with Hugh McKinney.

". . . be sticking your nose in where it doesn't belong," Hugh was saying.

"I'll do whatever I damn well please, and—"

Fiona hurried forward to place a hand on Phil's arm. "Darling, you're making a scene."

"Why should I care?" Phil growled.

"She's right," Hugh said. "This isn't the time or the place."

"Well, you just name the time and the place, and I'll be there."

Fiona gave her husband's arm a tug as she laughed a little

too loudly. "You fellows and your baseball rivalries! Phil, let's *go*."

Phil harrumphed, but this time he conceded to his wife's wishes and the two began walking toward the stairs that led to the cash desks on the floor below.

"I simply love this stained-glass ornament," Fiona said as Katie fell into step beside them. "I'm sure I could've bought a hundred other things, but Phil would have grouched at me all the way home." She lowered her voice conspiratorially. "Next time I'm in town, we'll have lunch, and then I'll come back and shop alone."

Katie merely smiled, wondering what Phil and Hugh had really been arguing about. She didn't buy the baseball rivalry bit for a minute.

~~~~~~~

Katie waved good-bye to the Lancasters and turned to speak with Rose. As she did, she stepped into Ray Davenport's path.

"Oops! Sorry, Ray." She smiled. "I'd better watch where I'm going."

"Yes, you had."

She was taken aback by his tone but decided to ignore it. "Were you coming to talk to me?"

"Nope. I'm on my way upstairs to see Vance."

A realization came to her. "Ah . . ." She looked around. "Who's with you?"

"Excuse me?" he asked.

"Which of your daughters is with you—Sasha or Sadie?"

"Neither."

Now Katie was really confused about Ray's behavior. "Well, do you have a second? I'd like a word with you."

Ray blew out a coffee-scented breath as he looked at his watch. "I'll come by your office when I've finished up with Vance. But I only have a minute, so you'll need to make it quick."

"Fine." She was about to tell him not to bother coming by

her office at all, but she really wanted to tell him how the post office manager had acted. She also wanted to find out what in the world was making her so-called friend behave like such a jerk.

She stormed into her office, slammed the door, and grabbed a peppermint. She unwrapped the candy, popped it into her mouth, and promptly bit it in half.

Her phone rang. It was Andy.

"Hey, Sunshine. How are you?"

"Okay, but I sure do have a lot to tell you about at lunch."

"Yeah . . . that's why I'm calling. I'm going to have to cancel on you today. Hopefully, I can make it up to you this evening."

"Sure. No problem."

"You're the best. Gotta run."

And that was the end of their call.

Swell. Just swell.

Katie decided she might as well walk to Tealicious when lunchtime came. Brad had been working on a delicious-looking seafood salad earlier that morning.

Finding it hard to concentrate, Katie was staring blankly at a spreadsheet on her computer screen when Ray came by a few minutes later. "What did you need to talk to me about?" he asked, sounding irritated.

Katie came this close to saying, "Nothing. Just go away." But, again, she hoped she could find out what was causing his boorish attitude.

"I went to the post office yesterday," she began.

"Good for you."

She pressed her lips together. "If you'd allow me to finish . . ."

"By all means."

"What's the matter with you?" she asked.

"Not a thing. Why?"

"Because you're acting like a jerk! Have I done something to offend you?"

"No," he said. "Do you have to have *every* man on Victoria Square at your beck and call to feel good about yourself?"

Katie's mouth dropped open—shocked and hurt by that remark. "Since when do I have *any* man on Victoria Square at my beck and call? In fact, Andy just called and canceled lunch."

"Then I imagine you'll have to run over to Tealicious and get America's Top Model Chef to whip up something and feed it to you."

"Is that what you're angry about?" Katie asked incredulously.

"I'm not angry about anything."

"You are! You're angry because Brad fed me a petit four yesterday."

Ray held up his hands. "Once again, I'm not angry about anything. If you want to fawn over your Chef Adonis, why shouldn't you? But, be warned. I mentioned to Sophie over the phone last night that Janine was out and Chef Brad Andrews was in, and she was over the moon. So, you might have some competition when she gets back to town."

"I'm not interested in Brad that way. And he's not interested in me, either."

"That's what you think. I know how a man looks when he's interested in a woman, and—believe me—he is."

"You're being ridiculous. Brad is a wonderful chef, and I'm lucky to have him working for me. That's *all*." She paused. "And he's too old for Sophie."

"That's what I told her. But I guess he's perfect for you."

"He's perfect for *Erikka*," Katie said.

"Yeah, well. I think his affection lies elsewhere."

"Well, you know what your opinion is like, Ray, and everybody has one!"

He drew his bushy brows together. "Tell me what you summoned me to hear so I can go on about my business."

Katie studied him for a moment, wondering why he was so angry about Brad. She had half a mind to tell him to go on

about his stupid business, but she wanted his opinion about
the post office manager.

"Are you going to listen to me objectively?" she asked.

He raised and dropped one shoulder.

She took a deep breath. The day was really wearing on
her patience. "I went to the post office yesterday and spoke
with the manager about Hugh McKinney's employment."

"And?"

"And all the guy would tell me was that yes, Hugh Mc-
Kinney had been an employee of the United States Postal
Service," Katie said. "You'd think he was a government agent
or a soldier, but instead of being instructed to divulge only his
name, rank, and serial number, the man was programmed to
say that Hugh McKinney was once an employee there."

"What did you expect, Katie? Did you think the man
would tell you that Hugh McKinney was doing something
inappropriate and that they let him take early retirement
rather than fire him?"

"Well, not exactly, but I expected him to be a little more
forthcoming than he was."

"Sorry to disappoint you, Your Majesty. The post office
manager was merely doing his job and failed to fall at your
feet like so many of your other conquests."

"Get out." Katie rose from behind her desk, determined
to throw him out bodily if she had to.

Ray stared at her for several long seconds, then pivoted
and walked away.

Katie slammed her door behind him. Then she opened it
and slammed it again, just to drive home her point.

What nerve! She had no conquests! What in the world was
the matter with him? She and Ray had been friends for years.
Okay, almost *a* year. He'd known almost since he met her that
she was dating Andy and hadn't minded the fact, yet now he
seemed downright jealous of Brad. Did he think maybe she
was cheating on Andy with Brad? But, surely he knew her
better than that! How dare he question her character!

She came down hard on her office chair and then got right back up. She was so angry she knew she needed to cool off before she could deal with work and/or her vendors. But she wasn't about to walk around Artisans Alley. Instead, she left her office and exited the building via the door to the vendors' lounge.

A few cars dotted the back parking lot and Katie headed for the perimeter. It was going to take more than a circuit or two to cool her flaming ire.

Fourteen

Katie finally calmed down and even managed a smile as she walked into Tealicious for lunch. It had only been two days, but she could already see how much Brad had improved the tea shop. By changing the music and tweaking the decor, the entire atmosphere had changed to that of elegance and class. The place had been entirely too laid-back with Janine in charge. Laid-back was fine for a diner or café, but people expected a different ambiance when they stepped into a tea shop.

The dining room was packed. Of course, it hadn't hurt that Margo had sent a press release to all the regional news outlets announcing the addition of world-class chef Brad Andrews to Tealicious. When Katie had first received Margo's email with the already-sent press release attached, Katie had been just a wee bit irritated. How dare Margo Bonner interfere with Katie's running of Tealicious? The woman had been given the option of a partnership, but she'd eschewed it in favor of providing Katie a loan to take over the shop.

Now that Katie saw the number of people waiting to be served, as well as those already seated in the dining room, she begrudgingly had to admit that Margo had done a brilliant piece of marketing. Maybe her former mother-in-law had wanted to ensure timely repayment of that loan, though she needn't worry about that—Katie felt sure she should be able to pay it off well ahead of schedule. Still, Katie realized she should be gracious and send Margo some flowers to show her appreciation. After all, it was entirely possible she'd simply been trying to help. And Katie certainly couldn't argue with the result.

A smiling Brad beckoned for her to join him. Katie sidled past the packed tables. Arriving at his side, she leaned forward conspiratorially. "Has it been like this all day? I mean, it was busy yesterday but nothing like this."

"It has. I've even signed a couple of autographs, believe it or not."

"Maybe people expect you to move on to bigger and better things soon—perhaps even a television gig," Katie said, with a smile. "I can see that happening. You have the face and voice for TV."

"You think?" He grinned. "What're you having today?"

"The seafood salad and hibiscus tea."

"Terrific. I'll add a shortbread cookie as well."

"Please don't. I'll have to walk two extra laps around the Square tomorrow morning as it is."

He scoffed. "Nonsense. You have to try one. They're tiny."

"Okay, but just *one*."

"Take a seat—that table over there is empty. I'll have one of the girls bring your lunch out."

Katie nodded and threaded her way across the dining room to an empty table by the window.

One of the servers, Emma, was bussing the table next to Katie's. She stepped closer and said softly, "Thanks for hiring

Brad. He's amazing to work for—at least, so far—and he's absolutely dreamy."

"I'm glad you're pleased." Katie tried to hide a grin as she shook her head.

"Is there anything I can get you?" Emma asked.

"Brad took my order." She heard a bell ringing in the kitchen. Emma hurried to answer and a moment later came out with a tray. Brad had done as she'd asked and only added the one cookie. Katie tasted her salad, which was every bit as delicious as she'd imagined it would be.

Katie eavesdropped on the conversations around her. Everyone seemed happy with the food, the ambiance, and she felt a flush of pride in her new business.

She finished her lunch—even the not-so-tiny shortbread cookie—and was debating getting more tea to take back with her to Artisans Alley, when Harper and Mary Jones came through the door. Katie cringed, remembering all too well Paul's unwelcome nighttime visit. She hoped the couple wouldn't see her, but her hopes were dashed.

Mary nudged Harper, and the two engaged in a whispered exchange. And then they headed straight for Katie's table.

The Harpers couldn't possibly accuse her of any wrongdoing. She was here first and in her own establishment, for goodness' sake. She had more right to be at Tealicious than anyone. She straightened her spine and lifted her chin.

"Hello, Katie," Mary said, and her voice actually sounded pleasant.

Katie didn't trust Mary's politeness not to be a trick. "Hello."

"Fancy seeing you here," Harper said, barking out a brittle cackle. Laughter coming from this man was as incongruous as roller skates on a zebra. "Just kidding. I know this is your place. Fine job you've done with it, too."

"Thank you." Katie was aware that her voice was flat and filled with suspicion, but she couldn't help it. She didn't trust these people.

"Paul said he came to see you the other night," Mary said. "He told us he accused you—to that meddlesome Detective Schuler, no less—of bothering us. I told my baby brother that you'd done nothing but come to express your sympathy over Ken's death and that you even brought me a lovely box of candy."

Katie shifted in her chair, trying to angle her body away from the Harpers and toward the door. "I appreciate your setting the record straight."

"Paul has always been a little overprotective of his family," Mary continued. "You wouldn't think that of the baby of the family, would you? But little Paul always was a bulldog."

Little Paul?

"What . . . what brings you to Tealicious?"

"Lunch—same as you," Harper said. "But, I imagine yours is *free* since it's *your* place."

Katie didn't appreciate his snarky tone. "Not at all. I pay for my food just like everyone else. I'm the owner, not a free-loader."

"Well, good for you," Mary said. "I just hope that doesn't mean you're paying for the food twice."

Katie merely shrugged, having no desire to discuss her business—or anything else—with Harper and Mary Jones. "I hope you enjoy your lunch as much as I've enjoyed mine." She stood. "If you'll excuse me, I need to get back to Artisans Alley."

"You know, if that newspaper article wasn't lying about how good the food is, I believe we will," Harper said.

Katie paid for her lunch and left her pretty little tea shop. As she walked back to Artisans Alley, she wondered why the Joneses had been so nice. The day she took the candy to Mary, the woman had practically thrown her out . . . and she'd definitely been hiding something. Harper had never been anything other than belligerent. Were they being amiable because they'd discovered she owned Tealicious? Ownership of the tea shop would, she supposed, lend her offer of buying their building—along with the rest of the interested Victoria Square merchants—more credibility.

No, there had to be more to their cordiality than the fact that they'd discovered she owned Tealicious. McKinlay Mill was a small town. Most of its residents didn't need to read in a newspaper that Katie had taken over the tea shop six months ago. More than that, Katie didn't trust either Harper or his wife. They'd been nice to her for a reason. But what could that reason possibly be?

~~~~~~~

Hours later, Katie was laboring over a stack of bills when Andy stopped in to see her. She smiled, stretched, and stood to embrace him.

"What a wonderful surprise." She noticed then that he held a small white bag. "What's that?"

"It's a cinnamon roll. I was afraid you didn't take time to eat."

"I appreciate your thoughtfulness," she said. "I did have lunch, though. I went to Tealicious. When I was there this morning, Brad was making a seafood salad that looked divine. So when you had to cancel, I decided to go try it."

Andy raised his eyebrows slightly. "Was it good?"

"Fantastic. You'll have to try it sometime."

"I will. You know, if you'd rather start going to Tealicious for our lunch dates, that would be fine."

Katie shook her head. "Absolutely not. There's a reason we don't normally have our lunch dates at either of our restaurants. Our lunch dates are for putting our work aside for an hour and focusing on each other."

Andy pulled her in for another kiss. And another.

Finally, Katie pulled back, a satisfied smile lingering on her lips. "Thank you for the cinnamon roll. I'll save it for later."

"That's fine. I really just needed an excuse to see you. Your smile always brightens my day."

"Wow. Is there any way we can play hooky for the rest of the day?" she asked, grinning.

Andy sobered. "I'm afraid not."

"Then, would it help get you through the day if I promise to give you a back rub tonight?"

He smiled. "Absolutely. You're the best."

"What's going on today? Did someone call in sick, or are you having an especially busy Tuesday?"

"Neither, but when Erikka came in, she told me that she got a letter from the school system saying that her part-time position has been eliminated."

"Oh, no," Katie said. "Poor Erikka. There goes her excellent benefits package."

He held up a finger. "Not exactly. There's a full-time position doing the same type of work that has become available, and the school system is offering that job to Erikka. They need to know by mid-July whether or not she accepts the position."

"Are you saying that Erikka is either going to have to go full-time with the school system or lose her job there altogether?"

"That's exactly what I'm saying." He sighed. "And if Erikka goes full-time, I'll most likely lose my assistant manager."

Katie hugged him. "Oh, Andy. I'm sorry."

And she was sorry that Andy was going to have to hire and train another assistant manager. But the thought of lovely Erikka leaving Angelo's Pizzeria for good made her heart soar. And even better for Katie, it actually was a wonderful opportunity for Erikka.

The crappy day had totally turned around. Nothing could spoil it now. But just to make sure, Katie crossed her fingers—hard.

~~~~~~

Things were definitely looking up. So much so that Katie was practically skipping later that afternoon when she left her office to stretch her legs and walk around Artisans Alley to see how everything was going. But when she passed the cash desks, she noticed Rose slumped on a stool at cash desk one with her chin lowered to her chest.

"Rose? What's wrong?" Katie moved around behind the desk, afraid that Rose was on the verge of collapse.

Rose raised her head, and tears shimmered in her clear blue eyes. "Shin splints. If my legs don't get better soon, I'll have to bow out of the walkathon. And I've trained so hard for it!"

Katie put an arm around Rose's shoulders. "Have you been to the doctor?"

"I saw him yesterday afternoon. He told me I have bone-related shin splints." She drew a shuddering breath. "I was afraid I had something worse—like a fracture. Dr. Peterson warned me that if I don't stop walking until the shin splints heal, I really *could* get a stress fracture."

"Rose, dear, you really need to be at home with your feet up."

"I've never been one to put my feet up and laze about. You know that."

"I *do* know that, but you have to take care of yourself," Katie said. "We want you to get well so you can participate in that walkathon."

Rose drew in a wavering breath.

"Are you okay to drive yourself home?"

"Of course. But if you don't mind, I'd like to leave now. I want to get home to my computer to look up what I need to do to quickly recover. I'm afraid my doctor isn't all that knowledgeable when it comes to how to fix this, other than advising rest."

"I can take over manning the cash desk. Keep me posted."

"I will, dear."

Katie watched as Rose gathered her purse and her current book, giving her a wave as she left Artisans Alley via the main entrance.

Katie looked around, comparing the foot traffic at Artisans Alley to that of Tealicious, and thought wryly that maybe she should talk to Margo about drawing up a press release to sing the praises of this establishment, too.

Even if the booths near the cash desks had been full of shoppers, Katie couldn't have missed the hulking form of Paul Fenton coming toward her. He carried a set of monogrammed towels he'd picked up from Rhonda Simpson's booth. Given his behavior the last time she'd seen him, Katie felt she'd be perfectly justified in refusing to serve him. But, then, that would only hurt Rhonda.

Paul placed the towels on the counter. "Hi."

Katie nodded, rang up the price of the towels, and gave Paul the total.

He handed her a credit card. "I want to apologize. I was out of line the other night."

"You think?" She blinked at him. "You forced your way into my home, threatened me to stay away from your family, and told the Sheriff's Office I'd harassed you. That's more than out of line. That's way the heck across the border and buying the souvenir T-shirt."

Paul's face hardened. "I'm sorry. I spoke with my sister, Mary, and she said I overreacted." He leaned closer. "What can I say? I'm grieving the loss of my big brother. I can't help being a little overprotective of my sister. Can I?"

Katie shrugged and ran the credit card, then handed it back to him along with the receipt, which needed his signature. "Could you sign this, please?"

"Of course." He signed his name and then handed back the slip of paper and pen. But then Paul made a grab for Katie's wrist. Eyes wide, she tried to pull her arm free, but Paul tightened his grip while caressing her skin with his thumb.

"There's no reason we can't be friends," he said softly. An underlying menace in his tone made the hair on the back of her neck bristle.

"I can't think of a single reason why we should," Katie said firmly.

He jerked her arm, pulling her closer to him, so close she could feel his breath on her face. "Because you don't want me as an enemy, Ms. Bonner."

"I thought I already was."

He smiled and let her go. "Not yet. But don't push your luck." He took the bag of towels and left the Alley.

Katie watched until he was out of sight before she sank onto the stool and rubbed her arm.

"What the hell was that?"

Katie started, not having heard Ray approach. "Ray, what's the matter with you? What are you raving about now?"

"I'm raving because from where I was standing it looked like Paul Fenton was trying to seduce you . . . and you didn't seem to be resisting him."

She rolled her eyes. "Shows what you know. Your detective skills have apparently gone to pot these days."

"I'm as sharp as ever!" He scowled. "Wait. What *was* he doing?" His expression darkened as realization seemed to sink in. "Threatening you? Of course. Damn it, woman, you make me stupid." He took out his phone.

"What are you doing?"

"Calling Schuler."

"Put the phone away. *Please*," Katie added.

"Just how bad a threat did Fenton make?"

"He didn't. Not in so many words. Besides, he'd turn it all around on me again and make me look like a fool to Detective Schuler." Katie told Ray about seeing Harper and Mary at Tealicious. "And then Paul strolls in here and buys monogrammed towels like it's the most normal thing in the world."

Ray squinted. "Did they have *his* monogram? I mean, what man buys monogrammed towels for himself?"

Katie ran a hand over her cheek. "I don't know what monogram was on them, Ray. I was trying to figure out what he was doing, not what he was buying. It's all just too weird. First, the entire family treats me crappy—even the one I'm doing business with—and then, today, they act like I'm the greatest thing since water slides."

"Or monogrammed towels. Huh. That *is* out there. Maybe I need to take a closer look at the entire Fenton clan."

"Why? And, more importantly, how? I thought the Sheriff's Office had cut off all communication with you."

"They're not my only source," Ray said sourly.

"Why are you here anyway? The last time I saw you, you were pretty rude to me."

"Yeah, well, I came to say I'm sorry." He lifted his hands and let them fall. "Like I said, you make me stupid."

Katie's stomach flip-flopped. "What's that supposed to mean?"

"You're a bright woman. Figure it out."

Katie sighed as Ray walked away. If she lived to be a hundred, she'd never figure that man out. Or any of the rest of them, most likely. All she knew was that she felt unsettled, and that wasn't a pleasant place to be.

Fifteen

~~~~~~~~~~

The shadows were lengthening when Katie closed Artisans Alley and walked across the Square to Sassy Sally's. She couldn't get Phil Lancaster's behavior toward Hugh McKinney out of her mind, and she was determined to find out how well Nick and Don knew the Lancasters.

Upon arriving, she found Nick perusing the bookshelves near the reception desk. He turned. "Good afternoon, madame," Nick said with a twinkle in his eye. "Would you like to make a reservation?"

"I'd *like* to reserve every night for the next year, but I can't afford it." She smiled. "Actually, I just dropped in to chat for a moment. Do you have time?"

"I always have time for the woman who brought Brad Andrews to Victoria Square." He shrugged. "I mean, I'd make time for you anyway, but I especially will now."

"Is Don around?"

"He's out running an errand. How are things going with Brad?"

"Great. I went to Tealicious for lunch and he'd made the most delicious seafood salad with crabmeat, tricolor pasta, peas, celery, and green bell pepper." She closed her eyes. "Amazing."

"That sounds fantastic." He squinted into the distance. "I wonder if I offered him a free night's stay, he'd make some for us."

"I'm sure he would. Or you *could* frequent Tealicious."

"And *pay* for it?" he asked, aghast.

Katie laughed, but then turned somber.

"Okay, what's up?" Nick asked.

"I'm not sure how to delicately broach the subject so I guess I'll just dive in."

"Do it."

"Okay. How long have you known Phil and Fiona Lancaster?"

"They were one of the first couples to book a reservation after Don and I appeared on that local television news program discussing the history of the mansion and detailing the renovations we'd made."

"Cool. From my own experience, I can see that it's easy to get to know Fiona. She's the loquacious one. But Phil is another story."

Nick arched a brow. "Spit it out. What is it you want to know, Katie?"

"How well do you know Phil?"

"Phil never says much until he has a drink or two in him," Nick said. "Then the man would debate sports, the stock market, or politics with a fence post—and there's only one opinion."

"His?"

"You got it. Thankfully, those are all subjects both Don and I avoid, and Fiona helps keep him under control. She steers him into safer territory when his mouth begins to run away from him."

"I took Fiona and Phil on a tour of Artisans Alley today," Katie said.

"I'm surprised they haven't been there before, as many times as they've visited the Square."

Katie wrinkled her forehead. "Yeah . . . that is odd. Maybe they've had other things planned to do and just hadn't gotten around to it."

"Maybe." He shrugged. "So, how'd they like it?"

"Fiona seemed to enjoy herself. And, it just so happens that Phil and Hugh McKinney—the new leather goods vendor—were Army buddies." She fell quiet for a moment, mulling over the things Phil had said about Hugh and the things they'd said to each other.

"What is it?" Nick prodded.

"Phil made me think that I shouldn't have allowed Hugh to rent a space at Artisans Alley," Katie said. "In fact, it was Vance who leased him the space, and I trust Vance's judgment . . . usually."

"But there's something about this McKinney fellow that creeps you out?"

"Not really. I didn't give the whole matter much thought until Phil started giving me ominous hints about Hugh McKinney's tenure at the post office, and surprise that Hugh hadn't been fired or wasn't making license plates."

"Did you ask Phil flat out what he was talking about?" Nick asked.

"No." She sighed. "I *did* go to the post office and asked to speak with Hugh's former employer."

Nick's eyes widened, but he said nothing.

Katie flicked a wrist as if to wave away his thoughts. "I know, I know. I didn't really expect him to provide me with any confidential information, but I'd hoped he might have at least said something along the lines of 'You sure made a good decision welcoming Hugh McKinney into your organization' or 'I'd keep an eye on that Hugh McKinney, if I were you.' The man could've been vague but still given me an idea of how he felt about Mr. McKinney . . . right?"

"Maybe he didn't have any particular feeling about McKinney."

"What do you mean by that?" Katie asked. "How could he *not* have any particular feeling about one of his employees, especially one who'd worked with him for years?"

Nick spread his hands. "There's a young woman on our cleaning staff who does an adequate job, doesn't converse with anyone, and guards her privacy. If you asked me about her, I could tell you her name, but that's about it. If you asked me for a job recommendation, I'd tell you the woman is reliable."

"That's the word you'd use? Reliable?"

"Yes. But, on the other hand, if you asked me about Leah, I'd tell you how much pride she takes in her work, how considerate she is of our guests and other staff members, and about how guests who've met her brag about her upon checkout. Unless she was leaving the area or something, I'd also beg you not to take our best worker."

Katie smiled. She'd met Leah. The woman really was a treasure.

"Was McKinney at Artisans Alley when you took Phil and Fiona on the tour?" Nick asked.

"He was. And they greeted each other rather like you'd expect old Army buddies to do: 'Hello, you old son-of-a-gun.' That sort of thing. But, later, Fiona and I came out of Chad's Pad to find Hugh and Phil arguing."

"About what?"

"Fiona said something about baseball rivalries, but I didn't buy it," Katie said. "I didn't hear much of what they were saying, but when Fiona began pulling Phil away, Hugh said it wasn't the time nor the place. Phil said for Hugh to tell him the time and the place and that he'd be there."

Nick made a confetti-tossing gesture. "It seems to me that

Phil gave you every opening to ask him what he knew about your newest vendor. You should've bitten the bullet and asked him."

"I know, but I didn't want to appear gossipy. Now I wish I had. How often do Phil and Fiona typically visit McKinlay Mill?"

"Every two or three months."

"If I don't have a better feel for Hugh's personality by the time the Lancasters return, maybe I'll ask Phil about him then," Katie said.

Nick grinned. "Just start pouring bourbon. He'll tell you anything you want to know . . . and then some."

Katie laughed.

As she walked back toward her apartment, however, Katie hoped she'd find out whatever secrets Hugh McKinney might be harboring long before the Lancasters returned to Sassy Sally's.

~~~~~~

Knowing Andy had been having a rough day, Katie decided to stop into Angelo's Pizzeria to see if he could come upstairs for a late dinner. The last time she'd made lasagna, she'd split it into two, freezing the extra. If he agreed, she would take it out of the freezer and then head to the grocery store to get a fresh loaf of bread.

As she entered the pizzeria, she made eye contact with Erikka, who narrowed her gaze at Katie and then quickly looked away.

"Hey, there, Katie!" Roger called to her from behind the counter. "Andy is in his office if you need to see him."

She smiled. "Thanks, Roger."

She walked on back to Andy's office, wondering why Erikka might be upset with *her.* She tried to push the notion out of her head as she tapped on the office door.

"Come in."

Katie opened the door and stuck her head in. "Hey, handsome. I came by to invite you to dinner."

Smiling, Andy stepped out from behind the desk and walked over to give her a kiss. He then tugged her inside the office, closed the door, and gave her a more thorough kiss.

"Wow," she said. "May I take that as a *yes*?"

"Yes, I'd love to come to dinner," Andy said. "It'll be later, though. The soonest I can get away is eight o'clock."

"That's perfect." She remembered Erikka's resentful glance and put some extra *oomph* into her good-bye kiss.

After taking the lasagna out of the freezer and putting it in the oven before she drove to the grocery store to get something for said dinner, Katie thought about Erikka. She'd thought the other woman might've had a crush on Andy, but now Katie wondered if it was something more. Was Erikka in love with Andy?

It doesn't matter, she told herself. *At the end of the month, Erikka will be gone . . . happily working for the school district. Or even* unhappily. *I don't really care, as long as she's away from Andy.* She knew that was uncharitable, but it was hard to have warm, fuzzy feelings toward someone who was trying to steal your boyfriend.

By the time she'd arrived at the store, Katie had decided on making a salad and lasagna for dinner. She headed for the produce section. There, inspecting bags of lettuce, was her friend and lawyer Seth Landers.

Grinning, Katie eased up behind him and said in the sultriest voice she could muster, "Do you come here often?"

He didn't even turn. "Only when I have to, Katie."

"Darn! I was hoping to fool you!"

"Never." He turned and gave her his best brotherly hug. "I actually despise grocery shopping. Luckily for me, Jaime enjoys it."

Katie looked around. "Is he here?"

"No. He's working late, and I'm on my own for dinner."

"Would you like to join Andy and me?" she asked.

"No, thanks. I appreciate the offer, but I have a deposition to read over this evening. I thought I'd make myself a salad and settle in for a long night of reading."

"Interesting case?"

"I wish it were," Seth said. "What about you? What are your plans for the evening?"

"I'm making lasagna for Andy. He's had a rough day. It appears Erikka will be leaving the pizzeria at the end of the month."

He nodded. "That's right. She works part-time for the school system, doesn't she?"

"She does," Katie said. "And they've notified her that they're eliminating the part-time position. If she wants to keep her job, she'll have to work full-time."

"I know a couple of members on the Greece school district's board of education, and they're adamant about getting their budget balanced. They're combining positions where they can and encouraging some of the older staff members to take early retirement."

"Speaking of early retirement, do you have any idea why a postal employee—specifically, Hugh McKinney—would be forced into early retirement by the post office?"

"I don't," Seth said. "But it was probably something as simple as a cost-savings measure."

"Hmm . . . I met someone who intimated that there might be another reason."

Seth smiled. "Take it from a skeptical attorney, but that other person might've simply been planting seeds to make you mistrust McKinney."

"Why would he do that?"

"Who knows? But in my line of work, I see a lot of strange, unreasonable things. It could be that the other person has a grudge against the guy and wants you to ask him to leave Artisans Alley."

"I wouldn't make the man leave without just cause," Katie said.

"Then I wouldn't worry about this other person's intimations. Observe McKinney to see if he gives you any reason to be concerned."

"That's good advice, Seth. Thanks."

"No charge. That's what pseudo-brothers are for. I'll have that merchants' agreement finalized within the next couple of days, and be sure and tell Andy for me that I wish him luck replacing Erikka."

"Will do."

And she had every intention of passing along Seth's regrets—even if she had none herself.

~~~~~~~

When Andy came through the apartment door and into the kitchen at just after eight, he closed his eyes and took a deep breath and sighed. "This place smells heavenly."

"And your place doesn't?" Katie asked. She stood at the counter, a serrated knife in one hand, about to slice a loaf of crusty Italian bread. She'd donned a cute vintage lace-trimmed eyelet apron because she knew it amused Andy to see her in it, calling it her Suzy Homemaker outfit.

"Yeah, sure, the pizzeria smells great, but this is different. This smells like Momma's kitchen."

Katie hugged him. "That's the best possible compliment you could give me." She knew how much Andy admired his mother and her cooking. His father—Ron—was the barbeque chef, but his mother was the maestro of the kitchen. Katie only crossed her fingers that the lasagna's taste would rival the aroma.

"How was your day?" Andy asked, after kissing the top of Katie's head.

She thought of telling him about Paul Fenton's visit to Artisans Alley, but she quickly dismissed the idea. Andy had been through enough today and had plenty on his mind without her adding to his distress. Plus, she certainly didn't want him to get into an argument—or worse, a fistfight—with Fenton. The man was menacing, to say the least. She'd prefer that she and Andy both stay as far away from him as possible.

"It was fine," she said. "I ran into Seth in the grocery store. He wanted me to wish you luck finding a new assistant manager. I didn't realize this, but he's friends with people on the Greece school board. He told me this shake-up is all about getting the budget under control."

Andy sighed. "It still sucks."

"I know, but what about training Roger for the assistant manager position?" Katie asked.

"Roger wants to work for that contractor doing construction and carpentry. Remember?"

"Sure, but he can still work for Angelo's while he's in school. And, since Erikka will be there until the end of the month, she could help you train Roger."

Katie felt Andy stiffen. He dropped his arms from around her and stepped away.

"You're glad Erikka is leaving, aren't you?" he asked.

She couldn't deny it. "Andy, I'm trying to help you solve your problem . . . to brainstorm. You'd do the same for me."

"You've been jealous of Erikka from the very start."

"If you'll recall, *I'm* the one who introduced you to Erikka and suggested you give her a job," Katie said. And that impulsive decision had come back to bite her again and again.

"Yes, you recommended Erikka for the job, but you've been jealous ever since."

Katie put her hands on her hips and glared up into Andy's face. "She's in love with you! Do you realize that?"

"We're friends. Period. I'm with you." He ran both hands through his hair. "Is she the reason you hired that golden boy to work at Tealicious?"

"I hired Brad Andrews on Nick's recommendation to manage Tealicious because Janine left me in the lurch, and

Brad is an acclaimed chef. He's already increased business tenfold. Why would you think I had an ulterior motive in hiring the man?"

"Because I believe you brought him in to get back at me for making Erikka my assistant manager. Even Ray Davenport told me this morning that I'd better watch that guy—that he was feeding you cake! Is that true?"

"Brad had me taste something he'd just baked. His hands were encased in gloves, and I'd taken mine off, so he popped it into my mouth! And since when do you put any stock whatsoever in anything Ray Davenport says?"

"Since he confirmed something that I noticed the first time I met Brad Andrews—the man likes you!"

"Well, I hope he *likes* me—we're going to be working together!"

"So, it's 'that woman is in love with you' when we're discussing Erikka, but when we're talking about Brad, everything is just hunky-dory fine."

"I only met the man last week."

Andy ignored her and paced around the small kitchen. "Sure, you suggested I hire Erikka, but you also went behind my back and advised her to apply for the job at the school district!"

"Fine," said Katie. "If you want Erikka at Angelo's so badly, offer her full-time pay and benefits!"

"Maybe I will!" Andy hollered, and slammed out of the kitchen.

Katie followed, but he was already heading down the steps before she could protest.

"What about this painstakingly prepared dinner?" she mumbled.

Mason brushed against her legs.

"No, Garfield, you don't get the lasagna." She bent and picked the cat up. "And my appetite is gone now, too." There was nothing to do but let it cool a little before she put it into the refrigerator.

As she wrapped the lasagna in foil, Katie wondered if Andy really *would* offer Erikka a full-time job. If he did, Katie knew the woman would take it. She wouldn't have been terribly surprised if Erikka had turned down the school system in order to stay close to Andy in the first place.

And the nerve of that man asking if she'd hired Brad because she was jealous of his relationship with Erikka! That was ridiculous. Andy knew Janine had quit suddenly, giving Katie only three days' notice. She'd had to do something. The fact that the *something* turned out to be putting Brad Andrews into the position was a godsend.

Why in the world had Ray Davenport stuck his big nose into her business and informed Andy that he'd better "watch that guy"? The fact that Ray and Andy had never gotten along but had now bonded over a sudden, shared, preposterous dislike of Brad Andrews was laughable—or, at least, it would be had Andy not thrown the entire matter into her face. She'd be giving Ray Davenport a piece of her mind the next time she saw him.

To think, this entire thing had begun over her desire to help Andy find a replacement for Erikka. Was it telling that Andy was so adamant about not wanting to replace her? Katie knew Erikka was in love with Andy. And now she wondered if he was in love with her, too.

Sixteen

Katie awoke Wednesday morning with a throbbing headache. She'd slept fitfully and wished she could simply pull the covers up over her head and stay in bed for the rest of the day.

Mason must have read her mind because he hopped onto the bed, butted her chin with his head, and then licked her forehead.

She groaned. "Okay, okay. I'm coming." She threw back the covers and swung her feet over the side of the bed. Della wound around her ankles just to make sure Katie knew she was hungry, too.

Katie allowed herself a wistful smile. Andy might not love her anymore, but Mason and Della did . . . at least, until she ran out of cat food.

Katie went into the kitchen and poured kibble into one bowl, wet food into another, and water in a third. That should take care of them throughout the day. She readied the coffee pot and washed down two ibuprofen tablets with a glass of water.

As she'd done off and on throughout the night, she checked her phone. Nope, still no message from Andy.

Fine.

She went into the bathroom and took a nice hot shower. She wasn't up to walking this morning, nor was she in the mood to go to Tealicious. Brad had made it abundantly clear that he was capable of running the tea shop fabulously. Maybe she'd go over to check in later that morning after her headache eased.

By the time Katie had finished her shower, the coffee was ready. She filled a travel mug and headed for Artisans Alley.

Had she thought her day would improve when she arrived at Artisans Alley, Katie was sadly mistaken. Vance met her at the door.

"Rose called. She won't be in today. She's at home resting and hoping to get over her shin splints."

Katie sighed. "All right. I'll be manning the cash desk if you need me."

"Ida or I can relieve you if there's something you need to do," Vance said. "Plus, Rose said to call her if we get too busy, and she'll come on in."

"No way," Katie said. "She needs to take care of herself. I hope you told her to let us know if she needs anything."

"Of course I did."

"Thanks, Vance. I'm going to grab my laptop from the office, and then I'll head to the registers."

Wednesdays weren't typically busy at Artisans Alley—particularly during the summer months—so Katie hoped she'd have a few minutes here and there to do some of the work she needed to do. She retrieved her laptop and a handful of peppermint candies, which she placed in her jeans pocket, and returned to the cash desk.

Moments later, Hugh McKinney came in. "Good morning, R—" He stopped. "I'm sorry, Katie. I'd started to say good morning to Rose. Force of habit—I've become accustomed to seeing her there every morning."

Katie nodded. "Rose loves to man the cash desk. She's taking today off, though." As a sudden pain shot through her right temple, Katie winced and put her hand to her head.

Hugh hurried over. "Are you all right?"

"I'm fine. It's only a headache. The pain relievers I took before leaving home haven't kicked in yet."

He frowned slightly. "May I see your hand?"

Katie tentatively stretched out her hand.

With his thumb and index finger, Hugh squeezed the webbing on Katie's hand between her own thumb and forefinger. "I get headaches frequently, and my acupressure therapist taught me this pain-relief technique." He released her hand. "You try it. Hold that pressure point like I showed you for twenty to thirty seconds while breathing deeply through your nose. Then switch hands. Repeat the whole process three times."

"And that will make my headache go away?"

He chuckled. "Sometimes it works, sometimes it doesn't. But, at least it'll take your mind off your headache for a minute or two."

"Good point." Katie squeezed the pressure point between the thumb and forefinger of her opposite hand.

"Take care of yourself." Hugh went on upstairs to his booth.

Katie tried to concentrate on breathing through her nose and willing her headache to ease, but instead she was assailed by two thoughts—one, that maybe Hugh McKinney was a good guy after all; and two, that after his behavior the night before, she didn't want to rely on Andy Rust any longer than she had to for a place to live.

Andy had behaved abominably the night before. He'd stormed out and presumably went straight to Erikka. And then what? Had Erikka confessed her feelings for Andy? Had he told her he loved her, too? After all, he'd gotten angry over practically nothing. Was it the idea of losing Erikka that had driven him over the edge? He'd behaved as if he'd do anything to keep Erikka from leaving. Remembering his insufferable behavior infuriated Katie. Could this be the end of her relationship with Andy?

If they were through, she couldn't possibly continue living in the apartment over Angelo's Pizzeria. But even if she and Andy somehow worked past this argument, she was far too independent to continue to depend on him for her living arrangements.

She applied pressure to the acupressure point on the other hand and considered her possibilities. She could turn the upstairs of Tealicious into an apartment, and then she would have the ideal situation. She'd be on hand to help get things going first thing in the morning, and she would have no additional rent. Of course, it would take a lot of work to complete the necessary renovations, but it could be fun, too. For once in her adult life, she could have the full authority to decorate her living space exactly as she wanted, making no concessions to anyone.

She smiled and released her hand, realizing her headache had eased considerably. Maybe there was something to Hugh's acupressure after all.

~~~~~~~

As it turned out, this particular Wednesday at Artisans Alley was busier than Katie had anticipated. Not only had she had no time at all to work on anything other than ringing up customers' purchases, she hadn't had the opportunity to check her phone. For that, she was grateful. Some of the anger and frustration she'd felt all night was easing as well. She'd made an important decision that would give her more independence and security, no matter what happened with Andy.

When Katie saw Ray Davenport heading her way, however, her ire was rekindled. He obviously didn't realize how peeved she was with him because he strode right over and leaned against the cash desk.

"I ran into Vance at Tanner's, and he told me about Rose," Ray said. "Is she going to be all right?"

Katie shrugged.

He tried again. "I hope she will be. I know she'd been looking forward to this walkathon."

Leaning to the side, Katie spoke to a customer who walked up behind Ray. "I can ring you up."

Ray moved aside so the young woman could place her purchases on the desk. Katie removed the tags and rang them up at a snail's pace.

"I know you're busy, Katie," Ray said when the customer finally departed, "but I need to speak with you. How about I buy you lunch?"

"No, thank you. I have plans."

"Can't you get somebody to cover for you for a few minutes? I really need to talk to you."

She turned a cold gaze on him. "No, I can't."

"Wait. Are you upset with me for some reason?"

"Wow, you really *are* Sherlock Holmes, aren't you?"

He flung out his arms. "What have I done now? I know I was an ass the other day, but I thought I'd been all right since then."

Katie faced him, eyes blazing. "What gave you the right to tell Andy he'd better keep an eye on Brad? Brad and I are business associates, and I'd like to consider him a friend as well. Nevertheless, my relationships are none of anyone's business."

"I was joking!" Ray shook his head. "I didn't intend the Dough Boy to take me seriously. I mean, when does he ever?"

"Regardless of your intentions, you didn't need to be discussing me with Andy . . . or anyone else for that matter."

"If I've caused trouble between the two of you, I'm sorry.

I'll go right now and explain to Andy that I was only kidding around."

"What you said didn't cause our problems, it merely fanned the flames," Katie said. "Please stay out of it."

"You know I'd never purposefully hurt you . . . don't you?"

Katie ran her hand over her forehead. "So, what did you want to talk to me about?"

He looked around to make sure there wasn't anyone close enough to hear what he was saying. "I spoke with a friend last night about Ken Fenton's murder."

"I didn't think you were supposed to be talking about that."

"I'm not. But my friend is also retired, and he knows I'm a suspect, so he wants to help me out," Ray said.

"Heaven help us—there are two of you."

"Don't kid yourself. There's only one of me, and you're glad of it."

"You're right about that," Katie muttered.

"Anyway, this guy told me that Paul and Ken didn't get along. He said they were together a lot, but that much of their time was spent arguing."

"Playing devil's advocate here, Ray; most siblings argue. That doesn't mean that Paul killed Ken."

"It doesn't mean he didn't, either. You've been on the receiving end of Paul Fenton's anger. Don't you believe he's capable of murder?"

"Yeah, actually, I do. I think he'd enjoy snapping me like a twig, as a matter of fact."

"I'm afraid you might be right about that," Ray said. "Please be extra careful until this murder is solved."

"You'd do well to heed your own advice," she said as another customer approached the cash desk.

This time, Ray didn't hang around and headed for the lobby exit. Katie watched him leave until the woman in front of her cleared her throat.

Katie forced a smile. "Did you find everything you need?"

~~~~~~~

Katie asked Ida to oversee the cash desk while she went to lunch. Not surprisingly, Ida was petulant, but she finally agreed to leave her beloved tag room to do it.

"Hurry back, though," Ida said. "Regan is coming in for another lace tatting lesson soon."

Katie smiled. "Good. I'll look forward to seeing her. Can I bring you back anything?"

"No, thank you. I have an egg salad sandwich in the refrigerator in the vendors' lounge. You know, more people should think ahead like I do. It saves time *and* money."

"Riiiight," Katie said, drawing out the word. "I'll be back soon!"

Katie stopped in her office and took her tape measure and a notepad from her desk drawer before heading for the tea shop. At Tealicious, she tried to be as inconspicuous as possible as she navigated to the back of the shop and the stairs that led to the second floor. She didn't want to get stopped by a customer or, worse, Brad, and drawn into a conversation when she had something important to attend to.

She realized that good contractors were booked at least two to four months in advance, but she wasn't in a terrible hurry . . . at least, she didn't *think* she was.

She looked around the spacious area and smiled. She was already getting excited about her new project and making it exactly how she wanted it.

Katie was kneeling on the floor anchoring the tape measure against one of the baseboards when she heard footsteps on the stairs. She thought it was probably Brad.

"Be with you in a second!" she called.

"So, there you are! I've been looking everywhere for you." Every muscle in Katie's body tensed. It was Andy.

"What are you doing?" he asked.

Katie stood and slid her palms down the sides of her

jeans. "Taking measurements. I'm going to renovate this space into an apartment."

He shook his head. "You always have to have a new project, don't you?"

She lifted her chin and said nothing.

"What are you going to do?" he asked. "Rent it out?"

"No, I'm going to live in it."

His eyebrows shot up. "Katie, sweetheart, I came to find you to apologize. I acted like a jerk last night."

"Yes, you did."

Andy reached for her, and she took a step back.

"Did you think we were through?" he asked, sounding puzzled.

"Are we?"

"Of course we're not. I love you, Katie. I just got angry, that's all." He opened his arms. "Come here. Please."

But Katie wasn't about to give in that easily. "Did you go see Erikka after you left me?"

"I did." His mouth tightened. "And I offered her a full-time job."

"Which she eagerly accepted, I'm sure," Katie said, her tone curt.

"Yes. I should've offered it to her in the first place. She deserves it. She's a hard worker."

"I'm sure she is. But I didn't deserve to be on the receiving end of your temper tantrum last night. All I did was suggest a replacement for Erikka. You acted as if I'd told you to fire her immediately."

Andy ran his hands through his hair. "And I'm here apologizing for that. I was frustrated, and I took it out on you. I should never have done that. You'd made that wonderful meal for me, and—"

"What did you do for dinner?" Katie asked. "Did you and Erikka go out to celebrate?"

He lowered his eyes.

"You did!" Katie gaped at him. "That's why I'm only now hearing from you."

"It wasn't like that. We went to a little restaurant near her apartment—that's all."

"That's all." Katie shook her head, too upset to say what she was thinking. "If you'll excuse me, I need to finish measuring this room."

"Katie, please don't do this. I love you. I really do."

She blinked back tears. "Just . . . please go."

Andy stood there for a long moment, then he turned and headed back down the stairs.

Katie swallowed hard and bit her lip, then went back to taking measurements.

Seventeen

Katie left Tealicious as inconspicuously as she'd arrived. Her stomach growled at the tantalizing aromas, reminding her that she hadn't had anything to eat that day except a couple of peppermint candies. She didn't stop, though. She wasn't in the mood for chitchat, and she was afraid that someone's—*anyone's*—kindness might make her cry.

She remembered she had a box of granola bars in her desk drawer. She'd have one of those. Plus, she wanted to call her tea shop landlord to see if the woman would be amenable to turning the upstairs portion of the building into an apartment.

As she dug around in her bottom drawer for the out-of-date granola bars, she wondered how best to approach Harriet Long. Harriet lived on the outskirts of McKinlay Mill, so it wasn't as if she would spread gossip all over the Square that Katie was planning on moving out of Andy's apartment.

Katie bit into the granola bar and thought wistfully of the lasagna in her fridge. She'd have that for dinner tonight. All by herself. And she'd enjoy every bite.

She dialed Harriet's number.

"Hi, Harriet. It's Katie Bonner."

"Katie, hello, dear. How have you been?"

"I'm great. You?"

"Yes, yes, I'm fine. The funniest thing—I've been meaning to call you and keep forgetting. What luck that you're calling me!"

Before waiting to learn why Katie was calling, Harriet plunged ahead with her story.

"You know, my younger sister lives in Florida. She loves it there, and she's invited me to come to live with her. Isn't that wonderful?"

"Well, yes, it—"

"But, to do so, I need to settle my affairs here in New York," Harriet continued. "I'm selling the house, of course, and all the furnishings—you'll need to come by and see if there's anything you'd like to put in a bid on. And, of course, your lease on the tea shop will survive the sale, but I thought I should ask if *you* might want to buy it before I put it on the market."

"Yes!" Katie practically shouted the word, afraid she wouldn't get the opportunity to speak again for several minutes. "What were you thinking of asking?"

Harriet told her.

Katie sighed. It was more than she thought the building was worth—and she'd need to get an independent appraisal before she made an official bid on the property, but she thought there might be some wiggle room when it came time to negotiate.

"I'll have to consult with my partner, of course, but I'll do that later today and call you back first thing tomorrow. Is that all right?"

"That would be lovely, dear. Until tomorrow, then."

Katie hung up the phone. Well, that was a surprise.

She finished the stale bar, grabbed another, and unwrapped it before heading for the cash desk, contemplating her upcoming conversation with Margo. She couldn't think of any reason why her mother-in-law wouldn't want to buy the building, but if she didn't, Katie could simply bow out of the other building purchase in order to acquire the Tealicious site. She hoped that wouldn't be necessary—she'd hate to do that to the other merchants and to Seth if he'd already finalized the contract.

She was nibbling the granola bar as she approached Ida and Regan, who were conversing at the cash desk.

"You've been gone all this time, and you're *still* eating?" Ida demanded.

Katie shrugged and said hello to Regan. "I'd like to talk to you when you're done with your lesson."

"Ms. Mitchell and I were just finishing up."

"Excuse me," Ida said. "I'm going to the vendors' lounge to eat my egg salad sandwich because, unlike some people, I have neither the disposable income nor the desire to go out to lunch *every* day."

As soon as Ida was gone, Katie laughingly told Regan, "Ida Mitchell could probably buy and sell every one of us. She's just cheap."

Regan grinned. "What did you want to talk to me about?"

"What's the name of the contractor Roger works with?"

"John Healy."

"Does he do a good job?" Katie asked.

"Excellent, according to everyone I've ever spoken with about him. I don't have any personal experience. Are you thinking of doing some redecorating?"

"Actually, I'm going to transform the upstairs of Tealicious into an apartment."

"I'm sure Mr. Healy will do a wonderful job." Regan took out her phone. "If you'll give me your number, I'll have Roger text you Mr. Healy's information."

Katie rattled off her phone number. "Thanks, Regan. I appreciate it."

"No problem."

"By the way, someone was telling me earlier today that Paul Fenton and his brother, Ken, didn't get along all that well." She knew she needed to tread carefully with Regan because Regan liked Paul. "I said, so what? Siblings argue. I mean, I don't have one of my own, but that's been my observation."

"Roger and I argue sometimes, but not very often. We've always looked out for each other. I mean, our parents weren't always around, so we had to take care of each other." Regan shrugged. "As for Paul and Ken, I only saw them arguing once. I came into work one morning, and Ken was there at Ink Artistry. He and Paul were arguing over some delivery Ken hadn't made. Paul said he wasn't going to take the blame for Ken this time."

"It sounds like Ken could be irresponsible. Paul's sister, Mary, told me that Paul is the overprotective one of the family. It sounds like he is also the more responsible brother."

"Maybe. Mary's right—Paul *is* protective of his family . . . especially of her. I get the impression that Mary acted as a surrogate mother to the boys."

Katie clucked her tongue. "That's hard. It must have made for a tough childhood for Mary, right?"

"Yeah." Regan said the word with such feeling that Katie knew the young woman had probably given up much of her formative years being a surrogate mom to Roger.

Before Katie could think of anything appropriately sympathetic to say, Regan said she had to run.

"I'll make sure Roger sends you Mr. Healy's information," she called on her way out of Artisans Alley.

~~~~~~

There was a lull in foot traffic at around two thirty that afternoon, so Katie took a walk through the lobby to check the front parking lot, where the number of vacant spots discouraged her. As she turned to retrace her steps, she passed an array of colorful nail polishes on display in Envy Day Spa's front window. She stepped up to take a closer look.

As she perused the various shades of berry, violet, blue, and rose, she was distracted by a familiar-sounding giggle. She looked up to see Sophie Davenport sitting in one of the hairstylist's chairs. Katie walked inside the spa to say hello.

"Sophie, hi."

"Hello, Katie." Sophie's tone was cool and detached until she turned back to look at her stylist, Debbie, through the mirror. "I think this is going to look good, don't you?"

"I think it's going to be beautiful," Debbie said. "Don't you think so, Katie?"

"I do." She tried to engage Sophie again. "Sophie, you'll have to stop by Tealicious and meet Brad Andrews. He's a wonderful chef, and—"

Sophie cut Katie off. "I've met him."

"Isn't he a dream?" Debbie asked, as she combed a strand of Sophie's wet hair up and snipped the ends. "Those looks *and* he cooks? I might ask him to marry me!"

Katie chuckled. It was clear she wasn't going to make any headway with Sophie, so she might as well return to her post. "I should probably get back to work."

"Those polishes you were looking at are buy one, get one free," Debbie said.

"Thanks. I'll check back later today or tomorrow morning." She held out her hands and looked at her nails. "I'm in desperate need of a manicure."

"Then why don't you treat yourself? We have openings all week."

"I might just take you up on that." Katie waved good-bye and strolled back to the cash desk. Debbie was right. She *should* treat herself . . . not that there was anyone to dress up for.

Despite her hands-on job, Erikka always displayed perfectly manicured nails. Was that an attribute that helped make her so attractive to Andy?

Katie didn't want to think about it.

~~~~~~~

When Vance came to relieve her about half an hour later, Katie was more than ready to leave the cash desk.

"I'm sorry it's taken me so long to get up here. I've been terribly busy," Vance said. "If Rose is out again tomorrow, I'll take full charge of the cash desk."

"Thanks, Vance." Katie picked up the laptop and hurried to her office.

It was heavenly to be able to close her door and shut out the world for a few minutes. She took another granola bar out of the box in the drawer and pondered the best way to approach Margo about buying the Tealicious building. She hoped her former mother-in-law was in her pleasant "I love you like a daughter" attitude and not her hypercritical "I always thought Chad could do better" mood.

She was never going to know unless she dialed the number. She took a deep breath and called Margo.

"Katie, what a nice surprise."

Katie was too cautious to feel optimistic by Margo's greeting. The woman's disposition could still swing either way.

"I'm calling to talk to you about the Tealicious building," Katie said. "I spoke with Harriet Long this morning, and she wants to sell the building. Harriet is giving us the opportunity to buy it before she puts it on the market."

"I certainly don't want someone coming in and raising our rent and dictating what we can and can't do. I can't imagine you'd want that, either. I say, let's buy it."

Katie released a breath she hadn't been aware she'd been holding. "I agree. Before speaking with Harriet, I was planning on going in with a group of Victoria Square merchants to buy, renovate, and lease a shop on the Square. Now that this opportunity has presented itself, I'll bow out of that deal and concentrate on the tea shop building."

"Nonsense. I see no reason you can't do both."

First hurdle passed.

Katie mentioned the purchase price and the need for an appraisal.

"Why don't I buy the building from Harriet, and we'll renegotiate the terms of our loan agreement in the same vein as our previous agreement—half and half. What do you say?"

Second hurdle passed.

"That's extremely generous of you, Margo. I think that's great." Katie bit her lip. "But there's something you should know. I want to turn the upstairs of the tea shop into an apartment."

"Hmm, I'm not sure that's a good idea . . . not unless there's a separate entrance. We wouldn't want a tenant having full access to the tea shop."

"I would be the tenant."

She'd spoken so softly that Margo had apparently not heard her.

"What was that?" Margo asked.

"I said I'll be the tenant." She spoke a bit louder and with more resolve.

"Oh."

Katie let the silence between them lie there for a moment before saying, "I feel it's time to reclaim my independence."

"Well . . ." Margo seemed at a momentary loss for words. "Um, what an interesting idea. Do whatever you'd like to the upstairs of Tealicious, and I'll look forward to seeing it the next time I come to Victoria Square for a visit."

I can hardly wait, Katie thought.

~~~~~~~

By the time Katie got caught up on the work she'd had to neglect in order to oversee the cash desk, she was late leaving

Artisans Alley for the day. She was tired and hungry as she trudged up the stairs to her apartment. Either she was hallucinating or the aromas coming from the pizzeria were particularly far-reaching this evening, because the closer Katie got to her door, the stronger and more tantalizing the smell. She closed her eyes for a brief moment and breathed in the scent as she fished out her keys. Tomato sauce, garlic, oregano . . . and was that basil? Yes, she believed it was. Had she not been so angry with Andy, she'd have gone back down to Angelo's and asked him to make her a calzone. But, no. She would heat up her lasagna.

She opened the door and her eyes widened when she saw Andy standing in her kitchen. The steaming hot lasagna and slices of garlic toast were on the table, along with a bottle of wine and a dozen red roses.

"I was a fool to leave the way I did last night," he said.

"Did you spend the night with Erikka?"

"No. You know I'd never do that."

"But I *don't* know," Katie said. "Last night, you flew into a rage at the mere thought of losing her."

He didn't deny it. "She's a terrific employee. I'd be hard-pressed to ever find someone else with her loyalty, dedication, and work ethic to replace her."

"And now you don't have to."

"That's right—I don't. Offering Erikka a full-time job was a savvy business decision."

"Is that all it was? Business?"

"Of course." He closed the distance between them and placed his hands on her shoulders. "Katie, I love you. You. Not Erikka. Not anyone else. You."

"But you left me for Erikka," she whispered.

"What?" He lowered his head. "I don't think I heard you correctly."

"Yes, you did. I said you left me for her."

"I didn't. If I need to, I'll call her and have her come up here right now and tell you that absolutely nothing happened between the two of us." He gently raised her chin so she'd look him in the eye. "I went and offered her the job. And she accepted. We ate a bland dinner. End of story."

"But you still walked out on me . . . on the dinner I'd made for you . . . on *our* evening . . . to go to her," she said quietly.

Realization flooded his face. "I'm sorry, Katie. I'm so sorry."

"Me, too."

"Please let me make this up to you," Andy said. "I'll do anything. Don't let my stupidity ruin what we have."

Katie was ever so tempted to tell him to go fire Erikka then. But, one, he probably wouldn't. And, two, he'd only resent Katie if he did. So she said nothing.

Andy crushed her against his broad chest. "I'm an idiot, Sunshine. I get single-minded when I've got a problem. You know that. Please, Katie, give me another chance."

"Fine," she said at last. "But know this. If you ever choose another woman over me again—for any reason—" She let the threat hang, knowing ultimatums should be a last resort.

Were they really at that point?

Andy pulled back. "How about a glass of wine? This is a celebration," he said and grabbed the bottle of red from the counter, cracking the screw cap.

Celebration? Katie wasn't so sure.

Eighteen

~~~~~~~

Katie awoke to find that Andy had put his arm around her and pulled her close during the night. She smiled slightly and nestled back against the solid warmth of his body before remembering that she was still upset with him. Last night she'd pretended to put the entire incident behind her, but she hadn't. Not really. The fact remained that Andy had left her in order to run to Erikka and ensure that the sycophantic young woman would remain by his side. He'd only made up with Katie yesterday after all was right with Erikka. And while it was Katie who was waking up beside Andy this morning, she knew all too well that Erikka would trade places with her in a heartbeat.

She gently moved Andy's arm from around her enough to slide out of the bed without waking him and grabbed some clothes before easing the bedroom door shut. After quickly dressing, she fed the cats and headed out to walk the Square. She was glad she had a valid excuse to slip out of the apartment this morning and hoped Andy would be gone when she returned. She was pretty sure he wouldn't—it was likely he'd still be asleep. But it was hard to face him when she wasn't exactly certain what she was feeling.

As she walked, she realized she had no easy fix for overcoming the pain Andy—and Erikka—had caused her. If she wanted to remain with Andy and foster their relationship, then Katie had to content herself with the fact that she would have to accept Erikka as a part of their lives . . . or, at least, as a part of Andy's life. Was she okay with that?

Seeing that she could make no progress with regard to her relationship status with Andy this morning, Katie turned her thoughts to Ken Fenton. Would Detective Schuler ever find the man's killer? Without Ray having his ear to the ground as he usually did, Katie had no idea what was going on with the investigation. It seemed to her, however, that finding a suspect—other than Ray—was taking an awfully long time.

After three circuits around the vast parking lot, Katie returned to the apartment to find that Andy was in the same position in which she'd left him. She studied his sleeping face for a moment. He was so good-looking. She resisted the urge to brush the hair off his forehead.

He must've sensed her presence because his eyes fluttered open and he stifled a yawn. "Good morning, Sunshine." He patted the mattress beside him. "Get back in here."

"I can't. I have to shower. I've just returned from my walk and I'm all sweaty."

"I could use a shower." He got out of bed, pulled Katie to him, and nuzzled her neck.

"Will you wash my hair?" She might still be ticked off at him, but she loved the feel of his big, strong hands massaging her scalp.

"Anything you want."

~~~~~~

Katie was a teensy bit late arriving at Artisans Alley. She came in through the lobby hoping to find Rose at the cash desk, but it was Vance who stood there greeting the vendors as they filed in and milled around before attending to their assigned tasks.

Katie went over to speak to him. "Isn't Rose any better?"

"Some, I think, but she's still staying off her feet as much as possible."

"I really hope she'll recover in time to participate in the walkathon."

"So do I," Vance said. "Ida has already informed me that she's too busy to help out at the registers today, but I can manage just fine."

"I need to work in my office for a little while this morning, but I'll be around if you need me."

As she was walking toward her office, she noticed two burly men coming down the stairs with motorcycle saddlebags.

Hmm . . . Hugh has already made two nice sales this morning. Good for him.

She stopped in the vendors' lounge for coffee and a doughnut from a box someone had left in the center of the table. After grabbing a couple of paper towels, she headed into her office and closed the door.

Her first order of business was to call Harriet Long. She took a bracing swig of her coffee to give herself a shot of courage. Harriet was a sweetheart, but she was lonely, and she could keep you on the phone half the day.

Fortunately for Katie, Harriet didn't answer her phone that morning. She was either still asleep or already out. Even more fortunate for Katie, Harriet had an answering machine.

"Hi, Harriet, it's Katie Bonner from Artisans Alley. I've spoken with my business partner, Margo Bonner, and we definitely want to buy the Tealicious building. I've given Margo your number and she'll be calling you later today about the details, but feel free to call me if you like." Katie then left her number and ended the call. Hopefully, Margo and Harriet could hammer out all the particulars on their own. She grinned to herself at the thought of her easily exasperated former mother-in-law dealing with Harriet. *C'est la vie!*

Before she had a chance to decide what to do next, Katie received a text from Roger with the contact information for John Healy, the contractor. Decision made. Katie called Healy. As she'd pretty much expected, her call went directly to voice mail. Again, she left her contact information, told Healy what she wanted and where she'd gotten his phone number, and said she'd like to speak with him at his earliest convenience.

She leaned back in her chair and took a bite of the gooey, cream-filled doughnut, pleased that she was making such excellent progress this morning.

Half an hour later, Katie was still ticking off her to-do list at breakneck speed when Vance called her from the registers.

"I hate to do this to you," he said, "but Janey just called and said that sparks shot out of one of the outlets at home. She's terrified the house will catch fire."

"I would be, too! Did she call emergency services?"

Vance chuckled. "As far as she's concerned, that's me. I don't think it's that big a deal. I'll check it out, likely replace the outlet, and be back as quick as I can."

Katie couldn't understand why he wasn't more concerned, but she supposed he knew what he was doing. She hurried to the cash desk to take over. Her first customer had picked out a pretty earrings-and-necklace set from Rose's booth.

"I love the color of your nail polish," Katie commented as the woman handed her a credit card.

"I had them done at Envy Day Spa just an hour ago."

Katie remembered all the shiny bottles of nail polishes on display at the salon and thought again that she really could use a manicure. As she said good-bye to her customer, Katie resolved to see if anyone could work her in after Vance returned.

In the hour that Katie manned the cash desk, she rang up two more motorcycle saddlebags. She wondered if there was some sort of biker convention in town or if there was a rally to raise money for some charity. If so, she hadn't seen anything about it on the news.

She opened one of the bags for inspection, finding it stuffed with the paper used to wrap more delicate items. Hugh must have scored a pile of it and was using it so that the bags would hold their shape. She'd have to speak to him about providing his own filler.

"Hey, I wasn't trying to steal anything," the burly male customer complained.

"Sorry. We're told to look through bags." He didn't have to know that it was her rule.

The man shrugged and handed her a wad of cash.

As Katie rang up the sale, she thought about the quality of the workmanship Hugh imparted.

She took out one of the large brown paper bags with handles that they used for large purchases and eased the saddlebags in. "Thanks for shopping at Artisans Alley."

The man's grin sent a shiver up Katie's spine. "Believe me, the pleasure is all mine."

~~~~~~~

Once Vance had returned and pronounced his house in tip-top shape now that the sparking outlet had been replaced, Katie wandered over to Envy Day Spa and Salon. A nail tech named Tana, who was new to the business, had an opening and was able to take Katie. She encouraged Katie to choose her polish and Katie decided on a pale mauve. She sat down across the table from Tana.

Even though the polish Katie had put on her nails two weeks ago was long gone, Tana cleaned her nails with polish remover.

As Katie watched Tana work around her cuticles with a damp cotton ball, she asked, "Is there a motorcycle rally going on this weekend? I know it's only Thursday, but I thought maybe some people were in town early."

Tana frowned slightly and moved on to the next finger. "Not that I know of. The Renaissance Festival in Sterling starts this weekend. I think that'll be a blast. I'm trying to get my boyfriend to take me, but even if he doesn't, I'm sure one or two of my girlfriends will be up for it. Do you enjoy Ren-Faires?"

"I've never been to one." Katie realized her question about motorcyclists had hit a brick wall with the young nail tech, but maybe she could see if Tana had heard anything interesting about Hugh McKinney. "But, you know what? I imagine Mr. McKinney—our new leather goods vendor—might have something suitable for a RenFaire."

"Yeah . . . I think I'll pass."

Although Tana went right on working nonchalantly, she now had Katie's full attention.

"Really?" Katie asked. "Why's that?"

"When I was a little girl, Mr. McKinney was our mail carrier. He was sorta strange. He'd spend way too much time in our neighborhood delivering the mail. My mom always said that if that man opened the mailboxes as often as he opened his mouth, he'd be the fastest mail carrier in New York."

They both laughed.

"Of course, he wouldn't be able to spend all his time visiting with people on his route if he carried the mail now," Tana continued. "These days they use some kind of electronic devices to keep track of where the carriers are at all times. My cousin has a mail route in Greece, and he hates that electronic thingy. He won't even take a lunch break before he's finished with his route because he's afraid he'll either get in trouble or suffer a pay cut."

Which made Katie glad she'd never taken a civil service exam for that job.

The women made innocuous chitchat for another ten minutes until Tana had finished with Katie's nails. As Katie paid the woman, she lamented that she hadn't learned as much as she would have liked about bikers—or Hugh McKinney. But at least she had pretty nails. It wasn't much, but it *was* something.

~~~~~~

Once Katie left the salon, she decided to have a chat with Hugh McKinney. As she approached his booth, she saw an overweight man and a petite woman, both in leathers, perusing the saddlebags on display in Hugh's booth.

When the man saw Katie approaching, he cleared his throat and said, "Well, we're going to look around for a few minutes and think about it, and then we'll be back." He took the woman's arm, nodded at Katie, and the couple walked away.

"I'm so sorry," Katie said to Hugh. "I hope I didn't cost you a sale."

"You didn't. If they're really interested, they'll be back." He smiled. "Did that acupressure trick work on your headache yesterday?"

"I believe it did. My headache went away soon after I tried it." Truth be told, Katie didn't know if the acupressure trick helped or if the pain reliever kicked in, but it didn't matter. "I treated myself to a manicure earlier today, and Tana from Envy Day Spa said you used to be her family's mail carrier."

"Well, how about that?" He grinned. "If she's young, I probably delivered her letters to Santa Claus."

"She is pretty young," Katie said. "She's a good nail tech, though."

"Good for her." He nodded. "I carried the mail for about fifteen years before I finally got a clerk's job."

"Which position did you like better?"

"Depended on the weather," he said. "I loved delivering mail during the spring and fall when the temperatures were mild and the days were sunny. I preferred being a clerk when it was sweltering, storming, or freezing cold."

Katie put out her hand and gently ran her fingertips over the saddlebag Hugh had been showing the couple who'd walked away. "You do fantastic work."

"Thank you." He promptly took the saddlebag and placed it under the table. "In case they do come back, I don't want to have to sold it to someone else."

"That's a strong possibility today," she said. "I've seen several of these come across the cash desk in the scant time I've spent there. Is there a motorcycle convention in town?"

"No. I give a presentation to area motorcycle clubs once a month and—well, not to brag—but when the bikers see the quality of my work, they start pouring in to buy the bags the very next day."

"That's an excellent marketing tactic," Katie said. "Would you mind talking to our Merchants Association about using speaking engagements to promote one's business sometime?"

"I'd be glad to."

Before they could make plans for Hugh to speak at the next Merchants Association meeting, Katie's phone rang. She looked at the screen but didn't recognize the number.

"Excuse me," she said to Hugh.

As she answered the call, she strode toward Chad's Pad, the small room where she stored her late husband's art.

"Ms. Bonner, this is Bill Parsons. I'm Ray Davenport's attorney. He asked me to give you a call."

Katie felt a chill run throughout her body. "What is it? What's wrong?"

"I'm afraid Mr. Davenport has just been arrested for the murder of Kenneth Fenton."

For a moment, Katie's legs felt weak, but then she put a hand against the wall and straightened. "You've . . . you've g-got to be k-kidding me. They . . . he . . . there . . . how?"

"Apparently, new evidence was found at the crime scene," Parsons said. "I'm not at liberty to say anything more at this time, and I need to get back to my client. He's being interviewed in a few minutes. However, Mr. Davenport was adamant that you go talk to his daughters."

"Me? But I . . . I—"

"In fact, he's asked that you stay with them until he's released."

"And when will that be?" Katie asked.

"Mr. Davenport's arraignment has been set for tomorrow morning."

Katie blew out a breath. That was a pretty tall order, considering the three Davenport girls liked Katie as much as a plate of uncooked liver. But Ray was her friend and she would do what a friend does in such situations: suck it up.

"Thanks, Mr. Parsons. I'll do my best. Where will the arraignment take place?"

Parsons gave her the address in Rochester. "I'll see you there tomorrow."

"I'll be there," Katie promised. Wild horses couldn't keep her away.

Nineteen

Katie pressed the "End Call" icon and managed to still her trembling hands long enough to call Vance.

"Hey, Katie! What's up?"

"Could you please come upstairs to Chad's Pad? Tell Ida you need her to take over, and then just walk away. Don't give her time to argue."

"What—?" He stopped before forming the sentence. "Be right there."

Katie knew Vance would realize that if she was barking orders like a drill sergeant, something was very wrong.

Katie was sitting on the uncomfortable, narrow bed where Chad sometimes slept when Vance came into Chad's. He stepped in quietly. "Are you all right?"

She nodded. "It's Ray. He's been arrested for Ken Fenton's murder."

"But that's ridiculous!"

"I wish it was, but I got a call from Ray's attorney. Apparently, he wants *me* to break the news to his daughters."

"Geeze," Vance said, and ran his hand over his whiskered chin. "How did this happen? What made the deputies decide to make an arrest now?"

"Mr. Parsons, Ray's attorney, said the Sheriff's Office found new evidence at the crime scene."

Vance gave a guttural growl. "I was afraid something bad would happen, but I didn't expect this."

"What do you mean?" Katie asked.

"Ray told me that someone broke into Wood U the other night."

"Nobody mentioned that to me." Not that it was any of her *personal* business, she supposed. But if someone was breaking into shops in Victoria Square, it was important for the head of the Merchants Association—and its members—to know. "Did Ray report the break-in to the Sheriff's Office?"

"He did," Vance said. "But since it didn't appear that anything was taken, the police wrote it up as vandalism."

"Vandalism?"

"Yeah, the door had been jimmied."

"Hmm." Katie frowned. "Maybe someone planned to break in but was scared off."

"I thought that at first, too. But now that new evidence has suddenly shown up at the crime scene—evidence that was significant enough to result in Ray's arrest—I have to wonder if the thief didn't get exactly what he came for."

~~~~~~~

After securing Vance's vow of secrecy, Katie went straight to Ray's house. She stepped onto the porch, took a deep breath, and rang the bell.

Sasha answered the door. "Dad's not here."

Before the girl could close the door in her face, Katie said, "I know. That's why *I'm* here."

Her face draining of color, Sasha stepped back to allow Katie entrance. "What is it? Where's Dad?"

As Sasha's eyes filled, Katie put a hand on her arm. "He's fine. Your dad is fine, Sasha. But he wanted me to come and stay with you and your sisters until he gets here."

Shaking her head as tears rolled down her cheeks, Sasha yelled, "Where's my dad?"

Sadie and Sophie hurried into the room. Sophie put her arms around Sasha and shot Katie a questioning glare.

"Your dad is fine," Katie said. "If we could all sit down, I'll explain everything."

Sadie led them into the living room where she, Sophie, and Sasha sat on the sofa. Katie perched on the armchair.

Katie cleared her throat. "A few minutes ago, I got a call from Bill Parsons, your dad's attorney."

A trio of gasps issued from the couch.

"Your dad has been arrested for the murder of Ken Fenton." The three girls started talking at once.

"This is *your* fault!"

"Why are you the one telling us this?"

"Dad absolutely cannot be in jail!"

Katie held up her hands. "Mr. Parsons said your dad wanted me to stay with the three of you until he can get home."

"I'm an adult," Sophie said, straightening her spine and drawing herself up to make herself as tall as possible. "We'll be fine with me here watching after my sisters. That is, after we go to the jail and check on Dad."

"Then I'll trail along behind you and sleep in the driveway in my car if I have to," Katie said. "Your father has been a good friend to me, and I'm not going to let him down. I think the *adult* thing for all of us to do"—she pierced Sophie with a look—"is to rally behind your dad and see how we can help him . . . starting with a visit to Mr. Parsons. If we can find out what evidence the deputies used to arrest him, then maybe we can help refute its validity."

"Okay," Sophie said. Before the younger girls could protest, Sophie turned her stern gaze on them. Both looked . . . not cowed, but effectively silenced. "Let's go see Mr. Parsons."

~~~~~~~

On the drive to Rochester and attorney Bill Parsons's office, Sadie and Sasha grumbled about why Sophie was so quick to give in to Katie. Katie drove with Sophie riding shotgun and the younger girls in the backseat griping as if their chauffeur couldn't understand every word of their angry whispers.

"Why did Dad have Mr. Parsons call *her* and not us?" Sadie asked.

"Or even Grandma and Grandpa?" That was Sasha.

"I don't know." Sophie sighed. "But the best thing we can do right now is to go along with *her* . . . at least to the attorney's office. Since he called *her*, she might be able to find out more than we can."

As soon as they entered the office, however, Katie saw that the battle was still raging. They filed into the reception area, and Katie started to introduce herself to the middle-aged receptionist.

"Hello, I'm Katie—"

Sophie muscled Katie to the side. "Sophie Davenport. We're here to see Bill Parsons concerning our dad, Raymond Davenport."

"Mr. Parsons is still at the jail meeting with Mr. Davenport at the moment," the receptionist said, giving them a pleasant smile. "If you'd like to sit down, he shouldn't be too much longer."

Fortunately, there was no one waiting in the lobby. Katie would have hated for a bunch of strangers to have overheard that Ray was in jail. She and Ray's daughters sat facing the door, so they'd be able to see Parsons when he came in.

Sasha wrapped her arms around herself and began to rock back and forth. "Our dad is in jail."

Katie leaned over to put a hand on Sasha's arm, but the

girl pulled away. Instead, big sister Sophie went to comfort her youngest sister and pulled her into an embrace.

Sasha mumbled something about Ray being handcuffed and fingerprinted. ". . . so humiliated."

"Humiliation is the least of Dad's worries right now," Sadie said. "If he goes to prison, all of those criminals he's put away for years will kill him."

"That's not going to happen," Katie said firmly.

"You don't know that," Sadie argued.

Katie looked into Sadie's bleak eyes and had to admit—if only to herself—that the girl was right. She didn't know anything. She'd never expected Ray to be arrested. She thought Ken Fenton's real killer would have been found long before it came to that.

Parsons walked in on a scene of three frightened young women and one adult who looked as if she might break into tears at any moment. "And you ladies are?"

The receptionist looked up from behind her computer screen. "Bill, this is Ray Davenport's wife and daughters."

"She is *not* our mother!" chorused from all three girls in strident tones.

Katie stood and stepped forward and held out her hand. "I'm Katie Bonner. We spoke earlier."

"Of course." Parsons shook her hand then gestured to the others. "Let's step into the conference room."

Once the women were seated around the rectangular conference room table—the Davenport sisters on one side and Katie on the other—Parsons closed the door and took a seat at the head of the table. He removed a yellow legal pad from his briefcase.

Katie could see that the first page of the pad was filled with notes. She tried to surreptitiously read them but couldn't make out anything. She made a mental note to call Seth Landers later to find out if Parsons had a good reputation in the legal community. Then she tried to tell herself that because of his years in law enforcement, Ray knew and had chosen a good criminal attorney . . . despite the fact that he might be concerned with the cost.

Parsons folded his hands atop the legal pad. "Thanks for coming into the office. Your dad's main concern is for you girls, and since your grandparents can't get here before his arraignment tomorrow morning, he has asked that Ms. Bonner stay with you until then."

"What will happen at the arraignment?" Sophie asked.

"The judge will read the charges against him, and your dad—through me, his counsel—will enter a plea of not guilty. Then the judge will determine the amount to set bail . . . if bail is granted."

"*If* it's granted?" Sophie asked, her voice rising.

Sadie and Sasha voiced their concerns about bail as well. Parsons raised a hand in a placating motion. "I feel confident bail will be set. Your father is an upstanding member of society, and since you—his family—and his business are here, he doesn't pose a flight risk."

"What new evidence did the police find that led to Ray's arrest?" Katie asked.

"That was . . . ah . . . Mr. Davenport's wedding ring."

"What makes the detectives so certain that it's Ray's ring?" Even if the ring had Ray's fingerprints on it, Katie reasoned, that still wasn't proof that it was *his* ring.

"It was engraved," Sophie said, her voice cracking. "It said 'Forever, Ray. Love, Rachel.'"

"Mom's ring was engraved, too," Sadie said. "And Dad never took his ring off . . . at least, not until *you* came along and started flirting with him."

"Wait." Katie ignored Sadie's dig. "If Ray wasn't wearing the ring anymore, then how did it get to the crime scene?"

"Not only the crime scene but the closet where Ken Fenton had been keeping his tools." Parsons wrote something on the legal pad.

Katie guessed he was noting the fact that Ray wasn't wearing the ring anymore and wanted to know when exactly

Ray had stopped wearing the ring. It could definitely help Ray's case.

"Did your father keep the ring in a jewelry case at home?" she asked the girls.

"He'd been wearing the ring on a chain around his neck," Sophie said. "But he'd have noticed if it got pulled off somehow."

"Actually, Mr. Davenport informed me that he often took the chain off and hung it on a hook near the door at Wood U when he was working so that it wouldn't get caught up on any tools," Parsons said.

Katie wished she knew what Parsons had written on the legal pad. She brightened. "That's it, then!"

The four other people at the table looked at her questioningly.

"Just this afternoon, my assistant manager, Vance Ingram, told me that someone broke into Wood U recently but didn't take anything. The deputies wrote up the incident as vandalism, but it had to be the real killer who broke into Wood U and stole your dad's wedding ring to frame him for the murder!"

"But how does that help us?" Sadie asked.

"Unless we can prove it," Sophie said sourly, "it doesn't."

~~~~~~~

Bill Parsons made it clear to Katie and the Davenport daughters that Ray didn't want any of them to come to visit him at the jail. He'd been adamant that he didn't want to see them until the arraignment the next morning . . . and preferably not then, but he "knows you're too stubborn to let him be arraigned in peace."

As if, Katie thought. She'd go see him now if she could stash the girls somewhere first. But, if she did that, he'd be disappointed with her. Ray wanted her with his daughters for a reason—whether that reason was their protection, his reassurance, or something else, Katie didn't have a clue.

Before driving back to Ray's house, she needed to go to her apartment, feed the cats, and pack an overnight bag. When she pulled into Victoria Square, Sophie demanded to know what she was doing.

"I need to go up to my apartment, feed Mason and Della, and get a few things." She took some money from her purse and handed it to Sophie. "You three go into Angelo's and order us a pizza for dinner. I'll be right back."

Sophie shoved the money back at Katie. "We've got our own money."

"Just take it and do what I ask you to do. I don't want to be in this predicament any more than the rest of you, but we need to make the best of it . . . for your dad's sake."

"Fine." Sophie got out of the car. Her sisters followed suit, and the three of them glumly stomped into the pizzeria.

Katie hurried upstairs. Mason and Della were thrilled to see her earlier than usual.

Her ringtone sounded, and Katie recognized the Artisans Alley number. "Katie?" It was Vance.

"Hi, Vance. I don't have a lot of time to talk right now. Ray has asked that I stay with his daughters. He's being arraigned in the morning. Have you heard any gossip in that regard?"

"No. And I haven't told a soul."

"I knew you wouldn't, but you know how news travels on the Square," Katie said gravely.

"Do you need anything? Is there anything I can do?"

She sighed. "No, but I appreciate your asking. Just cover for me if anyone wants to know where I am for the rest of the day. Say I'm running errands or something."

"Will do."

Katie said good-bye and ended the call. She opened the cat food can, dumping it into one bowl, and the kibble into another, and was filling the cats' water dish when Andy came through the kitchen door.

"So, what's going on with the Delightful Davenport Divas?" he asked.

Katie gave him a wan smile. "Good use of alliteration. I'm stuck with babysitting them tonight, so I asked them to get us a pizza."

"Babysitting?" He shook his head. "Sophie is—what? Eighteen—nineteen? Why do they need babysitting?"

"Her point exactly," Katie said. "However, Ray's attorney called and asked me to watch over them. I don't think Ray wants them to be alone."

"His attorney? What's going on?"

"Please keep this to yourself, but Ray has been arrested for the murder of Ken Fenton. He's being arraigned in the morning. Hopefully, the judge will set bail then, and Ray can get out of there."

"But why do *you* have to stay with his daughters?" Andy asked. "They have grandparents they can stay with. Besides, they can't stand you."

"I'm well aware of the fact that they despise me. They've made that abundantly clear. But their grandparents live too far away to get here before the arraignment. And I'm guessing Ray doesn't want to tell them anything until he has to."

"I don't like the thought of you staying with those spiteful girls."

"Yeah, I don't particularly like it, either. But it's just for one night. And what are they going to do? Murder me in my sleep?" Katie tried to laugh, but the sound came out hollow even to her ears.

"You don't know," Andy said. "The apple might not fall far from the tree."

Katie's mouth dropped open in shock. "Andy, you know as well as I do that Ray didn't kill Ken Fenton."

"That's just it—we don't *know* anything of the kind."

Twenty

After eating their dinner in stony silence, the girls tossed the pizza box and paper plates into the trash can and went into the den. They closed the door behind them with a slam, making it clear that Katie wasn't welcome.

She wandered into the living room and looked at the furniture. She was drawn to the overstuffed leather recliner, which she knew was Ray's chair. She walked over and saw that a magazine rack sat to the side of the chair. In it were law enforcement magazines, woodworking magazines, and a couple of crossword puzzle books. As she sank onto the chair, she plucked one of the puzzle books out of the rack. Ray's pencil marked his place.

Katie desperately wished she could talk to Ray. She knew it was impossible for anyone except Bill Parsons to see him, and even he would have to have a plausible reason at this time of the evening. Even if visitors were allowed, Katie knew Schuler wouldn't allow *her* to speak with Ray. If the detective truly believed Ray killed Ken Fenton, he might think it was at Katie's behest.

With a sigh, she picked up the pencil and looked down at the clues.

A five-letter word for aggravation.

"That's easy—g-i-r-l-s."

Nope. As appropriate as it was tonight, that was not the word. This particular five-letter word started with a T.

T-r-i-a-l.

She gulped. The thought of Ray having to endure a trial sickened her . . . especially when she considered that he might be wrongfully convicted and sent to prison. She put the pencil back into the book and returned it to the rack. Then she took out her phone and called Seth.

He answered on the first ring.

"Hi, Seth. It's Katie. I've got a professional question for you."

"Shoot."

"Are you familiar with a Rochester attorney by the name of Bill Parsons?"

"Yes. Bill is capable and highly respected. Is he the best criminal attorney in the business? Maybe not. But he is competent and will help Ray build a strong defense."

"How did you know I was asking about him on Ray's behalf?" she asked.

"I know because I saw Bill at the courthouse earlier. He was requesting that Ray be arraigned this afternoon, so he wouldn't have to spend the night in jail and away from his family. But, as you know, that didn't happen."

"Could another attorney have managed to get the arraignment this afternoon? Could *you* have done it?"

He chuckled. "I'm glad you have such confidence in me, but no. I'm a general practice attorney who does wills and real estate closings. It was just too late in the day, and the judge had a full docket."

"Oh. All right."

"Don't worry, Katie. Everything will get sorted out."

When Katie remained silent, Seth forced a jovial note into his voice and changed the subject. "I should have the Merchants Association contract ready tomorrow."

"Great. Thanks, Seth. But, I wonder, what if Ray needs help with bail? Is that something the Merchants Association could help him with?"

"Not a chance."

Ray had only been renting a home in McKinlay Mill. He had probably banked the money from the sale of his former home. How much of that would he have to pay to secure his bond?

Katie looked toward the closed door to the den. If Ray was refused bail, how would his daughters react? Just as troubling, what would Katie do and what could she do to remedy the situation without invoking Andy's ire?

She didn't want to think about it.

~~~~~~~

Katie didn't know how long she sat in Ray's comfy leather chair thinking and staring at the wall. As she pictured Ray miserable in his stark jail cell, her mind jumped to Andy—probably perfectly happy in his cozy pizza parlor with the lovely Erikka. Her eyelids got heavy . . . heavier . . .

She and Ray were on a tarmac . . . and the entire scene was in black-and-white. Ray was wearing a trench coat and a fedora, and Katie had on a prim suit with a skirt and jacket. She even wore gloves and carried a dainty purse.

"We're in Casablanca!*" Katie said.*

"I've been thinking, schweetheart."

Katie's eyes widened at Ray's terrible Humphrey Bogart impression.

"The problems of three little people don't amount to a hill of beans in this crazy world," Ray continued.

"Ray, what in the world are you talking about?" Katie was relieved that her voice sounded nothing like that of Ingrid Bergman.

"You belong with Andy. If you stayed here with me, you'd regret it. Maybe not today . . . maybe not tomorrow . . . but soon . . . and for the rest of your life."

At that moment, Erikka—wearing a tight white dress—sashayed across the tarmac behind Ray to the cheesy accompaniment of a slide trombone and a snare drum. She stopped and waved a lace handkerchief to someone out of Katie's line of sight.

"Yoo-hoo! Andy! I'm coming, darling!" Then, with a triumphant glare at Katie, Erikka flounced off to where Andy was presumably waiting.

Ray jerked his head in the direction Erikka had gone. *"Go to him, kid. That femme fatale will ruin Andy. You're the woman he needs. But first . . ."* He grabbed Katie, pulled her close, and then bent her over his arm for a passionate kiss.

"What the—?"

"We'll always have Victoria Schquare," Ray said. *"Here's lookin' at you—"*

Katie shook herself awake. She blew out a breath and wondered what in the world had been on that pizza. She involuntarily recalled Andy's words about "those spiteful girls," but she quickly dismissed the ridiculous notion that Ray's daughters had poisoned her pizza—everyone had eaten out of the same box.

She rose from the chair and went to find out what the "little angels" were up to.

The Davenport sisters were huddled at the kitchen table around a half gallon of fudge-swirl ice cream.

"Mind if I join you?" Katie asked.

Sophie lifted and dropped one shoulder. "Grab a spoon. They're in the drawer to the left of the sink."

Katie got a spoon from the drawer and helped herself to a taste of the creamy treat. She hoped it wouldn't lead to any more disturbing dreams.

For a minute or two, no one met anyone else's eyes . . . until Katie couldn't stand it anymore. "We need to put our heads together and figure out how to get your dad out of this mess."

"You got him into it," Sasha muttered.

"No, I didn't. He volunteered to go speak with Mr. Jones on behalf of the Merchants Association because he was acquainted with the man. None of us knew anything about Ken Fenton at that time. We didn't know he'd be there, that he had an explosive temper, that he'd slug your dad, or—"

"Or that he'd turn up dead," Sadie said flatly.

"What I *do* know," Katie said, "is that your father did not kill that man."

Sophie placed her spoon on the table. "But how do we prove that?"

"I have no clue." She looked around the table, hoping one of the girls had an idea. She was completely out of them.

"We could make a murder board like they do on some of those TV crime shows." Sasha lowered her head as she made the suggestion, certain that her idea would be shot down.

"That's an excellent idea," Katie said. "We need poster board and sticky notes . . . oh, and pens with different colors of ink."

The three girls pushed back their chairs and hurried off to get the necessary supplies.

They had a lot of brainstorming to do.

~~~~~~~

Two hours later, what was left of the ice cream had turned into a soupy mess in the center of the kitchen table. Katie noticed it and tossed it in the garbage. Then she got a sponge off the sink and cleaned the sticky goo that had seeped out of the carton. The melted ice cream served as the perfect metaphor for Katie. What had started out refreshing had now turned to trash.

When the girls had trudged off to their respective rooms minutes before, Katie still had no idea how to prove Ray's innocence. Now, standing in the middle of the kitchen with her hands on her hips, she took another look at their "murder board."

In the center was a circle with Ken Fenton's name inside it. Lines had been drawn from that circle to various squares—the suspects. Ray's square contained the words: *Heated argument leading to an assault on Dad*.

Paul Fenton had a square, and inside his was written, *How well did the brothers really get along?*

To be fair, they had listed other suspects that Detective Schuler had bantered about when talking with Katie. Vance Ingram had a square because he knew a lot about electricity. Hugh McKinney had a square because he seemed to know the Fentons *and* electricity. Katie hadn't told the girls that Phil Lancaster had warned her about Hugh.

Sadie had, at one point, put a square bearing Katie's name on the board.

"I'm a suspect?" Katie asked her.

She'd shrugged. "On television, they always say that everyone is a suspect."

Katie had declined to point out that "everyone" apparently didn't extend to the Davenport daughters, but the murder board work had still deteriorated from that point on. The girls got snippy with Katie and with one another, and Katie had finally said she was tired.

"We all need to look fresh for your dad's arraignment tomorrow morning," she told them.

Now Katie finished tidying the kitchen, but she left the murder board on display for the time being. Maybe something helpful would come to her or to one of Ray's daughters if each of them were to study it on her own at some point.

She went into the living room and found that someone had placed a blanket on the sofa for her. A blanket, but no pillow. But that, at least, was something.

~~~~~~~

Katie hadn't slept particularly well on the Davenports' sofa, but at least she hadn't had any more ridiculous dreams. After that dream kiss, how was she supposed to look either Ray or Andy in the eye today?

She folded the blanket and placed it over the back of the sofa before going to take a quick bath. She wanted to be ready when the girls got up.

After dressing in the black slacks and lavender silk blouse she'd brought with her and applying some makeup so that, hopefully, she wouldn't look as if she'd tossed and turned on a lumpy sofa all night long, she went into the kitchen and made a pot of coffee. She was wondering whether or not she should make the girls some breakfast when she heard an alarm go off.

The alarm was quickly silenced, and after a few minutes, Sophie shuffled into the room wearing her robe and slippers.

"Good morning," Katie said.

Sophie didn't return the greeting. "How'd you sleep on the couch?"

"Fine. Did you sleep well?"

"No. I thought about my dad all night long." Tears welled in her blue eyes, and Katie got up and moved toward her.

Sophie moved away from Katie. "I'm all right."

"I understand that as the oldest, you feel you have to be strong for your sisters," Katie said. "But I'm here. You can lean on me."

Sophie studied Katie for just a second, and then she turned away. "I need to go wake up Sadie and Sasha."

"Would you like me to make breakfast?"

"No, thanks. I doubt any of us will feel like eating," she said and shuffled out of the room.

She was right. Katie had no appetite and wondered how long it would be before this nightmare was over.

~~~~~~~

Katie, Sophie, Sasha, and Sadie sat in the courtroom with its muted blue walls and wooden accents, awaiting Ray's appearance. His was the third arraignment called. When the bailiff brought him into the courtroom, Ray looked drawn and pale. Katie's heart clutched at the sight of him. He kept his gaze trained straight ahead and didn't look toward the gallery.

Did he not expect the girls to be there? Was he ashamed to have them see him looking so disheveled and unshaven to hear the charges read against him? Maybe he couldn't bear the terrified expressions on their faces.

Before she could further consider Ray's reasons for not seeking out his family, the judge began to read the charges leveled against Ray.

Katie wanted to squeeze Sophie's free hand—Sadie had the other one—but she knew Sophie would rebuff her attempt to comfort her . . . and herself . . . so she kept her hands clutched tightly in her lap. She could have wept with relief when Seth Landers eased into the seat beside her and placed a hand on her forearm.

"Thank you," she whispered.

He gave her a crooked smile and winked.

"How do you plead?" the judge asked.

Bill Parsons spoke for Ray. "The defendant pleads not guilty, your honor."

Then came the subject of bail. The prosecution asked the judge to deny bail, but Parsons laid out all the reasons that Ray was not a flight risk. After asking for Ray's passport to be held by the court until after his trial, the judge set bail.

Katie thought it was an exorbitant amount, but Seth said that it wasn't that much considering he'd been accused of murder.

And it appeared that despite the fact that Parsons wasn't the most expensive criminal attorney in the county, he'd taken care of everything. Before long, Ray was free to go.

But how long would he stay free?

Twenty-One

The Davenport girls took the lead with Katie and Ray following a few steps behind. As they approached the parking lot, Sophie turned. "Thanks for everything," she said flatly, directing her comment at Katie. "We're good now."

"You're good?" Katie asked. "You mean you have a way home that doesn't include me?"

Ray gave a mirthless chuckle. "Yeah, kiddo, the cops escort you to the joint, but they don't give you a ride back to your house."

"Oh . . . well . . . I guess you can drive us home, then." Sophie turned and trudged toward the car.

"Thank you so much," Katie muttered.

"No, thank *you*," Ray told her, his voice subdued.

She let out an exasperated sigh. "You're welcome. Now get in the car."

On the drive back to McKinlay Mill, Katie told Ray that

Vance informed her about the break-in at Wood U, while the girls looked anywhere but the front of the vehicle and fumed in silence.

"Why didn't you tell me?" Katie asked and glanced askance.

Ray shrugged. "I didn't want to worry you."

"Didn't want to *worry* me? Hey, I'm president of the Victoria Square Merchants Association. I *need* to know when one of our businesses has been broken into or vandalized so I can pass a warning along to the other merchants."

"It wasn't a random thing," Ray said. "I was targeted. I thought that was pretty obvious from the arrest."

"I know . . . but we didn't know that before, and you still kept the information to yourself."

"Woman, if you're going to badger me, could you at least wait until after I've had a shower and a decent cup of coffee?"

"Oh, yeah? And why's that?" she challenged.

Ray seemed to shrink into his seat and turned his attention out the passenger-side window.

The rest of the drive was spent in an uncomfortable silence. When they arrived at Ray's house, the girls got out of Katie's car as if it were on fire.

Ray turned to Katie. "I'm sorry about the level of animosity being aimed at you. But could you come in for a few minutes? There are a few things I'd like to discuss with you."

"I dunno, Ray."

"Oh, come on. My girls don't bite."

"I'm not so sure." Still, Ray and Katie got out of the car and went inside. The girls were waiting in the living room, standing with their arms crossed, looking defiant.

"Go on and get cleaned up," Katie said to Ray. "The girls and I can get lunch started."

"That's not necessary." Sophie angled her body between Katie and her father. "I know what Dad likes, and *I'll* make lunch. We don't need you here. You can go on to work . . . or however you kill time during the day."

"Young lady, that's—"

"It's okay, Ray," Katie said, holding up a hand to stave off further protests. "Sophie's right—I have a lot to accomplish today."

"Still, I—"

Katie raised a finger to silence him. "You need to be with your daughters now. We can talk later."

He nodded. "Thank you . . . for everything."

"That's what friends are for." She managed a half-hearted smile and left the house.

As she got into her car to leave, she hoped Ray wouldn't be too hard on the girls . . . although their bratty attitude had grated on her last nerve for the past twenty-four hours. She was more than ready for some peace and quiet . . . and friendly faces.

Her first stop was Tealicious. She was hungry, besides the fact that she hadn't checked in at the tea shop in two days.

Upon her arrival, Brad came out to greet her with open arms and embraced her warmly. "Katie!"

This is more like it. So, there, Davenport girls.

"I'm happy you have such confidence in me, but I've missed seeing you," he said.

"Thanks, Brad. Something came up and I had to help out a friend for a little while. But, I'm back . . . and I'm starving."

"Ah, well, good. You're in for a treat. I have a wonderful salmon salad served on pumpernickel I'd like you to try. And also, I've got an egg and watercress served on sourdough."

"Great. Can I try both?" She peered into the display case to her right and pointed toward a platter of cookies. "What are those? I haven't seen those before."

"They're brown sugar cashew cookies."

"Yum. I'll have two of those, please."

"Coming right up." Brad motioned for one of his new hires—Amy, by her nametag—told her what to give Katie, and excused himself. "Be back in a second. I need to speak with this gentleman."

Katie glanced over her shoulder to see Paul Fenton standing by the front door, and her already high-anxiety level shot up about a hundred points. *What on earth is he doing here?* Fenton certainly didn't strike Katie as the dainty tea sandwich type.

Amy told Katie that if she'd like to be seated, she'd bring her plate and a pot of tea. Katie thanked her and sat down at a table near the front of the house that overlooked the parking lot.

As Katie watched, Brad and Paul walked outside to have—what appeared to be by what she could make out through the window—a pretty intense discussion.

What business could Brad possibly have with Paul Fenton . . . a man Katie considered a very real threat? But, then, what did Katie really know about Brad? She'd hired him on his superior credentials and Nick's recommendation. Still, he was admittedly an alcoholic and possibly even a drug abuser. Could it be that whatever shady business Paul and Ken Fenton were involved in was the *real* reason Brad had taken the job here at Tealicious? The man could have worked at any upscale restaurant in Manhattan. Why had he settled for a tea shop in a backwater like McKinlay Mill?

Amy interrupted Katie's reverie by bringing her food. She thanked the woman and tried to smile. She also tried to tell herself she was being ridiculous looking for underhanded behavior on Brad's part when she had nothing in the way of proof. But *was* she being ridiculous?

Her ringtone sounded. Katie pulled out her cell phone but didn't recognize the number. She decided to answer anyway. "Katie Bonner, how may I help you?"

"Hi, Katie. This is John Healy. You called for an estimate."

Healy. Who the heck is John Healy? Then it dawned on her: the contractor. "Yes, Mr. Healy. Thank you for returning my call."

"I'm in the area, and I can be at your tea shop in about fifteen minutes if you'd meet me there."

"I'm here now," she said, "and I'll definitely stay put. I'm looking forward to getting your thoughts on the renovation."

"Great. See you soon." The call ended.

Katie glanced out the window to see Paul Fenton walk away and a considerably calmer Brad turn back to enter the building. She didn't look in his direction as he abandoned the dining room for a direct line to the kitchen.

Curious.

Katie had just enough time to finish her lunch before Healy arrived. He appeared to be in his early fifties, with thinning salt-and-pepper hair and gray-green eyes. His face had the leathery appearance of someone who spent a lot of time outside with no thought of sun protection, and he wore a friendly smile. Healy gave Katie a warm handshake and asked her to call him John.

On the way upstairs, Katie explained to Healy that she wanted to turn the area into a loft apartment.

He nodded thoughtfully but kept his opinions to himself, other than to ask, "Will you be wanting a separate entrance?"

"I'd like an estimate both with and without a separate entrance," she said. "Ideally, I'd love a separate entrance, especially if, in the future, I ever decide to lease the apartment to someone else. But I'm not sure I can afford it."

Healy took a small notebook from the back pocket of his jeans and a pencil from behind his ear. He flipped open the notebook and jotted down, *Estimate with and without separate entrance.*

After inspecting the loft area, Healy retrieved a measuring tape from a front pocket and, other than asking Katie to hold one end now and then, he worked quietly. He listened to her suggestions and made a few of his own.

At last, he studied the notes he'd made and said, "For a job this size, I can use our design software to work up a couple of different plans for you. With each plan, I'll give you an estimate both with and without the addition of a separate entrance. But, for what it's worth, I believe you're going to get tired of coming and going through the tea shop all the time. Plus, it'll be a pain in the butt to put the entrance in later if you change your mind."

"I'll take that under advisement, John. Thank you."

He handed her a card. "On the back of this card is a website that's hidden from the public. It has a list of references on it, complete with phone numbers and email addresses. I'd appreciate it if you don't share it with anyone, but feel free to contact any of the people on the page to ask about my work."

"I'll do that."

"While I'll get the plans to you within the next few days, I wouldn't be able to start the job until at least September. Is that all right?"

She smiled. "If you could do it any sooner, I'd be concerned."

He laughed. "I'll be in touch."

~~~~~~~

When Katie entered Artisans Alley, she was delighted to see Rose back at cash desk one.

"Rose!" she cried and welcomed her friend back with a warm hug. "Are you better?"

"I am, but the doctor says I still need to take it easy for a few days in order to participate in the walkathon." Rose lowered her voice. "How are you? I heard about poor Ray."

Katie blew out a breath. "Well, I survived a night with the Davenport sisters. And that wasn't as easy as you might think."

"Oh, I know very well that girls can be spiteful when they think they're protecting their dad . . . or asserting their independence . . . or well, just about anything."

They both laughed.

"I'm so glad you're doing better," Katie said. "Ray is home now, and I hope this whole matter will be resolved soon."

Rose looked all around to ensure they weren't in danger

of being overheard. "You don't think . . . ? I mean . . . there's . . . probably no way Ray is guilty . . . right?"

"That's absolutely right."

"I . . . I agree with you . . . I do. But Nona . . . well, Sue told me that Nona has been visiting the other merchants on the Square trying to get Ray voted out of the Victoria Square Merchants Association."

Katie frowned. "What happened to innocent until proven guilty?"

Rose shrugged. "I suppose that when Ray got arrested, Nona took that as a guilty verdict."

"Well, it isn't." She groaned. "If she brings this nonsense to me—which she'll have to if she truly wants Ray kicked out of the association—I'll set her straight."

"You're a good friend, Katie."

Yes, she was Ray's friend. Period.

As she walked to her office, Katie wondered why it was so easy for some—namely Andy, Nona, and possibly even Rose—to believe Ray might have killed Ken Fenton. For goodness' sake, he had no motive whatsoever. And even if he had, Ray Davenport would never kill someone. He had his daughters to think of. He wouldn't want them to grow up alone. Second, he took an oath to protect and serve the people of Monroe County and became a homicide detective to put murderers behind bars.

But they say everyone has his limits.

Katie rubbed her eyes. *Good grief. They even have* me *doubting him. But I know better . . . I do.*

She sat at her desk and awakened her PC. She took out Healy's card and logged on to the hidden web page to which he'd directed her. There was an impressive list of client names. One stood out to her—Fiona Lancaster.

This was perfect. She could not only ask Fiona about John Healy's work, but she could also ask her why Phil didn't think Katie should have allowed Hugh to have a vendor booth at Artisans Alley. She picked up the receiver of the phone on her desk.

Fiona answered promptly. "Katie, dear, hello."

"Hi, Fiona. How are you?"

"Wonderful, thanks. You?"

"I'm fine. I'm calling regarding John Healy. I'm planning to renovate the upstairs of Tealicious, and John came to check it out today. He's going to work up a couple of different plans, and you're on his list of references."

"Of course I am! John is a genius. I adore his work. He's professional, direct, doesn't like surprises any more than I do, and he usually comes in not only on time but slightly under budget. I highly recommend him."

"That's good to know. Thank you. I was impressed with him, but it helps to hear you speak so highly of him."

"I know you'll be satisfied with his work."

"Fiona, while I have you on the line, could I please ask you a question?"

"Fire away."

"Why does Phil think I shouldn't have allowed Hugh McKinney to rent a vendor booth at Artisans Alley?" Katie asked. "Is there something about him I should know?"

"I don't think so. Phil merely likes giving people—especially his old Army pals—a hard time. I'll ask him, though, just to make sure."

"I'd appreciate that."

"I have to return to Victoria Square sooner than expected," Fiona said. "I'll be arriving on Sunday. Would you happen to be free for dinner?"

"Yes, that would be lovely."

"Good. I should be able to give you Phil's thoughts on Hugh McKinney—good, bad, or otherwise—then."

"All right. See you then."

After speaking with Fiona, Katie decided to wait until she had the estimates before talking with anyone else on John's reference page. Besides, she got the feeling they'd all be as complimentary as Fiona. She doubted he'd have his disgruntled clients' information on the page. But she had a good feeling after meeting Healy. That, coupled with Fiona's glowing praise and Roger's desire to work with the man, made her feel he was the man for the job . . . provided she could afford him.

She opened her email account and saw a message from Seth with the subject line *Jones Building*. The message had gone out to all the buyers in the contract, and Seth was asking each of them to come by his office that day at four o'clock to review and sign the contract.

> If you're unable to be here at four o'clock, please try to come in prior to that time to review and sign the document independently. This will facilitate my taking the contract to the bank on your behalf on Monday morning.

Katie was pleased that the building purchase was moving forward so quickly. When she thought about it, she had a lot of positives in her life right then. If she could only erase the two giant negatives—Ray's arrest and its implications, and Erikka.

She had no time to dwell on either her positives or her negatives just then, because the phone rang. Caller ID alerted her to the familiar number.

"Margo, hi. How's everything going?" Katie asked, charging her voice with positivity and praying her former mother-in-law hadn't changed her mind about buying and renovating the building.

"Everything's going swimmingly." Margo hesitated. "Classy people in the know still say that, don't they?"

Katie rolled her eyes. "Well, you would certainly know."

Margo gave a tinkle of laughter. "I'm calling to tell you

I'm having your friend Seth handle the arrangements for the Tealicious building purchase."

"Fantastic."

"I thought you'd be happy about that. He did a great job with our partnership agreement, so I thought it only natural that he'd take care of this for us, too."

"Exactly. I couldn't agree more," Katie said. "By the way, I met with a contractor today, and he's going to draw up a couple of different layouts and give me some estimates. Would you like to see the layouts before I choose?"

"Sure. I can take a look at them—if he has them ready— when I come to McKinlay Mill for the closing."

Every muscle in Katie's body tensed. "The closing . . . right."

"And, no offense, but I do believe I'll take those young men at Sassy Sally's up on their offer to stay at their charming B and B this time," Margo said.

"Right."

Thank goodness. No way did Katie want to give up her bed and, more importantly, her privacy for Margo. Then again, she'd sold her soul to get Tealicious, so it was only natural that Margo would want to be a part of its expansion and her financial stake in it.

When Katie ended the call, she mentally added Margo's pending visit to her list of negatives. She wondered if she should've mentioned Ray's predicament to her former mother-in-law but then decided she was right not to have done so. There was nothing Margo could do to help, after all, and— hopefully—this mess would be behind them long before she arrived.

But Katie didn't have to like it.

Twenty-Two

It was just after two when Andy showed up at Katie's office door carrying a small white bakery bag. He held it up and shook it slightly. "I thought you might be in need of a pick-me-up this afternoon."

Despite the closed bag, Katie closed her eyes and breathed in the scent of spices. "A cinnamon bun . . . just what I wanted." Actually, she was still full from lunch, but she wasn't going to say so after he went to the trouble of leaving work to bring her a treat.

Katie stood and, as Andy placed the bag on her desk, she stepped around her desk and put her arms around his neck. "I've missed you."

"It's only been a day," he said.

"And a night . . . a really lousy night." She kissed him.

"I'm glad you missed me," he said and pulled back. "Maybe it'll make you appreciate me more."

She cocked her head and scrutinized his face. "You think?"

"If not, maybe this will—I went by the apartment first thing this morning to check on Mason and Della."

She smiled. "You do know the way to my heart, don't you?"

"I sure do. They still had plenty of kibble, so I gave them a can of wet food and refilled their water dish."

"Thank you. You're wonderful, you know that?"

"Just to you," he murmured against her lips. "I'm an ogre to everyone else."

She knew that wasn't true—he was especially un-ogre-like to Erikka—but she let the thought pass and enjoyed his kiss.

"How was it spending time with the bad seeds?" Andy asked at last.

"I wouldn't call them *bad seeds*. They were just worried about their dad, that's all. But Ray is out on bail, so the girls should feel relieved . . . for now, at least." Katie wasn't particularly comfortable talking about Ray or his daughters with Andy, especially since Andy seemed willing to believe that Ray might have caused Ken Fenton's death. She changed the subject to something neutral. "Have you read the email from Seth?"

"I have. I thought I could drive us over to his office."

"That would be great. Thank you."

"And after we meet with Seth, I'd like to take you to dinner at the steak house, if you're up for it."

"I'm definitely up for that! A romantic dinner for two? How could I turn that down?" She frowned. "But we can't, Andy. I couldn't possibly keep you from Angelo's that long on one of your busiest nights of the week."

"Ah, but that's where a trusted assistant manager is invaluable. I talked it over with Erikka, and she's happy to run the pizza parlor until I get back." He gave her a smug grin. "See? I told you offering Erikka a full-time position was a smart move."

"You sure did." Katie hoped the sentiment didn't come out of her mouth as hollow and flat as it felt.

~~~~~

Between nibbling on the rich cinnamon roll and her semi-sleepless night, it was no wonder that Katie's eyelids were drooping, and her chin kept falling to her chest as she attempted to work that afternoon. More coffee didn't seem to help, so Katie decided to find someone with whom to chat for a few minutes . . . just until she could revive herself.

She stepped into the vendors' lounge, but since there was no one there at the moment, she strolled to the cash desks up front, smiling at shoppers on her way and asking how they were doing. When she got to cash desk one, Rose was sitting on a stool, holding another paperback with a buxom blonde in a full-length gown and a bare-chested Scot in a kilt and sporran on the cover. Katie was glad to see that there were no customers in line to prevent Rose from engaging in a quick conversation.

"Katie—I'm so glad you're here," Rose said. "Do you have one of those stain-removing wipes in your office?"

"I'm sorry, but I don't. Want me to check around and see if I can find one?"

"No, that's all right. I was ringing up a sale earlier and some white powder fell out of a satchel of some sort. It got all over me." Rose stood and showed Katie the white powder that she'd tried to wipe off her shirt but had only succeeded in rubbing in.

"Powder? Why was there powder in the satchel?"

"Who knows?" Rose shrugged. "The customer wasn't trying to steal powder by concealing it in the satchel or anything."

"It didn't fall out while you were checking the pockets to make sure they were empty?"

"No. It was after that—when I was handing the bag to the woman who purchased it. I don't even know where it came from. But I'm fairly certain it wasn't on the counter before I rang up the bag."

"Was the customer upset about the powder?"

"No." Rose flicked her wrist in dismissal. "She wasn't a bit upset about it . . . told me not to worry about it."

"I'll get you a damp paper towel," Katie said. "Maybe that will bring the powder out."

"All right. I'd appreciate that."

As Katie hurried back to the vendors' lounge, her mind was spinning. She'd checked all the saddlebags that had been sold when she'd worked the cash desk, and there hadn't been anything in any of them . . . especially not white powder.

White powder. A chill snaked down Katie's spine. Could Hugh McKinney be using Artisans Alley to traffic cocaine? Sure, it seemed like a far-fetched idea, but given the things Phil Lancaster had said—and the sheer number of saddle-bags that had been sold at Artisans Alley over the past couple of days—anything was possible.

Katie returned to the cash desk with the damp paper towel. Rose gratefully accepted it and managed to blot the majority of the powder off her blouse.

"Thank you, Katie. That helps a lot."

"You're welcome. I'll . . . um . . . be upstairs for a few minutes if anyone needs me."

She stiffened her backbone, headed for the central stair-case, and walked up the steps. Katie had no idea how she was going to ask Hugh about the white powder, but she'd come up with something. There was no way she would allow illegal activity to take place inside Artisans Alley.

Katie took a deep breath and approached Hugh's booth. "Good afternoon, Hugh."

"Hi, there." He straightened, looking up from the leather he'd been tooling. "I'd advise you not to get too close. This stuff gets all over everything."

The piece of leather over which he'd been working had a piece of paper on top of it. The paper was covered with—judging by the container on his worktable—baby powder.

"You're using powder on your leather?" Katie moved closer. "Why?"

"To etch in the design. See, I place the paper with the design onto the leather. I then take an awl and poke holes all around the design. After that, I put the paper back onto the leather and pour powder over it. And"—he lifted the paper—"*voila*. The design stands out, thanks to the powder, and I can tool the design into the leather."

"That's fascinating. But all that intricate work I saw come through yesterday and the day before . . . there wasn't any powder on those."

Hugh chuckled. "There had been. I take a sponge and clean the powder off after the design is etched in. But I know you didn't come all the way up here to watch an old man tool some leather."

"I'm actually just wandering around for a few minutes to keep from falling asleep," she said. "I didn't sleep very well last night. Besides, your leatherwork is really interesting." She forced a short laugh. "But, you're right, I can see how it would be messy. Rose said a woman bought a satchel earlier today and apparently got powder all over the cash desk."

Hugh shrugged. "I'm telling you . . . it gets everywhere."

Katie nodded, gave him a good-bye wave, and walked to the back stairs that led to the vendors' lounge and back to her office wondering if she'd overreacted about the powder or if she was right to think that there was more to Hugh McKinney's leather goods booth than met the eye. One thing was for certain, however; with all the possibilities swirling around in her brain, she was now totally wide-awake.

~~~~~~~

Later that afternoon, when Katie and Andy walked into Seth's conference room, she was surprised to see that every other member of the new Victoria Square Merchants partnership was already sitting at the table. She'd thought at least one or two of them would have come by beforehand to sign the paperwork. As Katie and Andy took their seats, Seth closed the door, dimmed the lights, and walked to the head of the table.

He clicked a few keys on his laptop, and the first page of the partnership agreement appeared on the projector behind him. "Can everyone see this okay?"

Amid a chorus of yeses, Nona Fiske asked, "Before we talk about the partnership agreement, can we take a moment to discuss Ray Davenport?"

"I'm sorry, Ms. Fiske, but no, we can't," Seth said. "Mr. Davenport isn't a partner in this venture, and as we have a lot of material to go over in a short amount of time, we can't venture off course."

Nona pressed her lips together and folded her arms across her chest.

Katie managed to hide her smile as Seth continued with the meeting. After the paperwork had been signed by all parties and Seth had dismissed them, he asked Katie if he could speak with her privately.

When everyone else except Andy, Seth, and Katie had left the conference room, Seth asked, "Have you spoken with Margo?"

"Yes. She told me she'd enlisted your aid in buying the Tealicious building." She scrunched up her face. "And she'll be here for the closing."

Seth chuckled. "That shouldn't be so bad."

"Let's hope not," Katie said.

Andy grinned. "Aw, come on. I like Margo."

Katie merely shook her head.

"Will she be helping you renovate the loft?" Seth asked.

"I'm not sure." Katie avoided looking at Andy. "Since the apartment will be for my private use, I'd rather incur the costs of renovation myself."

"Sure. That makes sense." Seth escorted them to the conference room door. "She can always pitch in if you need to make any changes should you decide to rent it to someone else."

Katie nodded. "Thanks for helping us make this happen, Seth."

"Just part of being your pseudo big brother."

Katie smiled. "Just be sure to send your bill to Margo—not me."

"She insisted on it."

Good old Margo. Maybe her visit won't be so terrible after all.

~~~~~~~

After the meeting, Andy took Katie to the Blue Star Steak House for a celebratory dinner. He raised his glass of beer. "To the new Victoria Square Merchants Partnership, LLP."

Katie clinked her glass to his. "To the partnership."

"And, I'll say again how lucky we are to have Erikka to allow us this opportunity for a romantic dinner," he said.

Katie's back stiffened but somehow she managed a smile. "True. But let's not ruin dinner by talking about work."

"Fine, then answer me this: Why do you still insist on moving to the loft above the tea shop?"

She shrugged. "It makes sense—that's all. I'd have my own place and not have to pay rent. I can decorate it however I want . . ."

"I've never said one word about your decorating the apartment over Angelo's," Andy said.

"I know. But, if you'll recall, I had a hard time talking you into leasing to me in the first place. Now, I'll only be a stone's throw away, I'll have my own place, and you—"

"Are you sure this isn't because you're still angry about the situation with Erikka?" he interrupted.

"I'm positive." It might have started out that way, but now the move was all about asserting her independence.

Andy blew out a breath, apparently unconvinced but not wanting to ruin the evening by discussing the matter. "So, why do you think Nona has a bug up her butt about Ray Davenport?"

"I'm sure she's been carrying a grudge against him since that whole ordeal with her nephew last December," Katie said. "She's probably still angry with me about that mess, too, come to think of it."

"I don't think that's it. I believe she's honestly afraid that Ray killed Ken Fenton."

"But that's ridiculous." Katie sipped her beer. "There are a lot of people who had a much better motive than Ray."

"Like who?"

"Paul Fenton, for one." She sat her glass down and rubbed her bare arms. "That guy creeps me out—I don't care how great Regan thinks he is."

Andy leaned closer. "Between you and me, Roger isn't a member of his sister's Paul Fenton admiration society, either. He confided to me that he feels there's something off about Paul. Roger doesn't trust the guy and wishes Regan would get a job somewhere else."

"I wonder what kind of shady business Ken—and probably Paul—were involved in. Do you think it could be drugs?"

"Finding out about shady businesses and tracking down killers are the responsibilities of the Sheriff's Office—not you. I'd appreciate it very much if you'd leave the detective work to them and stick around for more romantic dinners."

"Of course I will. But it's scary knowing there's a murderer running around McKinlay Mill."

"It is scary," Andy agreed. "It's also unnerving to contemplate the number of wolves running around Victoria Square in sheep's clothing."

Katie was well aware that Andy was warning her about Ray, but she believed the adage was far more applicable to Erikka.

~~~~~~

Andy parked his truck near the front of Artisans Alley and killed the engine. He turned to Katie, reached for her, and kissed her thoroughly. "I enjoyed dinner."

"So did I."

They got out of the truck and walked hand in hand to the pizzeria, kissed again, and Andy went inside while Katie climbed the stairs to her apartment. She was so happy to be home. It felt like she'd been away for a week.

She was still greeting the cats, giving them some much-appreciated attention, when a knock sounded on her door.

"Who is it?" she called.

"It's Ray. I need to talk to you."

Katie set Mason down on the floor and opened the door, letting Ray inside. "Is everything all right?"

He raised his bushy eyebrows in consternation. "Really?"

"Okay. Sorry. That *was* a dumb question."

Ray shoved his hands into his jeans pockets. "I saw the murder board."

"It was Sasha's idea." Katie turned for the counter and opened a can of cat food, putting it into a bowl and setting it on the floor. As Mason and Della huddled around their dinner, Katie invited Ray into the living room. "I went along with the murder board because it made them—and me—feel more productive. I left it up after the girls went to bed because I thought it might trigger something."

Ray sat on the armchair. "It was pretty good, as far as murder boards go. I was surprised to see you on there as a suspect."

"Yeah . . . that wasn't at my suggestion."

He smirked. "I didn't think it was."

"Did our murder board jog your memory about anything?"

"No . . . but I know you wouldn't brainstorm with the girls the way you would with me," Ray said. "I want the two of us to put our heads together and see what we can come up with."

"Then let's go back into the kitchen, get a legal pad and some markers, and see what we can accomplish."

Ray crossed the floor and was standing in front of her before Katie had time to turn. He put his arms around her and pulled her in for a hug. "I do appreciate everything you do," he said against her hair.

"You're welcome." She stepped back, feeling apprehensive. "We should get to work."

"Yeah."

Katie took a legal pad and a handful of markers of various colors from a drawer in the kitchen. She placed the items on the table and then put on a pot of coffee before sitting down to Ray's right.

"Let's start with the victim," Ray said.

"All right." Katie wrote *Ken Fenton* across the top of the pad in red ink.

"What do we know about him?"

"We know he's Harper Jones's brother-in-law and that his siblings are Mary Jones and Paul Fenton."

Ray nodded. "Write that down. Also, make note of the fact that he was working on the building for Harper Jones."

"And that he was involved in something shady."

"Don't write that," Ray said.

"Why not?"

"Because we don't *know* that Ken Fenton was involved in anything shady. We never saw him engaging in any sort of suspicious behavior."

Katie got up to get their coffee. "But other people did."

"It's still speculation. Besides, 'shady' is too vague. Nobody can say with any certainty whatsoever that Ken was involved with, say, planning a heist or dealing drugs."

Katie set the mugs of coffee on the table, along with sugar and creamer. "Still, the man's brother is a threatening jerk, and both siblings acted strangely about Ken's death. Fiona Lancaster said someone set her apartment building ablaze while Ken was working for her, and even Regan Mitchell overheard the brothers arguing about some kind of delivery."

"Again, those things are circumstantial . . . just like the evidence Schuler has on me." Ray captured her gaze with his own. "Now, if we're going to find Ken Fenton's killer, we need to discover the truth about him. Not hearsay—facts."

Katie nodded. "Then that's what we'll do. We'll learn everything we can about Ken Fenton."

Ray blew out a breath and scowled. "I only hope we can do it before I'm sent to prison for his murder."

Twenty-Three

Determined to find out all she could about Ken Fenton, Katie called Mary Jones as soon as she arrived at Artisans Alley on Saturday morning.

"Hello?" Mary asked, sounding cautious.

Katie didn't blame her. "Hi, Mary. It's Katie Bonner. Are you free this afternoon? If so, I'd like to buy you lunch at Tealicious on Victoria Square so we can have a chat."

"Actually, I have a busy afternoon ahead of me." Mary paused. "But I could do brunch."

"Terrific. Shall we say eleven o'clock, then?"

"That'll be fine. I . . . I'll look forward to it."

Katie ended the call. Wow. She had a lot to think about before she met with Mary. Until then, she decided to concentrate on the needs of Artisans Alley because she knew that if she distracted herself, her mind might come up with the exact ideas and words to convince Mary to share what she knew about what had gone on with her brothers prior to Ken's death. But there were other things to think about.

Vance had set the air-conditioning to a cooler temp and the main showroom tended to be just a bit chilly. Katie got up, grabbed her light blue summer cardigan, and walked toward the front of the establishment. She liked the sweater because it was comfy, adequately covered her white tank top, and it had pockets.

The Alley seemed particularly crowded that morning, and it was obvious her friend needed help. Poor Rose was swamped.

"I can take the next customer here," Katie called, going to the register beside Rose.

There was a flurry of activity as customers bought a variety of items: dolls, stained-glass ornaments, leather purses and satchels, jewelry, and embroidered pillowcases. They usually didn't see this much activity all at once until the holiday season.

At last, all the customers had paid for their purchases and Katie and Rose were relieved to get a break.

"Wow." Katie turned to Rose. "How crazy was that?"

"I know! I sold a couple of pairs of earrings and a necklace. I'm happy about that."

"Me, too. I'm always happy to see this place crowded." She smiled. "How are your legs holding up?"

"Much better. I feel confident I'll be able to participate in the walkathon."

"I'm glad." Katie checked the time on her phone. It was ten thirty. "I'm going to run back to my office for a few minutes, and then I'm going to get something to eat. Call me if you need me."

"All right."

Katie glanced down and saw a piece of fuzz on her sweater's hem. As she plucked it off, she noticed a dark blue pill on the floor between the registers. She bent and picked it up. It looked like prescription medication.

"Rose, is this yours?"

Rose leaned closer to see what Katie had in her hand. "No. I've been taking ibuprofen, but that's it."

Feeling somewhat disconcerted, Katie dropped the pill into her pocket.

"Call me if you need me," she said again and headed back to her office. Once there, she went online and searched for a picture of the dark blue elliptical-shaped pill. The photo that came up was an exact match for a high dosage of opioid oxycodone. Katie felt a prickle at the nape of her neck. Had someone simply dropped this pill or had it fallen out of one of the items she or Rose had rung up?

The idea left her feeling totally discombobulated.

~~~~~~~

Upon discovering the identity of the pill, Katie felt an urgent need to get the heck out of the office and seek fresh air. It was nearly time to meet Mary Jones, and she wanted to check with Brad before having brunch, so she quickly walked across the Square to Tealicious.

Brad smiled and waved when Katie walked in. He excused himself as soon as he could and came over to talk with her.

"How are you today?" he asked.

"I'm fine, Brad. How about you?"

"Super."

"I wanted to let you know that I'm planning on renovating the upstairs apartment," Katie said. "I'm hoping it won't be too disruptive for you or our patrons, but I'm sure we'll have to close the tea shop for a day or more during the most work-intensive renovations."

"Of course." He inclined his head, his smile ironic. "Whatever will I do with a few days off?"

"Maybe you could take a short trip. Is there anywhere you'd like to go?"

"Not particularly. But I'll figure something out."

"You have plenty of time. The renovations won't begin

until I acquire the property and get on the contractor's schedule."

"I'll do whatever I can to help." Brad waved at someone over Katie's shoulder.

Katie turned to see Mary Jones wave back at him. "Do you know Mary?"

"Of course. She's my friend Paul's sister."

"I didn't realize you and Paul Fenton were friends. Have you known him long?"

"Only since coming to work here. I'd like to say hello to her before I head back into the kitchen."

"Of course."

Katie watched their greeting for a moment before walking over to the display case. How had Brad gotten to know Paul Fenton so quickly?

Her mind flashed to the little blue pill she'd locked in her desk drawer. She did her best to shake off the thought as she strolled over to Mary and Brad.

"Hi, Mary. I was looking at the display case, and Brad has really outdone himself today."

"Thank you," he said.

"I'm looking forward to sampling several of those treats," Mary said.

The women settled at a table near the window. In no time the waitress arrived, and Katie and Mary ordered their food.

"Thanks for meeting with me," Katie said. "I wanted to see how you're doing. I'm sure that with everything that's happened, this is a horrible time for you and your family."

Mary blinked in response. "I appreciate that. Most people forget about the bereaved the day after the funeral, but for so many of us, it's after that initial flurry of activity surrounding the death that the pain truly starts to sink in."

"I only met your brother Ken once." She lowered her eyes. "You must have many fond memories of him."

Mary heaved a sigh. "He was always protective of us, even though I was the oldest. I was still the only girl, and his sister, so he thought he needed to look after me." She smiled wryly. "Once, when I was a freshman, I was on my way to school with some friends. The car broke down, and we were stranded on the side of the road. When Ken saw us from the bus, he had a fit until the school bus driver stopped to pick us up."

Katie smiled. "That's so sweet."

"It was. At the time I was mortified because my little brother had made such a scene, but looking back, I appreciate his thoughtfulness."

"Did Ken ever marry?" Katie asked.

"Yes. His wife died a few years ago. His son, Avery, is a freshman at RIT. He's studying computer programming and doing well in it. That boy is absolutely brilliant."

"I had no idea. Poor Avery must be devastated."

"He is. Harper and I encouraged him to stay with us for a while, but Avery didn't want to. He wanted to be at home." She shrugged. "I suppose I can't blame him. Plus, he has to return to school in the fall. I believe that will be good for him—getting back to his friends and his studies. It'll help get his mind off . . . well, everything." Mary looked away.

"What did Ken do for a living? I know he was doing some construction work for your husband—was that what he did full-time?" Katie asked.

"Yes. Ken was a self-employed handyman," Mary said. "He made a good living at it. He liked to call himself a jack-of-all-trades and master of none, but the truth is he could do just about anything he put his mind to. I was so very proud of him."

Katie reached out to pat Mary's hand.

Mary dabbed at her eyes with a napkin and gave a half-hearted smile. "Let's talk about you. What's it like to be a successful businesswoman? I imagine it must be incredibly empowering."

"It is. I've had some lucky breaks."

"And I'd wager you've done a lot of hard work."

"I have . . . and I'm happy that it's starting to pay off." She smiled. "I'm also happy to get to know you better, Mary. We'll have to do this again sometime."

And maybe they would. Mary was nicer than she'd appeared to be at first. Or was it possible that Mary was being so amiable because she still had something to hide?

~~~~~~~

After leaving Tealicious, Katie wanted to go straight to Wood U to talk to Ray. But she didn't want Mary to see her heading in that direction and guess her true motive behind the brunch invitation. Actually, even though she'd asked Mary to the tea shop to talk to see what she could learn about the woman's brother, Katie was glad she'd had the opportunity to talk with Mary a bit more.

She withdrew her phone from her pocket and called Ray. "It's me, Katie. I just had brunch with Mary Jones and learned more about Ken Fenton."

"Did she confess to killing him?" Ray asked.

Katie huffed. "No. She seems to have loved him a lot. But that's not why I called. Earlier, I found a dark blue elliptical-shaped pill on the floor at Artisans Alley. I—"

"That sounds like oxycodone."

"I looked it up and it is. Now I'm concerned that it might've fallen out of something leaving Artisans Alley."

"Don't jump to conclusions," Ray said. "It could just as easily have dropped out of someone's purse."

"It was behind one of the cash desks."

"It could've rolled. Have you mentioned the pill to anyone else?"

"Only to Rose. She was there when I found it, and I thought it might be hers."

"Did you tell Rose what the pill was?"

"Not yet. I haven't—"

"Don't. Don't say anything about it to anyone. I'll take

lunch as soon as I can get one of the girls to cover for me and head over to Artisans Alley." With that, he ended the call.

Katie frowned and wondered what had Ray behaving extra grumpy on that day.

She spotted Regan walking from the parking lot to the sidewalk ahead of her and called out to the girl. "Regan! Hi!"

Regan turned, shading her eyes against the afternoon sun. "Hey, Katie!"

Katie noted that Regan held a large, flat envelope. When they met on the sidewalk, Regan casually clasped her hands behind her back, effectively hiding said envelope.

"I'm on my way to Tealicious," Regan said. "It looks like maybe you've already been there."

"I have. And I ate way too much," Katie said and laughed.

"I'm hoping to find some cookies Roger might like. He's been working awfully hard lately, and I want to take him a treat."

"How nice! Why don't I go back with you and get the cookies? After all, Roger was so helpful in getting me in touch with John Healy."

"No, I'll get them. How did it go with Mr. Healy anyway?"

"It went well," Katie said. "He's been to see the building and said he'll get a couple of different plans with estimates drawn up right away."

"He will, too. He's known for being prompt."

"Cool. Are you sure I can't go to Tealicious with you and get those cookies for Roger?"

"Maybe next time. I don't want to hold you up. Bye!"

Regan started walking toward Tealicious, and when she moved her arms, Katie could see that Brad's name was boldly written upon the envelope Regan carried.

~~~~~~

The afternoon was waning when Ray gave a perfunctory knock on Katie's office door before entering with a bag of vending machine chips and a bottle of water. He closed the door and sat on the chair beside the desk.

"Show me what you've got," he said tersely.

"Hello to you, too," she responded flatly.

"Come on, Katie. We don't have all day."

Despite his brusque tone, Katie unlocked the desk drawer and took out the solitary pill, setting it on Ray's open palm.

Ray squinted at it. "Turn it over. I don't want to touch it."

"Why not?"

"I don't want my prints on the thing."

"But it's all right for *my* prints to be on it?" she asked incredulously.

"You've already touched it. Besides, you aren't a murder suspect."

Nudging the offending object with her index finger, Katie turned the pill over so Ray could see the indented numbers on it.

"That's oxycodone, all right. This is the dosage typically given only to people who have a tolerance for opioids."

Katie's brow furrowed. "What does that mean?"

"Anything sixty milligrams and above is prescribed only for those patients who already take opioids because they require higher doses for pain relief. For something like a toothache, you'd be given something much lower . . . say ten or fifteen milligrams."

"And how much is this pill?"

"That one is a hundred and sixty milligrams."

She gasped. "That's . . . that's a lot!"

"No shit, Sherlock."

Katie scowled at him. "Do you think someone could be trafficking drugs through Artisans Alley?"

Ray nodded toward the pill. "Lock that back in your drawer."

She did. "You didn't answer my question."

"I suppose anything is possible, but you need to keep your suspicions to yourself."

"No, I don't! I need to alert the Merchants Association, at the very least. What if—"

"Leave it alone, Katie. If someone *is* running drugs through Artisans Alley, and they believe you're onto them, they'll kill you. These people don't mess around. Besides, you could be way off base."

"Then what do I do?"

"Absolutely nothing . . . at least for now. I have a friend with the DEA. I'll have him casually come by with his dog." He opened his chips. "It's a drug dog, but in cases like this, it's trained to act as a service dog, so no one gets suspicious. Since Artisans Alley is closed on Monday, I'll see if my friend can come then."

"All right."

~~~~~~~

Given everything that was on her mind, it was no wonder that Katie started later that afternoon when a woodpecker-like knock rang out on her office door.

"Come in." She knew her voice sounded tentative, but she couldn't help it and was relieved when Sue Sweeney came through the door holding one of her distinctive candy boxes.

"Hi, there!" Sue gave Katie a bright sunny smile that matched the yellow and white polka-dot scarf tied at her throat. "I'm taking a poll. Would you try my new creation— chocolate fig squares—and vote on them?" She placed the box on Katie's desk and removed the lid.

The enticing aroma seemed to permeate Katie's office and she inhaled deeply.

"They smell wonderful," she said, as she plucked a square from the box. "You say they're chocolate and . . . fig?"

Sue nodded.

Katie bit into the square and closed her eyes with delight. "Mmmm!" she breathed and covered her mouth with one hand. "These are amazing!"

Sue giggled. "Thank you. Hugh adores them . . . or else

he's only saying that to boost my ego. That's why I wanted to get some additional opinions. Are you giving me your *honest* opinion?"

"I am." Katie swallowed and lowered her hand. "They're delicious." She popped the rest of the square into her mouth.

Sue took out a small notepad and pen, put a single mark inside the pad, and returned both pad and pen to her pocket. "I put you in the *yes* column."

"Darn. I see I spoke too soon," Katie teased. "I should've told you I need another one to make sure."

Laughing, Sue offered Katie another square.

"It sounds as if things are going well with you and Hugh," Katie said, refraining from eating the treat just yet.

"They are. He's a wonderful man."

"I've asked him to speak at an upcoming Merchants Association meeting about how he uses public speaking to drum up business. His talk at the motorcycle club meeting earlier this week resulted in his selling saddlebags to bikers in droves."

"Oh, Hugh is a master marketer," Sue said. "In fact, it was his idea to have people sample these fig squares. He said it would remind people that I'm here and that I'm innovative."

"Good thinking."

Hugh seemed to have knowledge on a lot of different things—marketing, acupressure, sewing . . .

What other skills did he possess?

Twenty-Four

It wasn't until almost quitting time that Katie realized how hungry she was. She called Del's Diner and placed a to-go order so she could take her meal home and eat it while relaxing in front of the television. She didn't do that very often, but she felt particularly lazy this evening. She supposed she still hadn't caught up on her sleep after Thursday's fiasco.

Walking into Del's, Katie got distracted by a squirrel dashing across the sidewalk in front of her. She smiled as she watched the bushy tail disappear behind a cluster of bushes. Still smiling, she turned her attention back to where she was walking, but not in time.

Paul Fenton grabbed her by the shoulders. "You need to be more careful."

She jerked away from him. "And you need to stop putting your hands on me."

"Just keeping you from tripping. You have no idea what

could happen when you're not concentrating on your own business rather than"—he nodded toward the bushes—"watching the squirrels. You pay attention to you, Katie. Those squirrels can take care of themselves."

With a glare, she stepped around him and walked into Del's. Her appetite had fled, but it wasn't the diner's fault. She paid for her grilled cheese and tomato soup and took them home to languish in the refrigerator. Maybe she'd feel like eating them later.

She fed the cats and then headed over to Sassy Sally's. She preferred not being home alone after her encounter with Paul, and she felt that walking to the other end of the Square would do her good to help blow off steam.

Don was sitting on the porch when she arrived.

He got to his feet. "Are you all right? You look a little pale."

"I'm fine," she said, stomping up the steps. "Just angry. I ran into Paul Fenton—or, rather, he made it a point to run into *me*—at Del's."

"Come on in, and let's get you a glass of wine." He ushered her into the kitchen.

Nick came in from the dining room. "Hey, Katie. I knew I heard your voice. What's going on?"

"Can't I come to visit without you two making a federal case out of it?" she asked with a wry grin.

"Not when your hands are shaking like that," Nick said.

"I got irritated when I ran into Paul Fenton a while ago," Katie said. "Maybe I'm being overly touchy—I've had a lot on my mind this week."

She was definitely *not* being overly touchy, but she didn't particularly want to discuss Paul Fenton at the moment.

"Margo and I are buying the Tealicious building, and I'm converting the upstairs into an apartment," she continued.

"Congratulations," Don said, handing her a glass. "That's wonderful."

"Yes, but we know that's not all you have on your mind," Nick added. "We heard about Ray Davenport's arrest."

"Has Nona Fiske been here trying to get your support for kicking Ray out of the Victoria Square Merchants Association?"

"She has." Don glanced at Nick. "But she won't get it."

"We know Ray is innocent." Nick shook his head. "I mean, the man dedicated his life to enforcing the law. He's not going to go off the rails without a darned good reason . . . and Ken Fenton wasn't a darned good reason."

"I can't image Ray ever going off the rails." Katie took a drink of the chilled Chardonnay. "He suggested to me last night that he needs to learn everything he can about Ken. I agreed, and I'm trying to help."

Nick rolled his eyes. "Of course you are. Sweetheart, sometimes you need to take a step back and let people fend for themselves."

"I'm a firm believer in helping my friends fend," she said, really wishing Nick hadn't just practically quoted Paul Fenton. "So, sue me. Anyway, I had brunch with Mary Jones this morning, and she was really nice. I get the feeling that Ken was a decent guy, too."

Don raised his brows. "I'm surprised to hear you say that."

"Well, Mary spoke so highly of him. Yes, he was her brother. But after Ken's wife died, he was the sole provider and caretaker of their son." Katie shrugged. "I could be totally wrong, but I get the feeling that the only malevolent person in that family is Paul."

"Even at that," Don said, "do you believe Paul was ruthless enough to kill his own brother?"

"I have no idea," Katie admitted. "The man appears to be devoted to his family, but he sure threatens me every chance he gets. He's the first person I've ever met who can turn what would appear to be an innocuous conversation into a warning."

"Is it possible that you're misconstruing Paul's comments because you find the man intimidating?" Don asked.

Nick playfully swatted Don's shoulder. "Honey, this is *Katie* we're talking about. Nothing intimidates her."

"Thanks, Nick," she said with a smile. "But, no, Don, I don't think that's it. I mean, Paul came to my home and threatened me . . . remember? And then he somehow made it look to Detective Schuler as if *I* were the bad guy."

"That's right." Nick rubbed his chin. "I wonder if Schuler is playing a bigger part in this whole situation than we realize."

Before the trio could debate that issue, Brad arrived. He was carrying the envelope Katie saw Regan delivering. Like Regan, Brad clasped the envelope behind his back, as if he didn't want them to see it.

"Good afternoon. You weren't meeting in here to talk about me, were you?" Brad teased.

"We were," Nick said. "And now you've gone and spoiled it."

"Did Regan find Roger a nice assortment of cookies?" Katie asked. "I ran into her when she was on her way to Tealicious."

"Yes, she certainly did. I imagine he was pleased with them. And I gave her a discount. I hope that's okay."

"Thank you. I wanted to buy him the cookies myself to express my appreciation for him fixing my lamp and passing along John Healy's information, but Regan insisted on getting them."

Brad nodded. "If you'll excuse me, I need to go upstairs to shower and change."

Hoping she'd given him enough time to get out of earshot, Katie asked Nick and Don if they were aware that Brad and Paul Fenton had struck up a friendship.

The men exchanged a loaded glance before Don answered, "Uh . . . no."

An awkward silence fell. Did Don look just a teensy bit guilty?

"Would you like to stay for dinner?" Nick asked.

"No, thanks. I need to be going," Katie said. "I'm guessing you have everything ready for Fiona's stay?"

"She's in her favorite room." Nick smiled. "She never asks for much more than that."

"Easy to please . . . that's nice."

"Nicer than you could possibly imagine," Don said. "Be careful walking home."

Katie's walk back across the empty Square to her apartment was perceptibly slower than the walk to Sassy Sally's had been. And while she was much less driven by emotion, she had even more to consider than she'd had before. She'd never imagined that Detective Schuler could be colluding with Paul Fenton. That would certainly explain why the man was determined to find Ray guilty of Ken Fenton's murder.

And what about Brad's friendship with Fenton? Don and Nick—or, rather *Don*—had claimed not to know anything about it, but they'd behaved suspiciously. Did the couple know more than they were letting on? If so, why hide it?

When she neared Angelo's Pizzeria, Katie could see Andy and Erikka working shoulder to shoulder, smiling at each other, their moves so well coordinated they appeared to have been choreographed. She sighed. Andy was right—he and Erikka made an excellent team.

Katie enjoyed cooking. She wondered if she'd be as happy working at Andy's side on a daily basis as Erikka seemed to be. She didn't know . . . but she didn't think she would. She prized her positions of authority at Artisans Alley and Tealicious. She would never again play "first mate" to Andy's—or anyone else's—"captain."

~~~~~~~

On Sunday morning, when Katie left her apartment for Artisans Alley, she saw Rose emerge from the back parking lot in her trainers, pumping her arms as she walked. Katie scrambled to catch up and fell into step beside her.

"Good morning, Katie."

"Hi, Rose. Did the doctor clear you for walking?" Katie asked.

"Yes, and I'm only doing one lap," Rose answered. "I don't want to overdo it, but I do feel well enough to resume my training."

"That's terrific. I'll keep you company if you don't mind."

"I don't mind at all. I'm glad to have somebody to converse with."

Katie had kept a furtive eye on the vendors because of the pill she'd found on the floor. Did anyone appear to be hiding anything? Was there anyone who wouldn't meet her gaze? Because of what Ray had told her, Katie didn't bring up the pill to Rose, and Rose seemed to have forgotten about it.

"Rose, what's your opinion of Detective Schuler?"

"I don't really know the man," Rose said, "but I guess he's all right. Why?"

"I don't know. I'm just having doubts about him since he turned that whole Paul Fenton situation around on me. Honestly, the man harasses me in my own home, I call the police, and they tell me that Paul has taken out a complaint against *me*? There's nothing right about that. Ray would have handled that incident much better."

"Well, sure he would have. Ray has a thing for you."

"He does not! And even if he did, he wouldn't have let that color his work."

Rose raised her eyebrows but simply kept walking.

Katie's steps faltered as she tried to make her case. "Ray would've warned me to stay away from Ken's family—just as Schuler did—but Ray would've taken the threat against me seriously. I can't help but wonder if . . . I don't know . . . if Detective Schuler and Paul Fenton are friends or something."

"I imagine they could be," Rose said. "Or it could just be that Detective Schuler doesn't fancy you, dear. He is married, you know."

"Rose, tell me truthfully—do you think I was wrong to feel threatened by Paul Fenton the night he came to my home?"

"Of course not. I'm trying to be objective, that's all. I

can't help but wonder if you got so used to Ray's treatment of you that it's made you believe Detective Schuler is biased in Paul's favor."

"I don't think that's it. When Ray and I first met, even though we didn't always get along, I always considered him to be fair."

"That's not quite how I remember things. Might you be wearing rose-colored glasses?" Rose suggested.

"I don't think so," Katie said, but the truth was she and Ray had not become friends until after he'd retired the summer before. A lot had happened since then.

Rose held up her hands. "I promise, I'm only playing devil's advocate to help you sort it all out in your own mind."

"Yeah . . . thanks, Rose."

After walking a lap with Rose, Katie went to her office. Was Rose right about Paul successfully playing the system once, or was there more to it? Was Detective Schuler in cahoots with Paul Fenton in whatever illegal activities in which the tattoo artist might be involved? Did Schuler have some sort of personal grudge against Ray? Or was Katie making a mountain out of a molehill?

She wasn't sure—not at all.

~~~~~~~

Since Artisans Alley was not terribly busy that Sunday morning, Katie decided to set aside all the detritus from her mind and concentrate on the one thing she thought could do some good—finding out more about Ken Fenton. Mary had said Ken had a college-aged son named Avery. And college-aged young men have social media pages. Katie did a search and found Avery's page within seconds.

There were a lot of photos of Avery with his dad, a few of him with Aunt Mary, but none of Avery with Uncle Paul.

Interesting.

Katie scrolled down the page and scanned the notes of sympathy Avery's friends had left about Ken's death. She felt a twinge of guilt at the impropriety of reading the young man's messages, but she reasoned that they were on a public forum. It wasn't like she was reading his email.

One message stood out to her. It was written by someone calling himself Racecardriver42, and it said: "I'm sorry about your dad. He was a good guy—always keeping your uncle Paul and me out of trouble . . . or, at least, trying to. If there's anything I can do, let me know."

So, according to Racecar, Ken tried to keep him and Paul out of trouble. Katie clicked on the name to view Racecar's profile. Clearly, Racecar liked to party. In several of his photos, he appeared to be inebriated. Racecar's list of friends included Paul; Ken; Ken's son, Avery; Mary; Hugh; Regan; Roger; and Andy.

Katie blinked. Racecar was friends with *Andy*? How was that possible? Katie had never met this man, and Andy had never spoken about him.

She took a screenshot of the page and texted it to Andy. How do you know this guy? she typed.

He texted back: We went to high school together. Haven't seen him in years. He doesn't seem to have matured much since high school. Why do you want to know about him?

Long story. I'll tell you tonight. XOXO.

Andy responded: Okay, but if he wants to lease a vendor spot at AA, tell him you're full up. He didn't have a stellar reputation in high school, and I'm guessing he still doesn't.

Then why are you FB friends with the guy? Katie asked. Were you close when you were in school together?

No. But I couldn't think of a valid reason to deny his friend request without coming across like a jerk. Plus, as a business owner, I don't want people to feel that I have a big head just because I run a pizzeria.

That's ridiculous, Katie fired back. You have a big head because you're still the best-looking guy in your graduating class.

Well, that does it.

Katie read the cryptic response. Does what? she wrote.

When Andy didn't respond, she decided he must've gotten busy. She gave up on Racecar and went back to Avery's profile page.

Minutes later, Andy burst into her office, came around the side of the desk, pulled her to her feet, and kissed her soundly.

"Does that answer your question?" he asked, sporting a wicked grin.

She smiled. "After that kiss, I'm not even sure what the question was, but I'll accept that answer."

He laughed. "You're beautiful, and I couldn't wait until tonight to see you. Now that I'm here, tell me why you wanted to know about Aaron."

Aaron? Oh, Racecar!

Katie explained that at brunch the day before, Mary told her about Ken's son. "Naturally, I was curious about the young man. Your friend Aaron had written on Avery's social media page that he was sorry about Avery's dad—that Ken had tried to keep Aaron and Paul out of trouble. That's when I clicked on Aaron's page and learned that you two know each other—or did."

Andy glanced down at her open laptop. "What does Paul's page look like? Is he as wild as Aaron appears to be?"

"I don't know." Katie sat back down and clicked on the link to Paul's page. The page contained one photograph—the one used as Paul's profile. Otherwise, his page was completely blank.

"Hmm, Paul must not want anyone knowing his business," Andy said.

"Then why have a page at all?"

"Remember, you need a profile in order to create a business page."

"That's right."

He shrugged. "And maybe Paul just wanted the private chat feature to talk with his friends."

"I suppose anything's possible."

Andy bent and kissed her again. "I've got to get back. I'll see you tonight. You should come by Angelo's for a calzone."

"As delicious as that sounds, I'm having dinner with Fiona Lancaster this evening."

"What? She doesn't like calzones?" He winked and left.

Katie resumed her social media spying on Avery Fenton. The young man with the curly brown hair had started working at the new Thai restaurant in Gates when it opened earlier this summer. Katie was guessing it was a part-time job that he'd leave as soon as he returned to college in the fall.

Avery confirmed Katie's guess with his most recent post: *Wanted to see a movie with my buds tonight, but I have to work. #dailygrind #moneyforschool*

So, Avery was working tonight. Katie took a peppermint from the jar on her desk and wondered if Fiona liked Thai food.

Twenty-Five

Katie heard Fiona's laughter as she approached Sassy Sally's door. When she entered the B and B, she could see that Nick was regaling Fiona, Don, and Brad with some wild story. She leaned against the doorjamb and folded her arms to wait for Nick to finish the tale.

He ended with, "And that was the fastest I'd ever seen Don run!"

This brought on another round of laughter by everyone except a sheepish Don, who merely shook his head. When he caught sight of Katie, his eyes sparkled as if he were ten years old and he'd just spotted Santa putting a shiny new bike under the tree.

"Katie! How nice to see you!"

"I'm sure *you're* happy to see me," she said sardonically. "Should I get Nick to tell me that story sometime?"

"No. In fact, I forbid him to ever mention it again."

"It involves Don and a skunk," Nick said, "and I'll be sure to fill you in later." He gave his partner a mischievous grin. "What? It's funny!"

"It really is," Fiona said. "But Katie and I have dinner plans. Would you fellas like to join us?"

"No, thank you," Brad said. "We . . . uh . . . we have some plans of our own."

"That's right." Don elbowed Nick, who was wrinkling his brow in confusion. "Remember?" He ran his hand up and down his forearm. *"Remember?"*

"Oh, yes!" Nick slapped his forehead. "Sometimes I'm so spacey. Hot dogs, nachos, and baseball!"

Were the Red Wings playing at home or would they watch a game on TV and fire up the grill?

"All right," Katie said. "Enjoy yourselves."

"We will," Brad called. "See you tomorrow!"

When she and Fiona got into Katie's car, Fiona said, "I adore those young men, but I'm glad it's just you and me for dinner. I've been looking forward to some girl talk for days."

"Me, too." Katie backed out of the parking lot. "How do you feel about Thai food?"

"I love it. I haven't had it in ages, though. I didn't realize there was a Thai place near Victoria Square."

"Well . . . it's a little bit of a drive," Katie said sheepishly.

"Why, Katie Bonner. If I didn't know better, I'd think you were up to something." She chuckled. "But, of course, I know better. Right?"

"Well . . ." Katie blew out a breath and explained that when she'd found out that Avery happened to be working at the Thai restaurant in Gates that evening, she decided to check him out. "I'd like to get an impression of the type of young man he is, you know?"

"Then let's do one better than looking at the boy from across a crowded room," Fiona said. "Let's request him as our server."

"B-but we can't! How would we possibly explain that? We don't know this kid."

Fiona grinned. "Leave it to me."

~~~~~~~

A diminutive hostess in a black cocktail dress greeted Katie and Fiona when they entered the elegant restaurant.

"Is Avery Fenton working this evening?" Fiona asked.

"Yes, Avery's here."

"May we please be seated at one of his tables? We'd like him to be our server."

"Of course." The hostess checked to see if Avery had an available table. He did, so she led them to it and handed them menus. "Avery will be with you momentarily."

"See?" Fiona asked Katie as the hostess returned to her podium. "Easy, peasy."

"But what are you going to—"

Katie was unable to finish her question because Avery Fenton arrived at their table.

"Good evening. My name is Avery, and I'll be your server. Would you like to hear our specials?"

"We would, Avery," Fiona said smoothly. "But first, I must tell you I asked to be seated in your station because I wanted to express my sincerest condolences. Your father did some work for me once. He was a wonderful man, and he spoke of you often. I'm sorry for your loss."

Avery gulped. "Thank you." He cleared his throat. "Sorry. I'm still—"

Fiona patted his forearm. "It's quite all right, darling. Time will dull the pain, but you'll never stop missing your dad."

"I know."

"Avery, I had brunch with your aunt Mary yesterday," Katie said, hoping to ease the heaviness that had descended. "She's so very proud of you."

"I appreciate that," Avery said. "She and Uncle Harper are awfully good to me."

"You mentioned the specials?" Fiona lifted her brows.

"Oh, yes."

As Avery rattled off the evening's specials, Katie felt like crawling under the table. This had been a terrible idea. Here the poor kid was trying to work to help pay for his college while his grief was still an open wound. So, what do she and Fiona do? Pour salt in it, of course.

Fiona requested the red curry duck from the list of specials. Katie hadn't even paid attention to them. She ordered the coconut chicken. They both ordered sparkling water.

When Avery had taken their order to the kitchen, Katie said, "I'm sorry. I shouldn't have brought you here."

"Nonsense," Fiona said. "It's nice for the young man to know his father loved him. And you chimed in about the aunt. Good job."

"It's true, though. Mary adores her nephew." She leaned closer to Fiona. "Did Ken really talk about Avery a lot while he was working for you?"

"Not to me. He did his job and kept his mouth shut . . . which was fine with me. I don't appreciate workers lollygagging on my dime, and I let them know that up front."

Katie's mouth dropped open.

"Come, now," Fiona said. "Don't let my firmness surprise you. You're a businesswoman. You know you have to be tough to avoid getting trampled on."

Avery returned with their drinks. This time when he left their table, Fiona commented softly, "I think that young man is very brave. You were sweet to want to come and check up on him." She flicked her braceleted wrist in Katie's direction. "Oh, I know you pretended—maybe even to yourself—that you merely wanted to see the boy, but you wanted to make sure that he'll be all right." She smiled sadly. "It has to be some comfort to him that the man who killed his father has been arrested."

Katie stiffened. "The police made an arrest, but they're looking at the wrong person."

"You think so?"

"I do."

"But how can you be sure?" Fiona asked.

"Because I know Ray Davenport and he's not like that." Katie kept her voice as quiet as possible, but she still looked around to make sure she hadn't been overheard.

Fiona reached over and gently patted Katie's hand. "I understand how hard it must be for you to learn that someone you know could be capable of murder, but sometimes the truth surprises us."

Katie knew she wasn't going to win this debate, and she certainly didn't want to conduct it here and now, so she changed the subject. "How was your drive to McKinlay Mill?"

"It was absolutely beautiful. I had lovely weather, and it's such a scenic trip. You really must come to visit me sometime."

"I'd like that," Katie said. "But I think I'm going to have my hands full for the next few months."

"Ah, yes. You asked about John Healy. He's a wonderful contractor. I believe you'll be delighted with his work."

"Thank you. I really liked him when I met him."

Avery interrupted their conversation by bringing their meals. "Let me know if you need anything else." With a nod, he left them to check on his other tables.

Fiona picked up the discussion right where they left off. "What are you having done?"

While they ate, Katie told Fiona about her plans to turn the upstairs of Tealicious into an apartment. "My partner and I are buying the building, so it makes perfect sense. I'm currently renting the apartment above Angelo's Pizzeria." She neglected to remind Fiona that it was Andy's restaurant. "It's cozy, but why pay rent when I'm buying my own building?"

"I agree. And if you ever decide to leave, you can rent out the apartment. I love entrepreneurial women. We're kindred spirits!"

Katie raised her water glass. "To kindred spirits."

Fiona clicked her glass to Katie's. "Seriously, I love what you're doing. You've diversified your businesses, you're buying real estate, and you aren't relying on a man. I got everything I have all on my own, too. Don't get me wrong—I adore Phil and he's very supportive, but my businesses are mine."

"That's fantastic. My aunt was a strong role model for me."

"She served you well," Fiona said.

"You mentioned Phil . . ." It wasn't the best segue, but it would have to do. "Why did he think it was a bad idea for me to allow Hugh to lease space at Artisans Alley?"

"Phil remembers Hugh as being a partier and a carouser." Fiona smiled. "And Phil was always jealous of me, even with his friends. These days, I'm afraid his thoughts are more rooted in the past than in the present."

Katie knew she had to tread carefully, but given the way Phil enjoyed tying one on, she found it hard to believe that he'd try to dissuade her from allowing Hugh into Artisans Alley because he had a drinking problem.

"Was Hugh a drinker, or was he into drugs?" Katie asked.

"Hugh experimented with a lot of things . . . things that Phil wasn't willing to try. That put a strain on their friendship."

"Do you—or Phil—believe Hugh was merely a recreational user or is it possible he was a dealer?" At Fiona's surprised expression, Katie continued. "I mean, Phil *did* say he was surprised Hugh wasn't in jail."

Fiona chuckled. "I believe Phil meant that given the wild life Hugh led in his younger days, he was surprised the man hadn't landed in jail. I'll up the ante and say that I'm surprised Hugh isn't dead."

Avery came to the table to check on them. "Would either of you ladies like dessert? The sticky rice with mango is delicious."

"I'm sure it is," Katie said. "But I couldn't possibly eat another bite."

"Neither could I. Do you have our check?"

Avery reached into his apron and produced their check. Katie tried to take it, but Fiona snatched it out of Avery's hand.

"This is my treat," Katie insisted.

"Nonsense."

Avery smiled. "I'll give you two a moment to sort this out, and I'll be back."

In the end, Fiona got her way. Katie noticed that she left Avery a very generous tip.

~~~~~~~~

When Katie arrived back at her apartment, she checked her phone. She'd turned it off during dinner and had forgotten about it until then. She had a message from Ray. His DEA friend would be at Artisans Alley at ten o'clock tomorrow morning.

She called him back. He answered on the first ring.

"Anything wrong?" he asked.

"No, I simply wondered if you'll be coming with your friend tomorrow . . . and, if not, can you give me a description so I'll know whom to expect?"

"I can be there if you need me," Ray said. "As for a description, look for the guy with the dog. That'll probably be him."

Katie blew out a breath. "What's the man's name?"

"Miles Patterson. The dog's name is Grimm. He's a German shepherd—Grimm, not Miles. Miles is from Jersey."

"You're just a barrel of laughs tonight, aren't you?"

"What can I say? So . . . do you want me there or not?"

"I can handle it just fine," she said. "It's probably better if you're *not* there. Is Grimm friendly?"

"He is if Miles tells him to be."

Lovely. That puts my fears to rest.

"Before I go, do you know whether or not Paul Fenton and Detective Schuler are friends?" Katie asked.

"Is that your new theory—that Schuler is targeting me because he's buddies with Paul?" He scoffed. "No. Whether the two of them are friendly or not, Schuler is a by-the-book cop."

"Are you sure about that? Would you stake your life on it? Because you might be, you know."

"I *am* staking my life on it, Katie. I know that."

"So, that's it, then? We leave it alone? Stay out of it?"

"Yeah." He sighed. "That's what we do. If I hadn't called Miles and had him work this little fiasco with Grimm into his schedule, I'd cancel that, too."

"Why?"

"Because I don't think he's going to find anything. And, if he does, then what? He can't make an arrest. He won't be catching anyone in the act."

"But, still—"

"But nothing. It's dangerous, and it's stupid. The only reason you're going out on a limb is for me, and—"

"Hold on," she interrupted. "I'm going out on a limb for *me*. If someone is selling drugs out of my building, I need to know it. I'm not about to put myself in the position of having all my assets seized because I was too blind to know what was going on right under my nose. I'm smarter than that, and you know it."

"I do know it."

"Good. Then you also know that if you cancel your friend's visit, then I'll call someone else. I'd rather end up looking like a fool than being one."

"Okay, okay. You win. Was that the bell? May I please go to my corner of the ring and have my manager shine a penlight into my eyes?"

"Be my guest. Just one more thing before you go."

He groaned.

"You're not the only person I'm afraid Schuler is biased against. You'd have never let Paul Fenton get away with charging into my home, threatening me, and then filing a complaint against me."

"Yes, I would have. I'd have had to. You *were* harassing his family."

Katie felt her jaw tighten. "I most certainly was not! Was having brunch with Mary Jones yesterday harassment? If so, maybe I should go to the police station and turn myself in."

"Maybe we'll get adjoining cells."

"I'm being serious," she said.

"So am I." He paused. "Had I been in Schuler's position, I'd have had to issue a warning to you to stay away from Paul and his family. We—the Sheriff's Office—are required to take all complaints seriously, even if we feel they might be frivolous."

"Oh, it was frivolous, all right."

"But I would have also warned Paul to stay away from you," Ray went on as if she hadn't spoken. "And I imagine that's exactly what Schuler did. The man *is* doing his job, Kate."

Kate? That was new. She let the comment pass.

"I'm just so afraid that you're going to find yourself convicted of a murder you didn't commit," Katie said.

"I'll be all right." His voice had softened. "I'll handle it."

"But—" Katie began.

"I'll handle it." Ray's voice was still gentler than it had been but was now firmer than ever.

"Okay. Thanks for getting Miles to come tomorrow."

"No problem. He'll be disguised as a blind guy so that anyone who sees him entering the building won't be suspicious."

"They won't be suspicious of a blind guy coming into the Alley on the day that it's closed?" Katie asked.

"No. He's a prospective new vendor. He's coming to check the place out to see if it'll work for him."

"All right."

"Have a good night," Ray said.

"You, too."

When she ended the call, she sat looking at her phone

until the screen went black. What was with him tonight? He'd answered the call in the guise of an angry old man. He'd finished the call . . . how? Deflated? Depressed? Defeated?

Katie felt as if Ray was trying to push her away. But why would he do that? Because of pressure from the girls? Or was there more to it? Was he afraid she'd get hurt if she continued trying to help him?

She started when she heard Andy's key in the lock.

"Hey, Sunshine!" He came into the living room and dropped onto the sofa beside her. He pulled her to him and kissed her. "How was dinner?"

Katie nestled her head against Andy's warm neck. "It was good. One thing about it, though—Fiona Lancaster is clearly not the sweet little pushover I imagined her to be."

Twenty-Six

Monday morning. Katie was seated at her office at Artisans Alley when she heard the side door open. She hurried into the vendors' lounge and saw a tall older man with an athletic build and a military bearing. He wore sunglasses and held the harness of a black German shepherd. The dog wore a vest announcing it as a service animal.

"Are you Miles?" Katie asked hesitantly.

The man raised the glasses up onto his head before sticking out his hand. "Yep. Nice to meet you."

"Katie Bonner." She shook the man's hand and then looked at the dog. "I understand that he's friendly . . . when you tell him to be."

Miles laughed. "I guess that little nugget of information came from Davenport. Where is he? I thought he was going to be here."

"No—" Katie began.

But before she could say anything further, Ray entered the lounge via Artisans Alley's main showroom. "I'm here," he said. "I couldn't miss an opportunity to see Grimm in action." He reached down and patted the dog's head.

"You can pet him right now," Miles told Katie. "It's when I slip the chain collar on him that he knows he's working. Then he's all business."

Katie wasn't sure she wanted to risk petting the big dog, but Miles instructed Grimm to shake her hand.

"Introduce yourself, buddy."

On cue, the dog sat and raised his paw. Katie smiled and shook it.

"What a good boy you are," she cooed. "Yes, you are."

Grimm happily wagged his tail.

"He's beautiful," Katie told Miles.

"Thank you. We're retired now, but he and I still do favors for crotchety old friends and we still come in handy with the local police now and then—missing person searches, narcotics investigations, that kind of thing—when they need us."

Ray harrumphed. "Crotchety old friends, huh? Takes one to know one."

"All right. Let's get started." Miles removed the service dog vest and handed it to Ray. "Make yourself useful and hang on to that." He slipped the chain collar and leash onto the dog, and the dog immediately went on alert. "Every room, Ms. Bonner?"

"Yes, please . . . and it's Katie."

He gave her a brisk nod. "Grimm, let's go."

Katie and Ray were quiet as they watched Grimm first inspect the vendors' lounge. Katie was sure there was a lot to smell there, but the dog didn't react to anything.

After they'd gone around the perimeter of the lounge and investigated the big Formica dining table, they headed for Katie's office. The room wasn't large enough for all three adults and the dog, so Miles and Grimm went inside while Katie and Ray watched from the doorway.

Grimm was immediately drawn to the small drawer in Katie's desk and sat. Miles glanced at Katie. "I thought this was your office."

"It is," she said. "There's an oxycodone tablet in there that I found on the floor Saturday. It's the reason I became concerned about drug trafficking."

"May I?" He nodded toward the drawer.

"Of course."

Miles opened the drawer and then rewarded Grimm with a treat.

"I didn't know what to do with the tablet," Katie said.

"After we leave, take it home, put it into a sealable plastic bag with either coffee grounds or kitty litter, and then put the bag into the garbage."

"Okay."

At Katie's look of confusion, Miles explained, "You don't want to be carrying narcotics around a drug dog."

"Oh! Of course not."

Miles grinned. "Let's see if we can find something else, Grimm."

The dog obediently left the office and resumed the search. After an extensive walk around the first floor, the group headed upstairs. To Katie's surprise, Grimm didn't show any interest whatsoever in Hugh McKinney's booth. Had she been wrong to suspect him? Had she suspected him mainly because it had been Vance to vet him and not her? Or was it solely because Phil had planted the seeds of doubt in her head?

"What's in here?" Miles asked, moving toward Chad's Pad.

Katie unlocked the door and explained that the room showcased her late husband's artwork. "It isn't for sale, but I display it in honor of his memory."

"Nice." Miles surveyed the paintings appreciatively as Grimm moved throughout the room.

And then Grimm sat down in front of an ocean landscape.

"What's he doing?" Katie asked.

"He's found something," Miles said.

"That's impossible. How could there be narcotics in a painting?" Her mind whirred with the possibilities. Did drug traffickers grind the opioids into powder, tint them, and use them in paint or something? She didn't see how that could work.

"Would you please take down the painting?" Miles asked.

Before Katie could react, Ray had taken down the landscape to reveal a cache that had been cut into the wall.

Katie gasped.

Miles took a latex glove from his pocket and slipped it onto his right hand. He reached into the cache and removed a plastic bag filled with blue tablets just like the one that was in Katie's desk drawer.

He arched a brow at Katie. "Good job. Your suspicions were right on target. Someone is using Artisans Alley to traffic opioids." He withdrew his phone and snapped a couple of photos.

Katie continued to gape at the wall. "How did they get in? I keep this door locked."

"Even I could pick that lock," Ray chimed in.

Katie frowned and addressed Miles. "What do we do now?"

"You must act as though it's business as usual around here," he said, pocketing the phone. "And for all intents and purposes, it is. I'll go to the authorities, and they'll likely implement an undercover surveillance and sting operation. I know you want these people out of your business as soon as possible, and I'll do my best to help get them out."

"B-but what about my friends . . . the vendors . . . the other merchants on the Square?" she asked.

"Say nothing to anyone," Ray said firmly.

"He's right. You don't know who's involved. And if the drug traffickers knew you or anyone else was onto them, it would be dangerous for everybody." Miles put the bag of tablets back into the wall and nodded at Ray.

Ray replaced the painting and then stood back to ensure it was straight.

"It's good," Miles said. "Let's go."

As they walked toward the staircase, Grimm stiffened and emitted a low growl.

Miles raised his index finger to his lips, slipped the vest back onto the dog, and put his sunglasses back over his eyes.

"I think you could get a lot of business here, Miles," Ray said, as they started down the stairs.

"And, of course, we'll give you a booth downstairs," Katie said. "I don't want you to be put off by the stairs."

"Stairs don't bother us," Miles said. "You don't need to make any special concessions for me."

"Oh, I know. Still, I feel that pottery would be a big draw downstairs." She could hear that someone was there. "I'm glad you came in today while the place was deserted so you could get the lay of the land. I do hope you'll decide to join us."

"I'll give you my decision in a day or so," Miles said. "I do appreciate the tour. Left or right at the bottom of the stairs?"

"Right, if you're going toward the vendors' lounge, and left if you're going toward the front door." Katie saw that their unexpected visitor was Fiona Lancaster. "Fiona, hi!"

"There you are," Fiona said with a smile. "Where is everyone?"

"I'm sorry for the inconvenience, but Artisans Alley is closed on Mondays."

"Oh. Well, that's fine," Fiona said. "I was actually looking for you. If I bring home another bauble, Phil might have my head."

"Fiona, this is Miles and Ray. Gentlemen, this is Fiona Lancaster."

"It's a pleasure to meet you," Miles said. "I'm afraid we must be going now. Katie, I'll let you know something definite in a day or so, but I am interested in leasing a booth here."

"Thank you," Katie said. "And thank you, Ray, for telling Miles about Artisans Alley."

"Always glad to help out a friend," Ray said. "Miles, let's go out through the vendors' lounge."

"Please don't let me interrupt," Fiona said. "Ever since Katie told me about her plans to renovate the upper level of Tealicious, I've been dying to see it."

"We can go over now," Katie said.

Fiona patted Katie's arm. "You finish up with your guests, and I'll meet you there."

"All right. See you in a few minutes." Katie smiled until Fiona was out the door. Then she turned to Ray and Miles and blew out a breath. "I'm sorry. I should've locked that door. But I left both entrances unlocked because I didn't know which one you'd use."

"Do you think she bought our act?" Ray asked.

"Why wouldn't she?" Katie asked. "She doesn't even live around here. She simply comes in and stays at Sassy Sally's every few weeks."

"Why's that?" Miles asked.

Katie shrugged. "It's just something she and her husband enjoy doing, I suppose. They used to own property in the area."

"That was quick thinking about the pottery," Miles said. "You're fast on your feet. You ever think about going into law enforcement?"

"Too much," Ray answered for her.

Katie ignored him and said to Miles, "Pottery was the first thing that popped into my mind. I tried to come up with some sort of craft a blind person would be able to create."

"That's our story, then, and we have to stick with it," Miles said. "Ray and I will leave together through the side entrance. I'll walk with Ray to Wood U, and then he can drive me to my car." He glanced at Ray. "I left it behind the empty warehouse across the back parking lot so no one in open view of Victoria Square would see a blind man get out of the driver's side of a car."

"Be careful," Ray told Katie. "And don't deviate from our cover story."

"I won't."

Miles patted her arm. "I'll be in touch soon. We're going to get these people, Katie."

"Thanks." She hoped he wasn't making empty promises.

~~~~~~~

After locking Artisans Alley, Katie marched across the tarmac and put a bright cheery smile firmly in place before entering Tealicious. She gazed around the dining room, spotted Fiona sitting at a table in the back, and made her way over to the table.

"These blueberry scones are divine," Fiona said as Katie took the chair across from her. "You must have one."

"I don't mind if I do." Katie helped herself to a scone as Emma, the server, brought over another teacup and saucer.

"I have to admit I was surprised to see that blind man and his dog there at Artisans Alley." Fiona winced. "Is it terribly antiquated of me that my first thought was, 'What's a blind man doing in an arts and crafts co-op?'"

"No. I was surprised when Ray called me and told me his friend was interested in a booth. But Ray spoke so highly of Miles's work."

"Have you seen any of it?" Fiona asked.

"Very little . . . but what I have seen is impressive." That much was true, at least. Miles and Grimm *had* been impressive.

"And what is it he does?"

"Pottery," Katie said simply.

"How very interesting. I suppose it makes sense, though. Pottery can be tactile as well as visual."

"Exactly."

"That other man . . ." Fiona began. "Ray, was it?"

Katie nodded.

"Wasn't he the one arrested for Ken Fenton's murder?"

"He was," Katie answered. Since she'd already professed her belief in Ray's innocence the night before, she didn't mention it again.

"According to the newspaper, they found evidence that linked him directly to the crime." Fiona leaned across the table. "You're so kind, Katie. I don't want you to end up hoodwinked by anyone."

"I've known Ray for ages," Katie said. "He's not a murderer." The first part of that statement was a bald-faced lie. She wholeheartedly believed the second.

"How do you explain the evidence against him? Do you think someone is trying to frame the man?"

Katie shrugged. "I guess it's possible." A change of subject was definitely in order. "I can hardly wait to get your suggestions for the apartment."

Fiona flicked her wrist. "I'm sure you don't need my input. Just by looking around this room I can tell you have a decorator's eye. Nick told me you picked out most of the furnishings at Sassy Sally's. But I simply adore seeing befores and afters."

"Me, too." Katie smiled, thrilled that they'd moved on from the awkward conversation.

～～～～～

After showing Fiona the office space above, the women parted and Katie went back to her apartment and wrestled with her conscience before she picked up the phone.

"Hey, Guy, I know it's not our usual lunch day, but could you please meet me upstairs at the apartment? It's kind of important."

"What's wrong, Sunshine?" Andy asked.

"I'll explain when you get here . . . if you can, I mean."

"I'll be there. Erikka isn't working today, but I'll leave Roger in charge."

When Andy arrived at the apartment, he let himself in

with his key and found Katie sitting on the sofa as still as a statue. He sat beside her and put his arms around her.

"Sweetheart, what's wrong?"

She chewed at her bottom lip while Andy waited patiently for her to begin.

"I'm not supposed to talk about it because . . . I don't know who I can trust."

She looked into his dark brown eyes. "I trust you."

He gave her a smile, hugging her tighter. "And?"

She shrugged. "I don't quite know where to begin."

"At the beginning, maybe?"

So, starting with finding the blue tablet on the floor behind the cash desk on Saturday morning, Katie relayed the pertinent events to Andy. Her tale ended with, "And that's when Grimm and Miles learned that someone had cut a hole in the wall behind one of Chad's paintings and filled it with oxycodone tablets."

"What did you do?" Andy asked, looking grim. "Because I didn't hear any police sirens this morning."

"No. We didn't call the police. Miles felt we should handle the matter quietly. We—or, rather, he and Ray—put the drugs back into the wall and hid them with the painting the way we'd found them. If we'd called the police, we'd have no way of knowing who the pills belonged to." She twisted her hands in her lap. "The drug trafficker would be out a bag of pills, but those could be replaced soon enough, and it would be back to business as usual."

Andy kissed her temple. "You must be terrified."

"Not really. Wary is more like it. Miles said the DEA would likely send in undercover and surveillance teams. The bad part is that I was instructed not to tell anybody."

"I'm glad you told me. You can't carry a burden like this alone."

"I hate it. I feel so helpless right now. I want to protect my vendors and our customers. I want to warn people like Rose and Vance. But Miles says it would be more dangerous for them to know."

"He's right. It would be particularly dangerous—to you and to everyone else—if the drug trafficker found out."

"I know."

Andy squeezed her shoulder again, and Katie closed her eyes. Right now, she felt safe and secure—a wonderful, if possibly fleeting, feeling.

"Maybe we can get away for a couple of days," he said. "Not a weekend—those are too hectic to throw on Erikka by herself just yet—but maybe an overnight trip in the middle of next week . . . somewhere fun and romantic. How does that sound?"

Katie looked into his big brown eyes and smiled. "Perfect."

~~~~~~

After Andy went back to work, Katie decided to clean her apartment. Housework was an excellent—and productive—way to dispel nervous energy. She gave the tchotchkes in the bedroom a thorough dusting, washed the windows, flipped the mattress, changed the bed linens, and alphabetized the stack of books on her nightstand.

Mason and Della watched all this activity with mild interest. However, when the vacuum cleaner came out of the closet, they both bolted under the bed.

Katie finished the job as quickly as possible in order to ease the cats' anxiety. When she turned off the machine, she heard the doorbell ring. She rolled the vacuum cleaner into the living room with her and then left it before going to the kitchen and looking through the peephole.

"It's me," came Ray's gruff voice. "Let me in."

She opened the door. As soon as Ray was inside, she re-locked it.

"Are you okay?" he asked, his voice a shade softer than it had been when he was standing on her stoop.

"Sure. I'm fine. How are you?"

"I'm well," he said. "I'm here to borrow a key to Artisans Alley. Miles spoke with someone at the DEA, and they want to set up surveillance ASAP."

"And why did they call you instead of me?" she demanded. "Whose idea was that?"

"I volunteered."

"Let me make sure I've got this right." Katie anchored her hands to her hips. "Last night after telling me that you can handle your situation by yourself, you're here trying to insinuate yourself into *my* situation? Well, guess what? You aren't a law enforcement officer anymore. Tell your friends to call *me* if they want access to my property."

"Look, as a detective, I can—"

"*Former* detective," Katie interrupted. "We're both adults who can take care of ourselves, right?"

Ray's mouth tightened into a thin, hard line. After a long moment, during which he lost the staring contest between them, he said, "I was only trying to help."

"I know the feeling. But you were quite clear when you said you didn't need my help. That works both ways," she said, keeping her voice level. "Please make sure you lock the door when you leave."

Katie walked back into the living room and turned on the vacuum cleaner to drown out anything else he might have to say.

Twenty-Seven

That night, vague, disorienting dreams haunted Katie's sleep. She awoke several times and cursed the fact that the one window in her bedroom faced the north end of Artisans Alley. She wouldn't see the lights of cars cutting through Victoria Square's main parking lot should the traffickers be counting on stealth. Then again, the Alley's security system was set. Whoever was dealing drugs out of the Alley was doing it during regular business hours. That thought wasn't of comfort, either.

She was up early, and Katie started off her day at the tea shop. It bothered her that she was still stinging from her argument with Ray the afternoon before, and she was determined that no one was going to get anything over on her. This morning, she intended to find out the exact nature of Brad's relationship with Paul Fenton. If that meant she had to fire Brad and work at Tealicious herself until she found a replacement, so be it.

When she entered the shop's kitchen, Brad was mixing up a crab salad. They exchanged greetings, and Katie tied an apron around her waist.

She pulled a clean mixing bowl from one of the shelves. "I thought I'd make some gluten-free chocolate chip cookies. Some of our patrons have been asking for more variety."

"Good idea. Sounds delicious."

"Thanks." She took out the appropriate flour and measured it into the bowl. "Um, Brad, we need to talk."

Brad let out a breath. "I'm listening."

"I need to be sure you're here on Victoria Square because you really want to work at this tiny tea shop and not because of . . . something else."

His gaze narrowed. "That's an odd thing to say. If I didn't want to work at Tealicious, I wouldn't be here."

It was time to show her cards. "Look, I realize you and Paul Fenton are friends, but he and I have had more than one unpleasant encounter," Katie said. "Frankly, I suspect that Paul is involved in some unsavory—if not illegal—activities."

Brad stepped closer to Katie. "And you think I am, too? Is that what you're saying?"

"No. You're doing a wonderful job here, and you've been a tremendous asset to Tealicious." She put down the measuring cup she held and turned to look Brad in the eye. "But if I find out you're using drugs or—"

"Stop," he interrupted, his voice hardening. "I'm not using drugs, and I'm not drinking." He removed his chef coat. Underneath it, he wore a sleeveless white T-shirt pulled taut against his muscular chest.

Katie gulped and tried not to stare, as she wondered what on earth he was doing.

He held out his forearm. On it, in harsh magenta ink, was displayed the name *Julia* in a free-flowing font.

Ah . . . the ex-girlfriend.

"I should've told you the truth about Paul from the beginning," Brad said. "I've asked him to transform this tattoo.

When Regan came to Tealicious yesterday, she brought me Paul's initial sketches." He lowered his eyes. "I didn't tell you because I was embarrassed."

"Why? We all have our regrets. Do you mind showing me the sketches?"

He shook his head. "That's not necessary. I didn't realize you had such a turbulent history with Paul. I can find someone else."

Feeling rather foolish for even bringing up the subject, Katie considered this. She didn't want to be unfair to Brad. "From what little I've seen, Paul appears to be an excellent tattoo artist. If you believe he can do the job for you, by all means, have him do it."

"Are you sure?" he asked softly.

"Positive." Somehow, she managed a smile. "And I *would* like to see the sketches if you don't mind. I'm interested to discover what Paul can turn a name into."

"They're impressive." Brad slipped his chef's coat back on. "And I'd love another opinion. Don and Nick are divided."

"Always," she said with a laugh. "I'm sorry if I offended you by asking about your relationship with Paul. Sometimes I simply can't believe my good luck that you're here. I wouldn't want anything to jeopardize that."

Katie felt the heat of a blush rise. *Oh yeah? Then why did you practically accuse him of falling off the wagon?*

"I'm happy to be here," Brad said with sincerity.

They stared at each other for long seconds. Katie was the first to look away. "I'd better get the rest of the ingredients for those cookies. They aren't going to bake by themselves."

~~~~~~~

Katie was in her office at Artisans Alley looking over the upcoming month's budget when she got a call from Miles Patterson.

"Good morning, Katie. I apologize for communicating with Ray instead of you last night. Since it was Ray who initially contacted me, it seemed only natural to convey my comrades' strategic maneuvers to you through him. I didn't mean to step on any toes."

"Thanks," Katie said. "It's just that this entire ordeal has me on edge."

"I can imagine. I'll be in later to accept the vendor booth and get it set up. Two of my former DEA colleagues—they're still active agents—will accompany me as my sister and brother-in-law. We're in the process of rounding up some pottery I can sell."

"All right. That sounds good." Katie hoped Miles didn't catch the tremor in her voice.

"We'll be there shortly after lunch. I'd like for you to give Beth and Cal—that's the names they'll be using—the grand tour. During that time, they'll be unobtrusively placing their surveillance equipment throughout Artisans Alley."

"Then what?"

"After that, it's just a waiting game," Miles said. "But, hopefully, we'll catch your drug dealer pretty soon."

Katie was silent.

"Are you up for this, Katie?"

"Y-yes." Then stronger, "Yes, I am."

"Good. Now, remember, to everyone else at Artisans Alley, I'm just another vendor."

"Right. Just another vendor."

"See you later," he said and laughed at his own joke.

Katie smiled as she hung up and hoped the supposed blind man would fool everyone—especially the traffickers.

Feeling restless, Katie left her office to get a cup of coffee in the vendors' lounge. She came back, grabbed a peppermint, popped it into her mouth, and bit it in two. She could do this. She'd handled worse. She could pretend that Miles was simply a normal guy who wasn't pretending to be blind so he could have his drug dog in tow. She could go along with Beth and Cal being Miles's family rather than DEA agents. She could even act as if there weren't bags of drugs stashed in a hole in the wall behind one of Chad's paintings.

She closed her eyes. Once this fiasco was over, she'd deserve an Academy Award—Best Actress in a Supporting Role.

Katie opened her eyes, took a bracing sip of her coffee, and decided to call Nick. Talking with him should be a good distraction, and afterward, she could get back to the budget.

"Hey, there, Katie!" Nick answered.

"You're way too bright and cheery for a Tuesday morning."

He laughed. "As my aunt Sally used to say, I've got the world by the tail on a downhill pull. The sun is shining, the birds are singing, and I've got a key lime pie in the oven."

"Key lime pies bake for only about ten minutes, right?"

He laughed. "Right. So, talk fast, sweetheart."

"I wanted to call and let you know that I spoke with Brad this morning. He confessed about the tattoo cover-up."

Nick blew out a breath. "Thank goodness! Do you know how hard it's been to keep that secret from you? Don and I hated it, but we'd promised not to tell."

"Brad shouldn't feel so embarrassed about his tattoo," Katie said. "I'm sure that when he got it, he thought he and Julia would be together forever."

"That's true. We all have our follies."

"I told Brad I'd like to see the sketches Regan brought. I'm curious to see how Paul can turn a name into something more decorative."

"My favorite is a feather," Nick said. "Not only is it beautiful, but it symbolizes that Brad has flown away from that toxic relationship to a better life."

"Ever the poet." Katie chuckled. "Brad said you and Don have a difference of opinion on how he should cover the tattoo."

Nick emitted a low growl. "Don prefers a cobra. It's huge and fierce-looking, and I'm not a fan."

"Brad is such a sweetheart that he offered to go to someone else when I told him that Paul and I have had words. I told him to stick with Paul."

"I'm glad Brad finally confided in you. He's a great guy."

Katie could hear a buzzer on the other end of the line.

"Pie's done, sweetie," Nick said. "I'll talk with you later."

"Save a slice for me."

As Katie hung up the phone, someone tapped on her door before opening it a crack and poking a white handkerchief tied to a carpenter's pencil into her office.

"Come in," she said.

She wasn't surprised to find that Ray was the bearer of the white flag.

"I surrender," he said. "Sorry about yesterday."

"Me, too. Come on in and have a seat."

Ray untied the handkerchief and stuffed it and the pencil into his shirt pocket before he sat on the chair beside her desk. He looked at Katie expectantly.

"Miles phoned earlier," she said. "He'll be in a little later today to set up his booth. He said his sister and brother-in-law would be in to help him arrange everything."

"Super. I know . . ." He chose his words carefully, probably in case anyone was listening. ". . . having a vendor like Miles might be tough at first, but I believe he'll be a great asset to Artisans Alley."

"I completely agree with you."

"If you guys need my help in getting Miles settled in, let me know."

Katie nodded. "All right."

Ray leaned closer and lowered his voice. "If you need me, you know where I'm at."

"Likewise."

He gave her a lopsided smile. "I appreciate that. I really do."

For the second time that morning, Katie stared at a man, feeling uncomfortable. This time, it wasn't she who looked away and then retreated.

~~~~~~~

A blast of chilled air greeted Katie as she entered the diner, spotted Andy, and then headed down the aisle. She slid into the booth across from the pizza man and took both his hands in hers.

Sandy—Del's best waitress—winked. "Somebody sure is happy to see you," she told Andy.

"I have that effect on her," he said with a grin. "Would you bring me a burger with everything on it and a side of fries?"

"Will do. Katie, what are you having?"

Katie ordered a chef's salad.

As soon as Sandy was out of earshot, Andy squeezed Katie's hands. "What's wrong?"

"Nothing . . . really. I'm just nervous. Our newest vendor is moving in after lunch. In fact, he should be there when I get back to Artisans Alley."

Andy nodded. "I realize you're nervous because Miles is blind. But don't worry, Sunshine. The man knows what he's doing. He wouldn't have rented the booth otherwise."

"I know, Andy. I'm just eager for . . . for him to settle in. That's all."

"You'll do great."

She was also ready to avoid speaking in code.

Katie caught a movement from the corner of her eye and turned to see Fiona Lancaster approach their table. "Fiona! What a nice surprise." It really wasn't, and Katie hoped Fiona couldn't tell how desperately she wanted the woman to leave so that she and Andy could dine in peace.

"I'm so glad I caught you," Fiona said. "I spoke with Rose, and she told me you were here. I'd like to run some ideas for the Tealicious apartment by you."

"That would be wonderful." The scent of Fiona's oppressive perfume instantly caused Katie's eyes to water. Without thinking, she dabbed at them with her napkin. "Unfortunately, I need to eat fast and get back to Artisans Alley. We've got a new vendor coming in today who needs special consideration. I'd be glad to come over to Sassy Sally's and talk with you as soon as I help him get situated."

"A new vendor . . . Would that be the blind man I met yesterday?"

"Yes. Miles, the potter." Katie smiled.

"Couldn't someone else help him?" Fiona asked. "After all, I'm only here until tomorrow."

Katie's smile faded. "Miles only called this morning to accept the vendor booth, and I neglected to mention it to Vance. I assure you, I'll come to Sassy Sally's as soon as I'm free."

"Of course." Fiona shrugged. "You'll both have to overlook my rudeness. I'm merely a silly old woman begging for attention."

"Nonsense," Katie said, having noted the edge to Fiona's self-deprecating words. "I look forward to hearing your ideas."

"See you later, then." With a little wave that encompassed them both, Fiona swept out of the diner.

"You handled that better than I would have," Andy said and coughed. "And I don't recall Fiona's perfume being that strong when I met her at Sassy Sally's."

"It wasn't. This scent must be new." In fact, the cloying aroma of lilacs still hung heavily in the air even after the woman had walked away, threatening to choke her. "Promise me something."

He grinned. "Anything."

"After you get off work tonight, let's have a nice, quiet, relaxing night—free of drama."

"You've got it, Sunshine."

Sandy arrived with their lunches and Katie was happy to

turn the conversation to more mundane topics. And she was glad she'd ordered the smaller salad, wondering if she might have a chance at a slice of Nick's key lime pie later that afternoon when meeting with Fiona.

Twenty-Eight

Half an hour later, Katie arrived at Artisans Alley to find Miles, Grimm, Vance, and an attractive brunette woman waiting for her in the vendors' lounge.

"Is that Katie?" Miles asked as she approached the group at the big table with cups of coffee before them.

"It is," she said. "Hi, Miles." She looked at Vance. "Thanks for welcoming our new vendor."

He nodded.

"Hey, Katie, I'd like you to meet my baby sister, Beth," Miles said.

The brunette was no baby but looked to be about the same age as Katie with blue eyes and a friendly smile. She stuck out her hand. "Nice to meet you, Katie."

"Nice to meet you." Beth's firm grip was what Katie expected from someone in law enforcement.

"My brother-in-law, Cal, is wandering around here some-where," Miles said offhandedly.

Beth smiled. "Everyone jokes about women loving to shop, but Cal enjoys it much more than I do."

"Beth and Cal are planning to take turns helping me out until I settle into a routine," Miles said. "Not that we need fussing over. Do we, Grimm?" He patted the dog and the massive German shepherd gave a woof in apparent agreement.

"That's a beautiful dog," Vance said.

Miles stroked the dog's ears. "So I'm told."

A sound at the door caused them all to turn. "And here's that shopaholic hubby of mine," Beth said.

Katie followed Beth's gaze to a tall blond man whose aviator sunglasses sat perched on top of his head. She could tell he was fully aware of his surroundings and carried him-self with an alert, ready-for-anything demeanor. In Katie's opinion, Beth could pass for Miles's mild-mannered sister, but it was also evident to her that Cal was every bit the fed-eral agent. Did he have anyone fooled?

Beth introduced Cal to Katie. He shook her hand and adopt-ed an air of joviality.

"Katie, this place is fantastic," Cal said. "I've been over it from one end to the other, and I'm impressed. I'll admit I'm a little concerned, though. This place is huge."

"Stop being such a worrywart," Beth said. "Miles will be fine. He doesn't have to traipse all over Artisans Alley, and Katie has kindly located his booth here near the side en-trance."

"Still, I want him to know the lay of the land. You never know what might happen."

Beth shook her head at her partner's faux worries. "That's why Katie will be showing both of us around." She turned to Katie as she hooked an arm around Cal's. "I think it's ador-able how protective Cal is over my big brother, but I've known Miles all my life. I know how capable he is."

They're really selling it now, Katie thought.

"Then, if you two are ready, I'd be happy to give you a tour," Katie said.

"I can do that if you're busy," Vance said.

Miles quickly took control of the situation. "Actually, Vance, I could use your assistance in setting up my booth, if you don't mind. I understand you're something of a jack-of-all-trades around here, and I'd truly appreciate your input."

"Sure. I'll be glad to help." Vance nodded to Katie and then began giving directions to Miles.

"Actually, if I simply tell Grimm to follow you, it will be easier," Miles said.

Vance shook his head in wonder. "Amazing. Wait until Janey meets this dog. My wife is a big-time animal lover, and this boy will definitely bowl her over."

Katie led Beth and Cal past all the vendors' booths on the lower level and then by the cash desks before leading them up the center staircase to the second level. She introduced the couple to everyone and asked the artisans to stop by Miles's booth and welcome him to the neighborhood at their convenience.

When the threesome stopped at Hugh McKinney's booth, the leather goods crafter narrowed his eyes at Cal. "You look familiar. Have we met?"

Cal smiled broadly. "I get that a lot. People tell me I bear a striking resemblance to a young Robert Redford. Do you think that could be it?"

Beth laughed and gave Cal a playful punch on the shoulder. "Don't mind him. *One* woman told him he looked like a young Robert Redford, and that woman was his mom!"

Katie caught the faint scent of lilacs. It smelled like Fiona's perfume, which had nearly gagged her at the diner. That fragrance had really lingered.

Cal's jaw dropped in mock outrage. "Aunt Mona agreed with her, Beth. That makes two people right there. Back me up here, Katie."

"I can see the resemblance," Katie said, forcing herself to

engage in the conversation when all she wanted to do was escape the overpowering scent of lilacs.

"I know I've seen you somewhere," Hugh persisted. "And I'm not talking about the starring role in *Butch Cassidy and the Sundance Kid*. Where do you work?"

"Beth and I are self-employed as eBay power sellers, which affords us the opportunity to help Miles sell his art online and get settled in here."

"We hit garage and yard sales, estate sales, and resell whatever we find," Beth added. "Is there anything we can look to buy for you?"

"Not that I can think of," Hugh said, but his brows were furrowed, his expression grim.

"It was a pleasure meeting you. I'm sure we'll see you around," Cal said.

"The tour wouldn't be complete without a visit to Chad's Pad," Katie said, leading the couple toward the tiny room where she showcased Chad's paintings. She unlocked the door and turned on the light in the claustrophobically small room. "Chad's my late husband. I keep his paintings on display in homage to him."

"That's so thoughtful," Beth said.

"He did beautiful work," Cal added.

The smell of lilacs had followed Katie into Chad's Pad. Had it gotten on her clothes at the diner? Was that why she couldn't escape it? As soon as she could get an opportunity, she'd go home and change. Fiona's perfume could turn what should have been a pleasant scent into an allergy-inducing nightmare.

Both agents studied the room, concentrating on the art-work. Katie noticed that they ran their hands over the frames. She surmised they were planting the surveillance. The devices must be tiny, though, because Katie couldn't detect them, and she was looking for them.

Finally, Cal gave Katie a slight nod. "I believe Miles will do well here."

"Isn't that what I said?" Beth asked. "Miles will be right at home here before you know it."

Katie understood that they were actually telling her that they thought the drug dealer would be caught soon. And if the drug dealer turned out to be Ken Fenton's murderer, as Katie suspected, all the better.

"I hope Miles *does* adjust quickly," Katie said. "I don't have any experience with Miles's special circumstances, but if there's anything I can do to help, please let me know."

"We sure will," Beth said. "Thank you."

When they rejoined Miles and Vance, they could see that Vance had helped Miles unpack his wares, turning empty shelves into an organized display of vases, plates, and mugs.

"Wow, this looks great!" Katie patted Vance's back to let him know how much she appreciated his work.

"I'll take your word for it," Miles said with a laugh.

As remarkable as keeping up the ruse was for Beth and Cal, Katie was doubly impressed with Miles.

"Hi, there!" It was Rose, and she was talking louder than usual. Did she think Miles was hard of hearing? "I'm Rose Nash. I sell jewelry and I'm usually working one of the cash desks."

"I'm Miles. This is my sister, Beth, and her husband, Cal."

"Nice to meet all of you. I won't keep you long. I'm training for my walkathon. I had terribly painful shin splints last week, and I was afraid I'd have to bow out of the event, but I'm better than ever now."

"I'm glad," Beth said. "Shin splints are the worst. I've had them before."

"My doctor told me I just have to be careful and not overdo it."

While Rose was talking, Katie realized she no longer smelled lilacs. "Rose, did Fiona Lancaster go upstairs when she was at Artisans Alley earlier today?"

"Not the first time she was here," Rose answered. "The first time, she just asked where you were at. I told her and she left. But when she came back a few minutes later, she went upstairs."

"Did she buy anything?" Katie asked.

"No. I guess maybe she'd made up her mind about something she was thinking of buying, because she certainly appeared to be a woman on a mission when she came back. But then she left empty-handed."

"That's odd." A shiver ran up Katie's spine and she glanced up to see that the agents were watching her.

Rose addressed Beth and Cal. "Oh, I've seen it happen a million times. Most of the items sold here are one-of-a-kind, you know. If you see something that strikes your fancy, you'd better grab it while you can."

Miles laughed and asked, "Rose, are you the head of Katie's marketing department?"

"I could be. Given all the jingles I've heard over the years . . ."

Katie tuned out Rose's chatter, distracted by thoughts of Fiona, and needed to sort things out. "I'm sorry, but I've got tasks I've got to attend to. I hope you'll excuse me."

Rose took up right where she left off as Katie sidled past the crowd and headed for her office, trying to remember every conversation she'd had with or about Fiona.

Fiona and her husband made frequent trips to McKinlay Mill for no other apparent reason than they *like* it here.

Fiona and Phil knew Hugh McKinney, and they'd hired Ken Fenton.

Based on the evidence given to Katie by her nose and the dull ache in her head, Fiona had been to both Hugh McKinney's booth and to Chad's Pad after seeing Katie and Andy at Del's. But how? The door had been locked. Fiona had lavished compliments on Chad's art, but she couldn't have entered the locked room. Could her return to the Alley have something to do with Miles? Did Fiona suspect he wasn't who he claimed to be?

When Katie had first met Phil Lancaster, he'd indicated

Hugh was lucky he wasn't in prison. Fiona had tried to blow it off as Phil's drunken ramblings, but what if it wasn't? What did Phil know? Were Hugh and Fiona working together in some way? Sure, it was a stretch, but Fiona was terribly proud of being a self-made woman. Just how far would she go to ensure her success?

There was a rap on Katie's door, and then Beth poked her head into the office. "Got a sec?"

"Sure," Katie said.

Beth jerked her chin toward the hallway. "Walk up the street with me."

Katie slowly rose from behind her desk and joined Beth in the vendors' lounge. The agent led her out the back door and into the rear parking lot. They walked in silence around to the front of the building and headed toward the east end of the Square.

Finally, Beth spoke. "What's up?"

"Excuse me?"

"You got pensive earlier when you were asking Rose about Fiona Lancaster. Why?"

Katie hesitated as they approached the uncrowded area near the building where Ken Fenton had been murdered. "It's stupid."

"I don't care how stupid you think it is," Beth said. "If you don't communicate with me, then I can't do my job."

Katie frowned. "When we were upstairs, I smelled lilacs. It reminded me of the perfume Fiona was wearing when I saw her earlier today. The scent lingered near Hugh's booth and I swear I caught a whiff of it in Chad's Pad. I was wondering why she'd been there . . . specifically, why she'd hurried back here after talking with me at Del's Diner."

"Do you think she's involved in the drug trafficking?"

"I don't know." Katie shook her head. "It doesn't make sense. Fiona is . . . well, she's *old*."

"Drug dealing doesn't discriminate. You'd be surprised at the array of people we've busted."

"I know, but the thought of Fiona being involved in anything illegal is ridiculous."

"Is it?" Beth asked.

Katie blew out a breath. "I don't know. But, either way, I have no evidence. All I've got is a gut feeling."

Beth looked pensive. "Trust that feeling."

"What do you mean?"

Beth let out an exasperated breath. "Cal's cover may already have been blown."

"What do you mean?"

"As you saw, Hugh McKinney wondered if he and Cal had met before. I may have been able to defuse the situation, but it had better be me the vendors interact with. Which also means *you've* got to be doubly careful as well. It shouldn't take us long to catch whoever is moving drugs through Artisans Alley, especially now that we have the surveillance equipment in place."

Katie wasn't sure she felt any better, but said, "Thanks, Beth."

"Thank *you*, Katie. I'm glad you chose to get involved."

Katie glanced at the building just beyond Beth's shoulder and hoped she wouldn't come to regret her decision.

Twenty-Nine

Katie and Beth returned to Artisans Alley, entering through the vendors' lounge. As Katie turned to go into her office, Beth caught her arm. "Cal and I will be here the rest of the afternoon, and I'll probably be the one helping Miles out over the next few days."

"That's good to know. I . . . I wouldn't want Miles to feel overwhelmed."

"Neither do we," Beth said, and with that, left the area.

Katie sat down before her computer and tried to resume work on the budget, but she found it impossible to concentrate. She wondered if she should call Fiona and tell her that something had come up at Artisans Alley and that she wouldn't be able to visit her at Sassy Sally's until later—maybe even the next morning. But would that alert Fiona to the fact that Katie was suspicious of her? She wanted to wait until she was sure she could act normally around the woman. She also wasn't looking forward to her next encounter with Fiona's overpowering perfume.

While she debated calling, her phone rang. She glanced at the caller ID before accepting the call. "Hi, Nick."

"K-Katie . . . I n-need . . . to s-see you." He sounded as if he might be hyperventilating.

"Nick, what's wrong?"

"I . . . I c-caught Don cheating on me."

"No. That can't be right. Don adores you. Are you sure you saw what you think you saw?"

Nick took a deep breath, and when he spoke again, he sounded more himself. "Don went down to the marina. I got everything caught up here, so I went over there to try to convince him to get that sexy snake tattoo we talked about—you remember, I told you how much I loved it."

"You mean, the huge, fierce-looking cobra?" Katie asked, confused.

"That's it." His voice was firm. He was trying to tell her something.

Just this morning, Nick had told Katie he wasn't a fan of the snake tattoo as a cover for Brad's ex-girlfriend's name. He'd preferred the feather. So, what was he saying?

"What happened when you went to the marina?" Katie asked.

"I saw him kissing another guy." He grunted, as if in pain. "Please, Katie . . . can you come and help me figure this out?"

"Of course."

"Now? And please don't tell anyone where you're going. I'll *die* if anyone else finds out."

"Okay, Nick. Sit tight. I'll be right there."

"I'm sorry," he whispered.

"Don't worry. Everything will be okay."

As soon as she ended the call, Katie pushed up and out of her chair and went directly to Miles's booth, intending to tell Beth and Cal what was going on and to enlist their help. But when she neared the booth, she saw that Hugh McKinney was there. Cal seemed preoccupied with unpacking more stock, while Beth chatted with the suspect, who turned to pierce Katie with a cold, fixed stare.

"Hey, there!" She forced a note of brightness into her voice. "It looks as if you're settling in well. How nice that the other vendors are welcoming you into the fold, Miles." She looked at Beth with what she hoped was a penetrating glare. "I have to run out for a minute—something *unexpected* has come up—but I hope to stop back by the booth later today."

"Uh, sure thing," Beth said, sounding decidedly unsure.

Katie bit her lip, hesitated, but then pivoted. She took the long route to the front exit, pausing in the Alley's lobby, hoping she'd been able to convey to Beth through her body language or telepathy or *anything else* that she needed immediate assistance. Still, Katie knew better than to count on something so uncertain.

Pulling out her cell phone, she sent a quick text to Ray: Call Miles and Schuler. Nick in trouble. Sassys—NOW!

Pocketing the phone, Katie walked out of Artisans Alley into the bright sunlight. Almost as soon as the text had gone through, her phone rang. Knowing anyone looking out a window at Sassy Sally's would be able to see her, Katie ignored her ringtone. Nick had made it clear that his captor had wanted her to come alone.

And who *was* his captor? Could it be Brad? Was that why Nick had used the cobra tattoo story? Or had he added that aspect—contradicting what he'd told her that morning—to let her know that his story was false?

Katie pushed through the wrought-iron gates and headed up the paved walk, climbed the porch steps, and entered Sassy Sally's to find the reception area and front room deserted. "Nick! Nick, where are you?"

"Up here!" His voice came from somewhere above.

Katie took a breath to steal her jagged nerves and climbed the stairs on leaden feet. What was she about to find?

At the top of the stairs, she asked, "Where are you, Nick?"

"In here. First door to your right."

Katie took another deep breath and approached the door, which was ajar. She pushed it open a teensy bit farther and saw a haggard-looking Nick sitting on the side of the bed. An already-darkening bruise colored his left cheek. His gaze seemed glued to a spot behind the door, letting her know where his captor hid. If Katie could use the door to hit the person with enough force to knock him or her off balance, then she and Nick could possibly prevail in the ensuing struggle.

Katie shoved the door open as hard as she could. It clanged against the wall.

Fiona stepped out from beyond the door, her unwavering right hand clutching a revolver. "Careful, Katie. You almost hit me."

Beyond Fiona, Katie could see Don gagged and tied to a chair. His chin was resting on his chest, a thin trickle of dried blood staining the side of his face. Katie's breath caught in her throat and she swung her questioning gaze around to Nick.

"He's all right," Nick said. The look in his eyes and the slight tremor in his voice told Katie that he wasn't a hundred percent sure that his partner was, in fact, okay.

"Don's just taking a little nap," Fiona said, her voice and expression both smug.

Katie decided to stall for time. She had to trust that help was on its way. "What are you doing with that gun, Fiona? Please don't tell me you and Nick are planning to kill Don. I mean, it was only a kiss, right?"

Fiona barked out a harsh laugh. "Don't insult my intelligence—or yours, either, for that matter."

"All right. Then what's this about?" Katie said with a calm she didn't feel.

"It was necessary to get you over here, and I figured that if one of your friends needed you, you'd drop everything and come running. And here you are." Fiona turned down the corners of her mouth. "You know what hurts my feelings, Katie? I was never really your friend. If I were, you'd have come over here to talk with me when I asked you to do so."

"Is that what this is all about?" Katie scoffed. "You're angry with me because I went to help my new vendor get settled in rather than come here to talk with you about the Tealicious apartment?" Although she strained her ears, Katie couldn't hear sounds of approaching vehicles or footsteps on the porch.

"Come off it, Katie. You know what this is about."

She *did* know what it was about, and it infuriated her. "Fine. You want to talk about hurt feelings? I'm hurt that you and Hugh McKinney are using one of my businesses to distribute drugs!"

"What?" The word emerged from Nick's throat as an outraged squeak. He obviously didn't know why Fiona had taken him and Don captive.

"You're delusional," Fiona told Katie.

Katie reined in her anger to appeal to the other woman's vanity. "I've got to hand it to you. How have you managed to run such a large operation? It *is* large, isn't it?"

Fiona couldn't seem to hide a smug grin. "One of the biggest on the East Coast. And it's being run by a seventy-five-year-old woman. Who'd have ever guessed that?"

"Who indeed?"

Eyes narrowing, Fiona cocked her head. "You, apparently. How'd you figure it out?"

"I didn't until I smelled your perfume at Hugh's booth and then in Chad's Pad this afternoon."

Fiona shook her head ruefully. "I'm slipping in my old age. Damn Phil for buying me such a gift and me for being so sentimental."

"It's a nice scent, but it lingers," Katie said. Still no sounds of an approaching cavalry echoed from below. The longer she could keep Fiona talking, the better chance of an outcome where no one got hurt.

Katie hazarded another glance at Nick. She could practically see the gears whirring in his head and wished she could find some way to assure him that help was on the way.

"Please put down the gun, Fiona," Katie said. "It isn't necessary. All I want is my share of the profits."

Fiona's eyebrows shot up, her expression darkening. "Oh, really? Do you honestly expect me to believe that?"

"Believe what you want. Artisans Alley is my business and it's in the red. If you're going to move drugs through it, then I should get a percentage of the profit. It's only fair."

"It's fair, all right, but I don't believe you."

"Why not? You said yourself I'm a savvy businesswoman."

"If all you wanted was a piece of the action, then why'd you call in the guy with the drug dog?" Fiona asked.

"Drug dog?"

"Miles is no blinder than I am," Fiona sneered. "I know a drug dog when I see one."

"Fair enough," Katie conceded. "On Saturday, I found a blue pill on the floor behind the cash desks. I looked it up online and learned that it's very valuable. I wanted to find out if there were more. Miles and I have a deal. He gets ten percent of the action for verifying what I already suspected—at least until I figure out how to cut *him* out."

"I wish I could believe you, Katie. In fact, I feel we could've been a great team had you and I met before I got tied up with all these incompetent men."

"You mean Hugh?"

"Hugh, Ken, Paul, Phil." Fiona still kept the gun trained on Katie. "They're all a bunch of screwups."

"I don't know. Hugh seems to be fairly adept at getting the product out the door through his leather goods, especially those motorcycle saddlebags."

"If he'd truly been good at his job, then you wouldn't have figured out what was going on." She waved the gun. "Come on. Get in here."

Katie heard the floor creak behind her and breathed a sigh of relief. "You're finished, Fiona."

"No, she's not."

Katie whirled to see Phil standing at the top of the stairs.

"I knew I'd have to come and clean up another one of your messes, Fi," he said. "So, here I am. I headed out this morning after you told me about this man you suspect to be a cop."

"Phil, you idiot." Fiona spat the words at her husband, who looked soberer and more collected than Katie had ever seen him. "I'm handling things just fine on my own."

"Really? Three deaths are going to be a lot harder to explain than just one." Phil spoke calmly as he walked into the room. "And we can't pin this one on the woodworker. If those two weren't gay, we could make it look like a love triangle gone wrong." He shook his head. "You really stepped in it this time, Fi. What's your plan?"

Fiona's expression faltered for the first time.

She doesn't have one, Katie thought. Her mind scrambled to come up with a scheme of her own. *Where is Schuler? Ray? Anybody?*

"Here's the plan." Katie's voice sounded so calm that it almost sounded foreign to her. "You and Fiona pay the three of us, and we keep our mouths shut." She gave Nick a pointed look. "This place is bleeding money. Don and Nick need all the help they can get."

"She's right. We do," Nick blurted, desperately nodding. "And we won't ask for anything other than a onetime payment. Right, Katie?"

"Actually, I won't even ask for that. All I want is what I was asking Fiona for before you got here, Phil—a percentage of the profit you make trafficking drugs through Artisans Alley. It's only fair."

"How do we know we can trust you?" Phil asked skeptically.

"You can't trust her, Phil!" Fiona shouted. "She's the reason there's a cop with a vendor booth at Artisans Alley!"

"What do you propose we do?" Phil stepped over and yanked the pistol away from his wife. "How many people do you think I can kill in this tiny town without it coming back to bite us? As it is, we're going to have to move our operations out of this burg."

"You don't have to do that," Katie said. "Not if you—"

"Shut up!" Fiona cried. "We're trying to think!" She whirled to face Phil. "I was handling this situation just fine before you got here!"

"Just like you handled the situation with Ken Fenton?" Phil demanded. "Had I not taken care of that, he'd have reported us to the feds and we'd both be in jail cells right now. You're far too reckless."

Katie noticed Nick's eyes widen. He held her gaze and mouthed the word, *Drop.*

Instantly, Katie fell to her knees, covered her head, and then rolled aside, hearing another thud as Beth yelled for Phil to lower his gun.

Time seemed to stand still, but then a shot rang out.

Katie risked opening her eyes to see Nick crawl over to her.

"Are you hurt?" she whispered.

He shook his head and put his arms around her, trying to shield them both from the chaos taking place all around them.

Another gunshot seemed to shatter Katie's eardrums and Fiona screamed. "Phil!"

"Get in here!" Beth shouted. "And we need an ambulance!"

Katie saw that Beth was bleeding from her left shoulder. Thank goodness Phil's aim had gone high. Beth's had not. Had her shot pierced Phil Lancaster's heart? His eyes were glassy, staring up at the ceiling. Fiona had flung herself across his chest. For a second, Katie thought the woman acted out of devotion, but then she saw her reach for Phil's gun.

"Beth!" Katie cried.

Arms splayed, Don toppled his chair onto Fiona. He'd managed to free his hands while everyone thought he was unconscious and struggled to subdue the older woman. Beth was instantly there and kicked Phil's gun out of the way. Grunting with effort, she managed to handcuff a winded Fiona. Katie and Nick scrambled across the floor and it took both of them to right Don and his chair. She let Nick attack the rope binding Don's feet.

"This'll sting," Katie said, touching the edge of the duct tape that covered Don's mouth. He mumbled something unintelligible and Katie ripped the tape off Don's mouth.

"Ya!" Don cried, and then swallowed. "It's better than being shot."

That it was.

Once free, Nick and Don embraced, leaving Katie to feel like a third wheel. That was okay. Halleluiah! She was safe.

Suddenly the bedroom seemed filled with uniformed deputies. They hauled a hollering Fiona to her feet and dragged her out of the room and down the stairs. With a lump in her throat, Katie watched as an EMT checked Phil's neck for a pulse. One of them looked up and shook his head at Beth.

"Let's get that shirt off you and take a look at that shoulder, Detective," another paramedic said.

Beth nodded and the two EMTs escorted the DEA agent over to sit on the bed.

"Let's give the lady some privacy," Katie told Nick and Don. They headed out the door, where she found Ray pressed against the wall, trying to stay out of the deputies' way. Once again, in his hand was the pencil with the handkerchief tied to it, which he waved enthusiastically.

"You got my message," Katie said unnecessarily.

Ray nodded.

"And that?"

"A surrender flag . . . damsel hankie . . . it's good for a multitude of things."

"You're off the hook," she said. "Phil confessed to killing Ken Fenton. We all heard it."

"Good to know."

Katie nodded to her left—the west—toward Artisans Alley. "Where's Miles?"

"Back at the Alley with Cal, who's probably already arrested Hugh," Ray said.

"On what grounds?"

"On the grounds that he and Fiona tried to move that cache of pills before Miles even showed up today."

"How did they know?" Katie asked. "I didn't think the surveillance equipment was in place until Beth and Cal arrived at the Alley."

"Miles didn't want to risk it. He put a camera in Chad's Pad yesterday."

Katie smiled. "Well, I'll be. What about Paul Fenton?"

"We've got nothing yet. Only time will tell."

Katie nodded. "Thanks for calling in reinforcements. I truly appreciate it . . . but what took you so long?"

He shrugged. "Aw, you know. I had to polish my shoes, get out my good damsel hankie . . ."

Katie scowled, but then gave a playful punch to his shoulder. "Jerk."

Ray grinned. "Come on, admit it; you wouldn't have it any other way."

Thirty

It was with a sense of relief that Katie sat down at her desk in Artisans Alley that next morning. Relief that the answer to the biggest of her questions—who had killed Ken Fenton and why—had been answered. But there was still so much she didn't know. And yet . . . she had a feeling she would find out fairly soon. She just had to wait to learn what crimes the Monroe County DA charged Fiona Lancaster and Hugh McKinney with.

A knock at her door caused Katie to look up from her computer screen. "Can I bum a cup of coffee off you?" Ray asked, sounding contrite.

"You know from your vendor days here at the Alley that everyone has to *pay* for their coffee."

"You couldn't spare a friggin' quarter?" he asked, sounding annoyed.

Katie shrugged and sighed. "I suppose I could." She dug

into her jeans pocket and came up with a couple of quarters. She was about to rise, but Ray waved her back to stay seated. "I'll get it."

Was it telling that he knew just how she liked her second-favorite caffeine drink of choice?

Ray returned with two mugs, setting one on the desk in front of her before appropriating the tiny office's guest chair.

"What's on your mind?" Katie asked, picking up her cup.

"I just thought you might like to know how things stand in the Ken Fenton murder investigation."

"You mean everything not already mentioned on the channel ten news?"

Ray sipped his coffee. "Uh-huh."

"I'm a *little* interested."

"Bull! You'd probably sell a few pints of blood to learn what I know."

"Blood?"

"Sure. There's a plasma center right in Greece. You want the address?"

"I don't think they'd have any information on Fiona, Hugh, and Paul, other than they're in jail awaiting arraignment."

"Eh, you're probably right."

Katie sipped her coffee, but Ray didn't seem in a hurry to spill the beans. "Oh, come on. Tell all."

Ray shrugged, looking smug. "Well, okay. Fiona and Hugh are up for murder. On the other hand, Paul Fenton is up on lesser—but still serious—charges. He's cooperating with the district attorney to strengthen their case against Fiona and Hugh. It seems he tried to break away from the group after realizing one of them was responsible for his brother's death, but Hugh threatened Paul's remaining family to keep him in the drug-distributing fold."

"Imagine that."

Ray cocked his head, looking smug. "I got to wrangle an invitation to sit in on the interrogation."

"Just a courtesy for an old, retired colleague?" Katie asked.

"You got it."

"So that's why you've been among the missing for the past couple of days."

"The girls can handle the store if I have to be away for a few hours."

"Lucky you." She took another sip from her cup. "And?"

"It seems Paul hadn't realized the scope of the operation until it was too late. He'd bought some pot and a few prescription drugs from Hugh when Hugh had a mail route. Paul told the DA that he was just out of high school at that time and was easily led down the wrong path."

"Did someone play a tiny violin in sympathy?" Katie asked, nonplussed.

Ray scowled at her and continued his recitation. "When Hugh looked him up a few months ago and said he knew how Paul could earn some extra money, Paul was eager to find out more. It seems Fiona came up with the idea for dealing in prescription drugs after Phil hurt his back and was sent his medication through the mail from the Veterans' hospital. All she needed was a greedy doctor and a lot of fake names. She already had the addresses—those from her real estate holdings. Finding a shady doctor wasn't that hard, but Fiona was afraid that having a large volume of drugs coming to her apartment buildings would attract too much attention.

"That's where Phil's old military pal, Hugh McKinney, came in. As you know, Hugh worked for the postal service and made sure no one batted an eye at the number of prescription medications delivered to Fiona's fake patients. But he wasn't content with the money she paid him and he decided he wanted a bigger role."

"And where does Paul fit in?"

"Paul got cold feet but he realized he knew too much about the operation for Hugh to wish him well and send him on his way. So, Paul went to his brother for advice. Ken made the fatal mistake of confronting Hugh."

Katie winced.

"When Hugh told Fiona Ken had threatened their operation, she had Phil take care of the problem."

"By killing Ken."

"You got it. Phil knew how to rig the saw to short out and hoped that it would appear Ken had simply picked up a faulty piece of equipment. But if anyone had suspected foul play, Phil anticipated that it wouldn't be too hard to point the finger at Hugh for the murder. Then he and Fiona could close up shop on Victoria Square and move elsewhere."

"Paul didn't tell you that."

"No. Fiona admitted that straightaway. She isn't the tough old broad you first met. Now she's just a little old lady with chafed thighs wearing an orange jumpsuit."

"I can't say I feel sorry for her," Katie stated.

"Nor I."

"What's going to happen to Paul?"

"He'll likely cop a plea and get off with a light sentence, but unless he makes bail, he won't be back at his tattoo shop anytime soon."

"I wonder if Regan can run it without him?"

"That's not the DA's call."

"No, but . . ." Katie didn't voice the fact that Brad would either have to wait for Paul to get out of jail or find another ink artist to transform his *Julia* tat to either a cobra or a feather. Personally, she preferred the feather.

"I haven't heard anything about Agent Beth. How's she doing?" Katie asked.

"Already back on the job. She won't be in the field until she's a hundred percent healed, but she's dedicated to the work. I kind of know how that feels."

Katie bet he did.

Another knock on the door drew Katie's attention.

"Hey, Sunshine. Need a breakfast break?" Andy proffered a white paper bag with a grease stain on its side. That could only mean one thing: cinnamon buns! He looked in

Ray's direction. "Sorry, old man, but I only brought enough for Katie and me."

"That's all right," Ray said, stood, and polished off the last of his coffee. "I've got a business to run." He nodded in Katie's direction. "Talk to you later."

She knew it was a promise he'd keep, too.

Once Ray sidled past Andy and out the door, Andy commandeered the office guest chair, handing Katie the bag. "How did you know I skipped breakfast today?" she asked.

"A lucky guess."

She spread the goodies, still warm from the oven, onto a couple of paper napkins, wrapped one, and handed it to Andy before doing the same for herself.

"So what was Davenport doing here so early?"

"He thought I might like to know what's happening to the bad guys—and gal."

"And?"

"They're bad."

Andy grimaced and didn't seem all that interested in learning the dirty details. "Now, as I recall, just a few days ago we talked about going away for a few days."

"And?"

"And I've been thinking about it—a lot."

Katie leaned forward, her lips just inches from Andy's. "Why don't you tell me all about it?"

Epilogue

It was a bright, hot Saturday in late August, and each shop on Victoria Square had shut down for the two hours between nine and eleven a.m. so everyone could stand along the walkathon route and cheer on Rose. Katie, Andy, and a crowd of Artisans Alley's vendors stood in front of the former applesauce warehouse. Katie wore shorts, a T-shirt, and an Angelo's Pizzeria baseball cap with her ponytail pulled through the hole in the back. Holding Andy's hand with her right, she held a sweating bottle of water in her left to hand to Rose when she passed.

"I kinda wish I'd have walked with Rose," she said as the crowd cheered for another throng of walkers.

Andy shook his head. "Nah. This is Rose's big event. It's good that she doesn't have to share her glory with anyone."

"Apart from the other hundred and forty-nine walkers, you mean?"

He squeezed her hand. "You know what I mean."

"Yeah." Katie smiled. "Who needs glory when you've got peace of mind, anyway?"

"What's that?" He leaned closer to be able to better hear her.

"I said you're incredibly handsome, and I'm a lucky woman."

He grinned. "I doubt that's what you said, but I'll take it."

Katie laughed. She did feel lucky. There were no drugs in Artisans Alley. There were no drug *dealers* in Artisans Alley. Nor were there any drug enforcement agents posing as vendors in Artisans Alley. Sure, she had a couple of vacant vendor spots, but those would soon be filled. Poor Sue Sweeney was heartbroken, but she was also relieved to find out the truth about Hugh before she fell too hard for the man. Life went on, and Sue had brought her big popcorn popper outdoors and was selling bags of it to the crowd.

Katie spotted Ray and his daughters standing on the porch outside Wood U. She smiled at him but didn't wave. The Davenport girls still weren't on friendly terms with her and she didn't want to disturb what appeared to be a happy day for the family. All three girls were laughing and cheering on the walkers.

Catching Katie's gaze on him, Ray took a carpenter's pencil from his pocket. Tied to it was a white handkerchief. He waved it like a flag.

Katie laughed.

"What's so funny?" Andy asked.

"Nothing. I'm just happy."

Recipe

~~~~~~~

Katie's Gluten-Free Chocolate Chip Cookies

> 2¼ cups all-purpose gluten-free flour blend
> ½ teaspoon xanthan gum
> 1 teaspoon baking soda
> 1 teaspoon salt
> ½ cup cream cheese, room temperature
> ¾ cup unsalted butter, melted
> 1 cup packed light brown sugar
> ½ cup granulated sugar
> 1½ teaspoons vanilla extract
> 2 egg yolks, room temperature
> 2 cups semisweet chocolate chips

In a medium bowl, whisk together the gluten-free flour, xanthan gum (omit if the flour blend already has xanthan or guar gum), baking soda, and salt. Set aside.

In a large mixing bowl, place the cream cheese, pour in the melted butter and brown and granulated sugars, and mix on medium speed for 2 minutes. Add the vanilla extract and egg yolks (one at a time), mixing on low-medium speed until well blended. Add the flour mixture, beating on low until just combined. Add the chocolate chips and mix on low or by hand, until thoroughly mixed. Cover the mixing bowl with plastic wrap and refrigerate for a minimum of 4 hours, and up to 4 days.

When you are ready to bake, remove from the refrigerator and let sit for 15 to 60 minutes, or long enough for the dough to soften enough for easy scooping.

Preheat the oven to 375°F (190°C, Gas Mark 5). Line baking sheets with parchment paper or silicone liners. (Do not spray with cooking oil.) Use a scoop to make even mounds of cookie dough spaced several inches apart. Bake the cookies for 11 to 12 minutes. Remove when the edges are set and just beginning to brown. The centers will look undercooked but will continue to cook as they cool. Let the cookies rest on the baking sheet for 2 to 3 minutes before removing to a wire rack to finish cooling.

YIELD: ABOUT 20 COOKIES

Ready to find
your next great read?

Let us help.

Visit prh.com/nextread